MW01593671

Cruelty:

The Daughter of Anger and Revenge

A German in a Foreign Land

LUCINDA HECK

FriesenPress

One Printers Way
Altona, MB R0G 0B0
Canada

www.friesenpress.com

Copyright © 2022 by Lucinda Heck
First Edition — 2022

All rights reserved.

No part of this publication may be reproduced in any form, or by any means, electronic or mechanical, including photocopying, recording, or any information browsing, storage, or retrieval system, without permission in writing from FriesenPress.

Images were purchased from Alamay or Shutterstock, personal photographs of the author, or are accredited at the bottom of the images.

ISBN
978-1-03-913666-3 (Hardcover)
978-1-03-913665-6 (Paperback)
978-1-03-913667-0 (eBook)

1. FICTION, LITERARY

Distributed to the trade by The Ingram Book Company

DEDICATION *and* ACKNOWLEDGMENTS

I cannot thank John enough for his support during the process of writing this book. He accompanied me to Serbia to see the mass grave of my relatives in Jarek, one of the most moving experiences in my life. When I bought hundreds of books for the research, he didn't complain. His faith in me never wavered.

This is also for my granddaughters, Jessa and Ellie, so they may know of the courage and passions of their family and find inspiration in their story.

"The Harper's Songs"

Wer nie sein Brot mit Tränen ass,
Wer nie die kummervollen Nächte
Auf seinem Bette weinend sass,
Der kennt euch nicht, ihr himmlischen Mächte!

Ihr führt ins Leben uns hinein,
Ihr lasst den Armen schuldig werden,
Dann überlasst ihr ihn der Pein:
Denn alle Schuld rächt sich auf Erden.
(Johann Wolfgang von Goethe, 1749–1832)

He who has never eaten his bread with tears, or during a night of grief has never sat on his bed crying, does not know the powers of heaven. You, God, brought us to life. Yet you let the poor and wretched be indebted to you. And then you abandon him to his own agony: for all guilt is avenged on earth.

TABLE OF CONTENTS

INTRODUCTION

When the two-year Austro-Turkish war ended in 1718, the Banat region of Hungary became part of the Habsburg Monarchy and thus would be under the rule of Austria. The region had been conquered in 1716 by Prince Eugene of Savoy. The history of animosity between the Turks and Austria was long. The Turks had laid siege to Vienna previously for three weeks in 1529 and again in 1683 for sixty-two days. The Turks knew that Vienna was the gate to Europe, and they called the city "The Golden Apple." Maria Theresa, Empress of the Habsburg Empire from 1740 to 1780, was an "Enlightened" ruler whose reforms made Austria a modern European state. She doubled the size of the army and created a military academy to build a corps of highly trained officers, the Theresian Military Academy. She abolished tax exemptions for nobility and the Church. She made education for children compulsory, abolished torture and serfdom, created a postal system, began building projects to beautify Vienna, and created a sewage system to aid in public health.

Her reforms included giving land grants to poor German farmers three times in the Banat region. Some money and a plot of land to start a farm were offered to them. These new settlers were also not to be taxed for the first six to ten years. Her reasons for this initiative were to increase the population of the Empire and in so doing increase the military ranks. The soldiers were necessary to keep the Ottoman Empire away from her front door. And lastly, with new crops and eventually more money from taxation, the economy of Austria would be helped.

By 1787 approximately 150,000 ethnic Germans had moved into the Banat area. There were stipulations given to these early settlers. During the first two periods, 1718 to 1737 and 1744 to 1772, only Catholics would be able to leave Germany and settle in the Banat. Maria Theresa, although an "Enlightened" monarch, persecuted Protestants. In the 1750s she deported 2,600 Protestants from Upper Austria to Transylvania. Laws forbade the possession of any Lutheran books and the holding of Protestant religious meetings in homes. There were also conversion prisons to "entice" conversion to Catholicism. By permitting only Catholics to settle in the Banat, she was ensuring the expansion of Catholicism. If anyone who was not Catholic attempted to make the journey, they were either beaten and sent back or made to convert. During the last period of colonization, 1782–1787, this religious stipulation was withdrawn when Joseph II, Maria Theresa's son and heir, issued the Edict of Tolerance and allowed Protestants also to become colonists. The colonists were to remain German, speak the German language, keep German traditions, be educated in German, and reside within the German communities they established.

The Banat Today

CHAPTER ONE

Going to a Strange Land

The Story of Stefan Fritz

Many songs have tried to express the feelings of leaving one's homeland forever. They have a sorrow tinged with beauty that makes one feel wretched. A heartbrokenness that, no matter how much a life improves, can only be described as a displacement. They say you are putting down new roots. But do the roots ever take hold, and are you nourished by the new growth? Or are they weeds, growing but producing nothing? I often thought it was like the feeling I had as a child when I lost my favorite toy. My mother told me I could get a new one, which I did, but it was never the same. It was not filled with the memories and love that I had with the older, more used toy. The peculiar sounds, smells, sights are gone and only linger in the memory. A memory which is of course faulty but truer than any fact. For it was these inarticulate moments that forged the memories that had made life livable. The lure of land, home, and money was the enticement for me to leave my homeland and settle in a distant land. A land between two rivers, where I sat and sang sad songs.

My wife, Sophie, and I left for Vienna in the spring of 1763 to register for and receive our papers. It was raining; I hoped the dreary day was not some ominous sign about our departure. Sophie's mother was crying, and the rain only added to the amount of water on her face. Her handkerchief was soaked and of little good. Our move would be exceptionally hard on Sophie's family, as they had grown to depend on her for help and support and, as importantly, she and her mother had become friends. Sophie cried only after we turned our backs and started on the trek to Vienna. My parents were excited for us to begin a new life with hope. Sickness and lack of material goods had taken a heavy toll on my parents and the people of our village. They embraced us heartily, wished us a safe journey, and gave us a sack of food, and my mother gave Sophie some new embroidery works she had done, to place in our new house. I promised that we would write and tell them all about this new land to which we were traveling. I hoped that eventually some of my family would join us. My reports of good land and people would inspire them to pull up roots and plant them in the new land.

The road was passable, and one could smell new growth, a wonderful scent of nature's regeneration. The fragrance came from deep within the earth. It reminded me of hay freshly cut as well as land that had been recently tilled. The kind of earth you would rub on your face and hands to be closer to it, smell it, and revel in being dirty. Proud to be dirty.

"Sophie, you mustn't cry. Please stop. You are making this trip difficult. We will be able to keep in touch with family. They may even join us."

"But, Stefan, we are leaving them forever. You know that! Life will be horrible. We have no idea what we will face."

"But we have a better chance of making a life. We can grow our own food and put to market the crops we cultivate. Life will surely be better. A new start."

"You are just dreaming. How will my mother survive alone if there is another famine or outbreak of influenza? Children died because the fevers were so high. I was two when it broke out, and I remember seeing mothers bathing their children over and over to bring the fevers down. The tiny bundles they carried out of the house to be buried. The tears. The mothers became weak themselves with coughing and lack of nourishment." Her tone had become more insistent and almost desperate. Her cheeks reddened from emotion.

I did not answer her questions but replied, "With six children in my family, I would have received such a small portion of land that we would have barely been able to subsist if we had stayed in Germany. Please understand that I am doing this for us and the children we hope to have. We are tenant farmers who pay high taxes and have little left for life. I am tired and I am only twenty-four. Please stop! You are only upsetting yourself and making the journey unbearable. There are already settlers there. We are not going into some wasteland."

"*Ja*, and how do you know that? Who do we know that has come back and shown us their good life?"

Of course, we knew no one. Although we were traveling with fellow Germans, we were all from different villages. At least we had a common language and traditions. Sophie and I were hiding the fact that we were Lutherans because Maria Theresa wanted only Catholics to form the new colonies. If we were quiet and kept our feelings to ourselves, we might pass for Catholics. We took nothing with us that would identify our religion. When we had to write our religious affiliation, I wrote "Catholic." I am sure that part of Sophie's angst was due to this deception.

We had both lived secluded lives in the beautiful Black Forest region of Germany. I loved the winter. During the day, the forest shimmered as light penetrated through the trees. As a child I thought that diamonds could be harvested from the trees. The streams and waterfalls appeared laced with silver bracelets. To a child's imagination the world seemed rich and beautiful, the place where magic happened. And of course, the forest was alive with unknown creatures who came out at night to play. These creatures' laughter was muffled by the snow but could be heard by sleepless children. We could sled and make fortresses in the snow. Those great snowball fights!

In the summer, the large fragrant trees gave shade and shelter from the heat. Lazy and carefree days could be spent looking for mushrooms and other edibles. I would spend hours climbing trees and using my slingshot to scare girls and other moving things. Sometimes I would shoot berries that would stain the girls' clothing. I am sure their mothers were not happy, but the girls were never able to identify their mysterious attacker. As I got older I would toss wreaths made of flowers in hope of gaining their attention. Eventually their attention and mine turned to other things.

These images, scents, sounds, and the tactile pleasures of snow, flowers, and young love would remain with me always. They were the images of a life and a childhood that was never far away from the sun and the earth.

Even when we relocated to a new land, I could smell the scents of the forest. I hoped that I would find other cherished places in this new land, places that in old age I could return to and remember our new life as I was now remembering my homeland. Yes, I did have hope.

Once we became adults our lives became hard, in our homeland, and there was no hope of improving our station in life. We had all become bound to our homes, the land, and the endless sameness. We loved our families, but we all became stagnant. Our lives had small expectations: no drought, no sickness, no accidents, no fires, and the hope that death would not be harsh. Most homes had thatched roofs and were half-timber and brick, and we had one large living area. We also brought in the livestock at night and stored the hay inside. We ate only what we grew or raised, and we made our own clothing, cooking utensils, farm tools, baskets, and furniture. Most villages had one mill, a smith, and a carpenter.

But I was to learn that hope and despair are different sides of the same coin. Also that I could not see beyond my own desires. I had seen pain, death, and hunger, but I had never lived with these emotions. They belonged in other people's lives. The tragedy of a "good life" is that it is different from a "full life." The fullness of life includes those things we keep locked inside us, that break us every day, as well as the joys of the simple and beautiful.

Sophie, who was never adventurous, had only fear. Her home near the Black Forest was all she knew and all she wanted to know. She had been born there, played, grew up, and fell in love there. The bad times were only small episodes that were quickly forgotten. She loved the smells of baking bread, fresh cut herbs and flowers, and of course the air that was always clean and clear. She could imagine nothing else and wanted nothing else.

That I was able to persuade her to go on the journey was nothing short of miraculous. It had taken me months. I believe that her love and faith in me became the deciding factor. She would not believe that I would lie to her or put her in any kind of danger.

I knew there was a large and wondrous world that I had never seen. I wanted to see this world, have my own piece of land, live in amazement. The dullness of my life became oppressive as I got older and had to spend my entire day in the field or repairing tools. I could not see endless hours doing the same things over and over, talking to the same people, hearing the same gossip, and watching the same events, without losing my sense of worth. I was worth more than the sum of my life so far. I wanted to believe that I could make a mark and create a better life for our children.

My life prior to 1763 afforded me a little education, which enabled me to read parts of Luther's Bible. I was a curious child, which is necessary to learn, but I was undisciplined. Boys grew up to be their fathers and girls their mothers, so I was unsure what an education would provide. My imagination was captured by the places in the Bible. Where was Jerusalem, where was Rome, what did the Sea of Galilee look like, and where were the places that St. Paul visited, were all questions I could never ask in church school. Church school really only consisted of reading Luther's Catechism and finding places in the Bible that supported his doctrines. And, of course, memorization. I was always behind in my memorization of Bible verses and Luther's Catechism. I would daydream and pretend I was traveling with Jesus to see the places and meet the people. My mother and father were unable to persuade me that this was not what an education was. The pastor would shrug his shoulders and say: "Stefan, your mind must be held captive by the messages of Christ and His teachings! You are wasting your mind on these things that will not increase your faith. Do you know the Ten Commandments yet?" Of course I did not, and I did not know what they meant.

Sometimes I would wander into the pastor's rooms and look at his books. I pretended I could read them, and then little by little I was able to read more and more words. I think the pastor knew what I was doing but allowed me this little pleasure because it would keep me out of trouble. Eventually I had to go to work and leave behind the books and questions.

Sophie, on the other hand, did know the Ten Commandments and their meaning and often said that my desire to learn more was a kind of envy. I was meant to be a farmer and I should not envy those who were able to go to university. Sophie believed that there was knowledge that should not be known.

"Look at the fate of Adam and Eve when they wanted knowledge. Stefan, you are able to make the earth fruitful, and that is a wonderful thing. This is how God has blessed you."

But still I had such curiosity. I did not equate yearning for a better life with a form of envy. Nor did I believe that knowledge could somehow hurt a person. Without knowledge, people passed on superstitions and outdated ideas. They feared anything new, and what I saw was the lack of knowledge hurting people. People only knew what their parents knew or what the pastor had taught them about life. I believed that there could be better circumstances. I also understood that if I failed our circumstances would be dire. It was more like willingness to take a gamble than envy. Of course, I did not talk about this gamble. What was really important was my desire to know more and see more. How could anyone lack this desire? I told Sophie that the children of Israel traveled forty years for a better life. They underwent hardships but they prevailed. Our journey would be easy in comparison.

When we were courting, she and I would meet at the edge of the forest in the evenings to plan our futures after we married. It was there we first made love. Our first meetings had been filled with soft kisses and caresses.

Sophie was amazed at her depth of feeling for me. She told me that days passed so slowly and the wait for our time together at night seemed endless. "You make me feel loved and beautiful."

I was the first boy Sophie had ever kissed, and these kisses were the most affection she had ever experienced. As time went on, I became more sexually aroused by our love making and we both became more curious with our bodies. I always made sure that I never overstepped boundaries when she would pull away or suggest we stop. One evening though neither of us wanted to stop.

"I love you so much Stefan. I think I want to consummate our love. You have been with other women, and this will be my first time. I am afraid. Please be gentle."

"Of course, Sophie. Are you sure of this? It will be painful for you. I think you should think this over. Your parents will be disappointed in you and probably mad at me."

"You're right. Let's meet tomorrow night and we can talk some more."

The next night we met, and Sophie told me that as long as she had my promise of marriage, that this was something she wanted. I will tell my parents of our plan to marry tomorrow. Come to my house and we can discuss plans with them. I am hopeful that all will go well. My mother seems to like you very much."

"I will bring my grandmother's ring that my mother has saved for me."

Our love making was gentle, but Sophie was surprised by the pain. She had brought a change of clothes. We cleaned ourselves in the pool a few feet away. The water felt wonderful on our bodies. We held each other and kissed more.

"I feel wonderful! Even though it was painful I know that we are now one." Sophie started to cry as she said these words.

"Yes, I am one with you Sophie."

I helped her get dressed and walked her to her house. We kissed at the door. "I will come by tomorrow evening."

The next evening, I dressed in my best clothes and brought flowers. When she opened the door, she was smiling. "I assume this is a good sign. The smile I mean."

"Yes, I have told my parents why you are coming to see me tonight. My father expects you to ask him for my hand."

"Of course. I have even prepared a little speech."

I was offered a glass of wine by Sophie's mother. I was so nervous I didn't drink it. After some very insignificant conversation I stood and went over to her father.

"Herr Haller, I am here this evening to ask for Sophie's hand in marriage. We love each other very much and I promise to provide for her. I would like her to live with me in our family house until we can build our own. My parents have agreed, and my mother is delighted that she will have some help. I would now like to place my grandmother's ring on her hand."

"Stefan, you are a good man and I believe Sophie and you are both in love. I see no reason why the two of you should not marry. When do you plan to have the ceremony?"

Sophie, unable to contain her excitement loudly exclaimed, "Next week!"

Her mother came over and hugged her. "Well, we have a lot to get ready then. I suggest you talk with the pastor tomorrow. I know he is found of you Stefan. I am sure he will be thrilled that about this next step in your life."

Sophie was a small young woman, five-foot-one. She was slight and trim. Her usual clothing was a dark skirt, an apron, and a white blouse, often heavy and bulky, with the obligatory babushka. She would wear a cloth belt that showed off her small waist. She had long, brown, curly hair and green eyes. Her cheek bones were high, and her cheeks were often flushed with emotion. Her upper lip had a delicate curve that made her lips noticeable. Her face, although simple, was appealing because it radiated her good soul. She was kind and soft-spoken. She laughed often with a low, rather crackling sound. She sang in the church choir and surprised everyone with her warm alto voice.

I, on the other hand, was tall, nearly six feet. I was proud of my height and walked with a strong, straight back. My hair, bleached by the sun, was a warm, rusty brown. However, my blue eyes appeared out of place with my dark, tanned skin. I was muscular and loved showing off my firm, trim body. I was often accused of vanity, but that was an insult that could be ignored. I always had many friends around me. As shy as Sophie was, I was gregarious. I could not carry a tune, and my singing often embarrassed Sophie because I sang with such gusto. People tended to move away from me, but I did see many smile and laugh, especially when they saw Sophie's cheeks redden. We were the perfect match; the pot had found his lid.

As was the custom, we went to all the houses in our small village and gave personal greeting and invitations. Everyone was excited and happy for us. On the wedding day Sophie chose to wear a white dress with a white apron. She looked like a doll.

When the wedding procession got to her house and I saw her I burst out, "Sophie, you are the most beautiful woman I have ever seen." I was going to give her a kiss, but her father lightly pushed me away. "You can save that for latter!" Everyone laughed.

We were married and settled into a normal life as farmer and wife. Now we were Herr and Frau Fritz. Nights were spent in tender kisses and talking and holding each other. Eventually Sophie felt the same passion that I felt. We now understood what the Bible passage meant about the flesh becoming one. We were now more closely tied to each other than to any other person in our lives. It was a mystery and a joy. At night I also began reading poetry to her.

My life was changing in ways that I had never imagined. I knew what it meant to share a life with someone. That there was a purpose to the daily grind—a warm home and heart waiting. I began to notice small things of beauty and thought about ways of pleasing Sophie; I was no longer merely thinking of myself. Poetry was a door into this new life. I found worlds of new ideas, and sentences that caused me to question what I knew of life. There was no topic that poetry did not tackle. Love, death, the countryside, music, God, all were part of poetry. I must admit that much of the poetry I did not understand, but the words in my head sounded wonderful.

The pastor as a wedding gift had given me two books of poetry. They were poems by Haller and Klopstock. The pastor, Herr Schmidt, hoped that my curious mind would remain curious and that I would grow to love German literature. I received the books with great appreciation and said they were the most wonderful gift I had ever received: I had my own books.

"Stefan, if you have any questions about the words or the poems, please come to me. Since coming here, I have not found many people with an interest in poetry, and I would love to talk to you about them. Luther was right, I believe; education is necessary to become a good person."

"Of course, sir. It will be my pleasure to meet with you often."

We set a date for Thursdays after lessons.

My favorite poem was one by Klopstock.

"The Rose Garland" by Fredrick Gottlieb Klopstock
In the shades of spring I found her
And bound her hair with rosy ribbons
She did not feel them; and slumbered on.
I looked at her, and within this glance
My life hung upon her life.
I truly felt this, but did not understand it
I whispered speechlessly to her
And rustled the rose garland.
She looked at me;
Her life hung upon my life within this one glance,
And all around us was Elysium.

After we were married, I would read the poems from these books to Sophie. She listened carefully, but I could tell when she was losing interest. I tried to explain them to her as best I could, and she was kind by asking questions, but I was not going to win her over to the art of poetry. Once we settled into our new home, built by the men of the village, Sophie loved keeping the house clean and inviting her new friends over for coffee and cake and gossiping while they knitted or worked at the spinning wheel. She was not sophisticated or intellectual but a kind, loving person.

Sophie complained about being so far from family. We had been able to build a new house at the edge of town, and it was a long walk to her parent's house. Her hope was that we would be able to visit them, or they could visit us. She would walk to visit a few hours and return exhausted after her walk home. She would help her mother with the house chores and other things that needed to be done, the washing, mending, and shopping.

The longing for home never left her. One time after we had moved to the Banat, I saw her starring out our bedroom window.

"Sophie, what do you see out there?"

"I am imagining the Black Forest where we played as children. I can see our homes and smell our mothers' cooking. I do yearn for our homeland."

"Sophie, Sophie. Is there nothing I can do to make you see this as our home? Doesn't our love make a home no matter where we are?"

I got the book of poetry the pastor had given me and turned to the "The Rose Garland". I laid down next to her and read the poem. When she turned to me, she hugged me so fiercely that "Oh, Stefan, this is about our love! How did he know about our love."

"It doesn't matter, does it? What matters is that it is our love."

"Stefan, what is this 'Elysium' though?"

"It is heaven. Yes, yes, we are in heaven with our love."

I was glad I had found a trade when I was fourteen, I had been taken in as an apprentice to the cabinetmaker in the village. I would spend the mornings on the farm with my father and the afternoons at the wood shop. I actually enjoyed the work. In using my hands to create and mend, I saw a different meaning to the idea of work. I also learned the value of striving for just the right shape of a curve in a surface, finding a perfect piece of prime wood to be planed, learning how to make carved ornamentation. Of course, I rarely was allowed this kind of work. My days were spent chopping the wood and planing it. I did watch carefully and took pieces home to work on at night. Eventually I spent all my time in the shop. I became a well-known cabinet maker throughout the Banat. It would change my life forever.

Once we had moved to the Banat, we heard through letters what was happening back home. Marriages, births, deaths etc. We knew that in the past there had been terrible outbreaks of plagues that had rampaged through the villages in Germany. In the years 1708, 1712, and 1732 there had been several. In 1729 there was a pandemic that in six months spread from Russia to all of Europe. The mortality rate was extremely high. The plague did not spare royalty or peasant. By 1732 many peasant farmers and their families had lost their very young and very old.

An outbreak in 1758 had affected only our village in Germany and a few of the surrounding villages. Sophie's father died, leaving her mother destitute with three children to feed and raise. Within a month Elisabeth's health and spirit were broken. She managed only because women came to help her and brought food, which enabled her to take her husband's place on the farm. It was necessary that the crops were taken care of, the livestock fed, the cows milked. She left many of the household concerns of baking, sewing, cleaning, and washing clothes to her older girls and the women of the village.

My family had not been able to resist the influenza outbreak. My grandparents had been taken seriously ill and my mother had the added burden of caring for them. They both died, and at some level, despite the sorrow, there now was less work and worry.

"It is so hard not to be able to go home to visit family and help them in these hard times. My mother has written about my brother and sisters." She read me the letter and her shoulders began to shake as tears clouded her eyes.

> Little Michael was so weak that he had stopped crying and
> merely slept in the crib. One afternoon your sister went to
> pick him up and realized he was dead. She was unable to
> tell me what happened for an entire day, that tiny Michael
> had died alone in a crib. She bundled her brother up in
> some clean linens and carried him out to the fields where
> I was working. We buried him in a grave where other
> victims had found their rest. The village believed that they
> should not be buried in church cemeteries, to help contain
> the virus. But there was no rest for the survivors. Houses
> smelled of fever and excrement. Shops were nearly empty

or filled with hacking sounds, the fields were not being cultivated, and taxes could not be paid. The influenza outbreak had not left many dead, but every household was attempting to recover not only their health but their spirits.

After a few months in the Banat, I began to notice that Sophie was beginning to show signs of enormous fatigue and she was losing weight. Her cheeks were sunken, and her waist was noticeably thinner. Between the hard work, the loss of contact with her family, and her desire to help me with work at the shop and our farm, she could barely get out of bed in the early hours of the morning to make breakfast. I worked from sunup till sundown. When I came home, Sophie was almost always asleep. She always left dinner for me under a cloth on the table. I did my own dishes and put them back. I did not wake her but rather sat next to her on the bed with a candle and read from my poetry book or write in my notebook.

I learned that women needed different things than a man to be happy. With Sophie it was little things: a bouquet of flowers I had picked, a pastry I bought, a small doily that a neighbor gave us, a walk in the evening to have a beer, friends over for dinner. It was when I was thoughtful and did the dishes at night or swept the floor that Sophie seemed to brighten. Slowly Sophie began to have more energy and talked less about her desire to return home.

Often after our small home church service on Sunday, I would pack a picnic lunch for us to eat out in the fields and often made love. It was during these times that I realized how little things are the most important. When we would go to the shop after our picnics, I could hear Sophie humming hymns as she cleaned the shop and helped me organize my tools and receipts. Coming up behind her to hug her when she was humming produced a high note that I would often laugh about. "You could sing on the stage with those kinds of notes."

"O Stefan, stop that. I am too shy to step out on a stage. I am only comfortable singing at church." She would then kiss me on the cheek and go back to work.

Our new life had started, and I could feel hope. The worst part of our trek to Banat was over once we settled in our home. But the journey down the Danube was difficult. Sophie had heard of the brutality of the Turks towards

Christians and knew that they were on the borders of Austria and Hungary. She feared a harsher life in establishing a new home with no one for support. She feared everything because she knew nothing. She heard the other travelers talk about the rumors they had heard from those who had returned from the first colonization. There were few left, and all were in need.

Swamps and the diseases that came from swamps had decimated the population in the Banat. Sixty thousand Turks pillaged the region in 1736 and by 1738 had overrun the population. Of the twenty thousand settlers, only ten thousand remained. The Turks also brought the plague. In all, twenty-eight of the villages had been destroyed. Sophie was justified in her fear. What was ahead of us was hard, backbreaking work, and this, along with malaria, gave the Banat region the nickname "The Grave of the Germans." The land to which Sophie and I were going could only be conceived as a wasteland. Although the swamps had been drained, all the towns needed to be rebuilt and the fields cultivated. What awaited was the fulfillment of the saying *"Der erste hat den Tod, der Zweite hat die Not, der Dritte erst hat Brot."* (The first had death, the second had need, the third had bread.)

I carried a small notebook with me to record our travels. I wrote that we were traveling from our home to Ulm by horse-driven cart "with our mattress and linens; a trunk of clothing; some dishes, pots and pans; and the few books we owned, the most precious being our Luther Bible, as we started our adventure. We wrote our family history in the front. We changed the cover as best we could and hid the Bible with the linens. The books of poetry I found here and there are a great comfort to me. I love the sounds of the words even if I often don't understand what they mean. Our livestock consists of a goat that we use for milk, butter, and cheese. At Ulm we will get a boat to Vienna and then travel down the Danube to our new home."

At night we recounted to each other stories of the Black Forest. We had both grown up with the stories of "The Big Man" and "King Mummelsee." We hoped that none of the water nymphs of the King would be found in the Danube. We laughed as we remembered our childhoods and how our parents would scare us into behaving by telling these stories. Our parents would say, "Watch out or the Big Man will get you and you will never return to your safe home." However, we did fear that the water nymphs might get angry, as the passenger boats were carried downriver by currents, and cause water levels to seethe and dash us on the cliffs. Each night we read a passage from the Bible and then said the Lord's Prayer. I finished by reciting a short love poem. This nightly ritual appeared to soothe Sophie. I had never been as religious as Sophie, but I believed that God would not give me the desire to start a new life in a foreign land without somehow blessing the endeavor.

In both Ulm and Vienna, we saw the boats on which we were to travel. They were merely rafts, known as Ulm Boxes. Each had a ten-foot-high shack covered by a canvas roof, in the middle of the boat, that was able to offer some shelter. Depending on its size, a boat could carry between twenty and one hundred people. Long poles were used to push the boats downstream, and they could only go in one direction. There was no turning back. The crews appeared friendly, but passengers feared that their kindness would depart once on the trip.

The people who had gathered at the river were nervous and anxious to get on the way. Many had waited over a week to board the boats. They heard rumors of a plague outbreak in the area of Hungary to which they were going. Also, there were horrible stories about the Turks and how they had destroyed many villages and murdered many of the first colonists. I kept Sophie away from the talk as best I could, but that night, waiting to board the boat, she was again crying.

"Stefan, I won't have children in such a horrible place. Please, let us return."

It was too late to return. With twenty-nine other people, and all their worldly possessions and animals, we boarded the boat. There were two other married couples, a family of eight that included grandparents, two families of four, a couple with a newborn baby girl, and a family of six. It was May and the weather was beautiful. The Danube seemed peaceful, and I dared to wish that this was a good omen. The grandparents and the new mother took a place in the shack. The young couples found places for themselves and their children, who were well-mannered. When the boat left the dock, however, the excitement was too much for them and they began running the length of the boat, watching as the men walked back and forth with their poles. Growing tired, they soon sat by their parents. The older boys asked if they could help the oarsmen, who willingly taught them the task.

The first day was beautiful, and seeing new sights brightened our thoughts. The gentle wave movement and rocking made everyone tired. We dozed peacefully in the sun and ate the fruit and nuts we had brought with us. Others began to talk amongst themselves, and I joined in their conversations. Sophie listened closely and I sensed she was becoming less frightened.

"I have heard it called the land of milk and honey, with large areas for crops, homes, and villages. We only need to work hard, which we are all used to," said one traveler.

"I heard from one man who returned that the Turks are no longer a threat," said another. "They destroyed everything that was built, but the plague killed them as well as the settlers. We will start again. Our own land using our own hands for ourselves. We won't have to pay taxes for three years."

"What we grow and make will be used to make our lives better. We will be servants to ourselves. We will be able to eat our bread and drink the wine that our hands have made. Build our own houses and businesses and thrive."

"We can only wait and see."

People began to ask the oarsmen what they knew or had heard. They confirmed that the first settlement had all but been destroyed. New settlers, however, had started to go there by the hundreds and had not returned. The oarsmen laughed and said that the Danube's hidden cliffs and bad weather were as much a danger as the Turks. The area was mostly populated by live-stock and soldiers who were Serbs. The land had not been cultivated.

"You Germans will be good for the land. You know what hard work is and how to grow crops and make the land fertile. Hard work and hope will be rewarded."

On the first night, we made a camp on the shore of the Danube. We started fires and cooked dinner. We took turns keeping watch, being unsure if there would be robbers. The little we had with us was precious. The children had a difficult time settling themselves. If this was because of fear or excite-ment, I wasn't sure. After dinner I took out my notebook and wrote about the day's conversations. I also put to paper my own fears: "Will Sophie have the courage to start this new life and hopefully a new family? The oarsmen did tell the men about the colony that was started for undesirables who begged and robbed. They were sent to Hungary in hopes that their departure would clean up Vienna. About two hundred of these undesirables were sent to the Banat every year. The practice has been stopped, however, because the Queen was rightfully afraid that people would not emigrate if they knew there were such lowlifes. I cannot worry about what might be!" I closed the notebook and moved closer to Sophie, who was almost asleep. I curled in behind her and placed my hand on one of her breasts. They were so soft and firm. Within seconds we were both aroused. Amazingly, Sophie had gained her vigor back on the trip to Ulm. It was wonderful that our lovemaking had become so heated and passionate again. We got up and moved a safe distance to enjoy a beautiful night of love. We both laughed as people watched us move. They knew what young people do.

At daybreak we left for the next leg of the trip. It took four weeks to reach Temeswar. The days were clear and beautiful, the river calm, and the nights cool. We made friends with a few of the young people who were journeying with us. Sophie was immediately taken with the baby girl, Helga, whose mother, Gretchen, and father, Wilhelm, became our friends. We had many talks and shared our life stories with Wilhelm and Gretchen Müller. Their dreams were ours.

We sang songs and talked about our "former" lives. The journey down the Danube was a moment out of time. As many sayings go, our life flowed like the river, quietly moving onward. I thought of all the Psalms that promise wonderful things near the water. I guess some of the memorization work had been important. We would build our new homes by the water and plant our crops and our lives by this beautiful river.

During the day we prepared food, cleaned our living areas and clothing, mended tools, and fished. The days passed quickly and we were always aware of our own trepidations. I tried to keep my thoughts on the beautiful surroundings and land that we passed each day. During the occasional days when the waters were rough, we had to scramble to keep things and people from going overboard. But there was much to laugh about afterwards. The eggs we tried to keep from rolling off the sides, the collisions of children as they tried to walk, the minor bumps and bruises all seemed to turn into stories of great heroics. The women always appeared to be much braver than the men in these stories, or at least to have more brains.

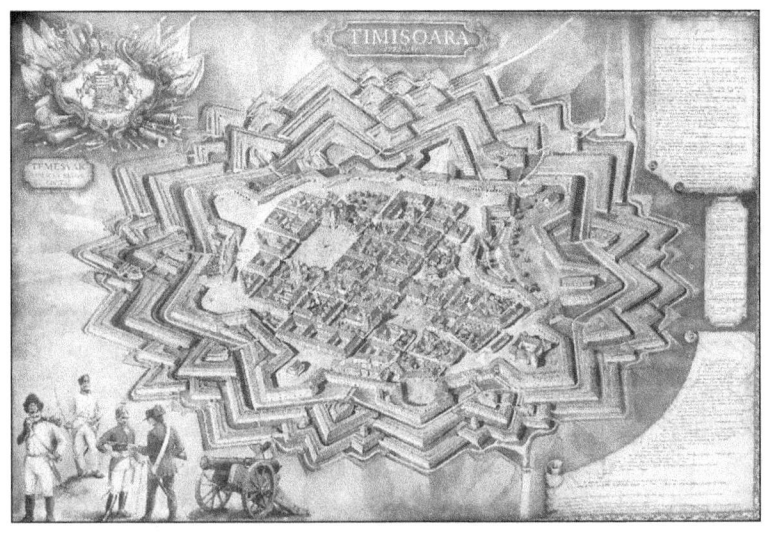

Personal photo of old map of Timisoara

When we arrived in Temeswar, or Timisoara, we found a thriving town with pubs, inns, and a city hall that served food and held dances. There was a cathedral, a mosque, a synagogue, a hospital, schools, and more than we could have imagined. One of the oldest pubs, called the White Ox, had been established in 1718. This pub proved to be a wonderful place to meet people and learn the goings-on of the town. We could listen to music, dance, tell stories, and get to know our fellow travelers and colonists.

The former Governor, Count Mercy, had drained the marshes and encouraged agriculture. As the oarsmen had related, our agricultural skills were much more advanced than those of the Serbians who lived alongside us. We felt safe from the Turks, as there was a fortress. However, there was still an atmosphere of a wasteland, because much of the land was fallow. At first, Sophie was only able to see the amount of work that lay ahead of us. I told her to think only of this one day and not to worry about the next day. We knew what hard work was, and we would certainly do our part to make this new homeland our own. We were not giving up who and what we were.

However, the work was backbreaking. There were still swamps and all the diseases they carried. Many families had at least one person get sick or die from them. This was why our destination became known as the German

Graveyard. People were homesick, and the illness only made this worse. Some did return home after a death, but this number was low. We started to make friends and have meals together. We heard that altogether there were ten villages around Temeswar. Amazingly, by the final year of the second migration there would be more than five thousand families and fifty-six villages.

There was a total of two hundred houses in our village, so we became a very tight-knit group. Families wrote home in hopes that some of their relatives would join them. I had decided that after the first year and when we had begun to prosper I would invite a couple of my brothers to join us. Sophie's letters home were filled with the gossip of the village: what each woman was like and how she was treated by her husband, who was pregnant, and who made the best bread and strudel. Women helped each other as much as possible, especially if a family member was sick. Life became exactly like the life their mothers had lived, except that it was our home and we were servants to no one.

For our household we received a cow, a hoe, dried fruit, a water tub, a grave shovel, a rug, a spinning wheel, a milk pail, and a butter barrel. This allowed me to set up a shop, and the garden provided us with food. During the first three months, people utilized my skills to build things for their houses or do repair work. It was very hard to keep body and soul together, but we all helped each other and worked together. These bonds would become strong and important.

Personal photos of house in the village Schowe. The houses are the same as when they were first built.

The houses in the village were built perpendicular to the large street and were designed with long, adjoining rooms. Long porches were on one side of the houses. Women decorated the outsides of the houses with personal touches so that each house could be unique and welcoming. Each dwelling had a fenced-in area for a garden of flowers and vegetables. Fruit trees and grapevines also dotted the landscape.

Sophie eventually began to see progress and took great pride in her management of the house inside and out. Our house was immaculate and always smelled of fresh bread and baking. Herbs and flowers were hung to dry over the sink. Flowers adorned the side yard where the porch was located. Pieces of embroidery and tatting were on tables and chairs. Sophie had also begun to make a quilt for us. She was never idle, and this helped her with her bouts of sadness.

The women brought lunch to the men—a meal of bread, sausage, and cheese. In the evening a large meal of meat, potatoes, and vegetables with wine or beer was enjoyed, and then we sat on our porches.

Our love making in the fields of the Banat proved rewarding. In ten months, Sophie and I had our first child, a boy we named Johann. We baptized him the next day at the Catholic church. Even though we both were Lutheran, I believed it important to have an official record of his birth and that he be baptized into the Christian faith. I hoped there would not be questions about why the priest never saw us in church. He only looked quizzically at us. If he asked us anything, I had planned to tell him Sophie's pregnancy had been hard and I needed to stay home with her, but now we would be able to attend regularly.

We were thrilled when she became pregnant. She was nineteen, and the pregnancy was hard on her. The women of the village were excited about her pregnancy and gave her heartfelt advice on how to care for herself and the little baby inside her.

Sophie listened to the women and in trying to please all of them often did nothing and hoped not to offend them. One piece of advice that she did follow was that the husband was to give in to his wife's whims. I did not object but did have to laugh at some of her whims. She also avoided alcohol and anything that could startle her. She yearned for strudel, chicken soup, pudding, and plum jam. Since she was sick every morning, all the women agreed that the child would be healthy. I made her a birthing chair and made sure that the house was always clean and tidy. She seemed to have less energy than usual, and she claimed this was because she was carrying such a heavy weight around with her. During the last month, she stayed inside the house and only cooked, baked, and dusted, which was more than enough work for her.

When her water broke, I called the midwife and a few of her closest friends to help. We darkened the room and closed all the windows, and one friend gave her a crucifix to hold to gain comfort when the pains were the most severe. As is the custom of all men, I left.

The women told stories of their own birthings and how everything they endured was forgotten once they had their babies in their arms. Sophie learned about which side the baby should lie on after it was born, how to get her milk to flow, how to wash the baby, how to get him to sleep through the night, and how to swaddle him and carry him with her. Gretchen reminded Sophie how much joy Helga had given everyone on the Danube and to keep her mind on such joys. Sophie and Gretchen began laughing because Helga had also kept everyone awake many nights.

When the cries of a baby could be heard outside, I ran in and saw our baby boy. Sophie was beaming as she held him out to me to hold. The ladies cleaned up the linens and began their duties of washing the baby, tying and cutting off the umbilical cord, and helping with the afterbirth. Sophie quietly said, "I now believe that our journey has been blessed by the arrival of our Johann."

"So, you have already decided on the name without me! Well, it's a good name, strong. So, Johann it will be. Do we even have a Johann in our family?"

"No, a new name for a new start."

The baby was happy and grew daily. Sophie doted on him, and strapping Johann to her back she took him everywhere with her. She cleaned, cooked, made clothes, took care of our small garden, and planted vegetables. The home and porch were always spotless, and the neat rows of our garden gave her great pride. She made our home wonderful so my hard work of starting a furniture shop did not seem a burden. We had built the shop on the back of our house and slowly we started to make a living.

Johann was a happy child, which made some of the difficulties in starting a new business manageable. Sophie could bring him to the shop and help me, since he was not fussy or in constant need of attention. When he was two, he often walked through the house to come to the shop and entertain our customers.

Our house was usually full of the furniture that I had made and became a small store for people to look at what could be bought. I also made small wooden toys for Johann and his friends. With the addition of Johann, our home was warm and full of promise. Both Johann and I gained weight. Our friends remarked that I must be eating for Johann also.

We had our second boy, whom we named Thomas, a year later. The delivery was again difficult. It was a breech birth, and the midwife told us that damage had been done to Sophie's womb and she could have no more children. Sophie was confined to bed, as was the custom, but after three weeks she was refusing to get out of bed.

"Sophie, please get out of bed," I said. "You must take care of Johann and our new angel. The midwife has said you are able to move around. I am getting so far behind in work and there is only so much Johann can 'help' me with. People have been wonderful, staying with Johann a little each day, but they have their own children and families. I count on you for so many things!"

"I don't want to. I am so tired, and it takes everything out of me to just feed him. I don't think I have enough milk, and all he wants to do is feed. Maybe one of the *omas* [grandmothers] can take Johann in for a while. You can give them some furniture to pay for their help. Please just let me be!"

"Let me help you out of bed. Maybe some fresh air and sitting out on the porch will help. I am sure Johann can play on the porch while you take care of Thomas. Please try, Sophie!" I tried not to let my anger and anxiety into my voice, but we all needed Sophie. Little Thomas was not growing and seemed lethargic. Gretchen had come over several times with meals for us and would sit with Sophie and try to cheer her. She told me that she had seen women become this way sometimes after childbirth, especially hard births.

"I've seen women not care for their babies. It is like they don't exist and they wither away, the poor little ones. I would like to get someone who is still nursing and bring them over to help, but they say they are so busy with their own. Some have twins and just can't. I will do what I can, but I think we need to use goat's milk to help Thomas."

We took a large handkerchief that we soaked in warmed goat's milk to try to get Thomas to drink. It was a long and tedious process. Thomas did drink, and he seemed not to be losing any more weight. Gradually, Sophie stopped eating and her milk flow became less and less. My only thought was to save Thomas and help Sophie get better. Johann thankfully seemed not to notice too much of the goings-on. He did often cry that Mama seemed not to want him and would not read to him anymore. He would get in bed with her and in a pleading voice say, "Mama read." Sometimes he would take a cookie to share with her, but she only ate a bite and said, "Thank you, Johann."

At wit's end, I swaddled Thomas and took him to the Merciful Hospital Church that was run by Misericordian monks. As the church and the hospital were connected, I entered the church first. The smell of candles and incense was strangely calming to me. My hope was that they would care for Thomas until I got Sophie well. I was prepared to offer anything. Having never been in a Catholic church and did not attended the Catholic services as I had promised, I at once became aware that it had similarities to the Lutheran church I had grown up in. A nave, a baptismal font, an altar, candles—all was familiar except for the icons and statues of Mary and other saints to which Catholics prayed in acts of idolatry. Although we had lied about being

Catholic at Johann's baptism, I was sure that this deception would be revealed and Thomas would receive no care. I was also aware that I now had to rely on God for the care of my child.

Many thoughts passed through my mind. I had no idea where the sick and dying children were taken in Temeswar, or those unfortunate babies born out of wedlock. These were things that men never talked about, and since Johann was never ill, I had no idea what choices I had. I knew that babies were often left on church doorsteps at night, but I could not do this with Thomas. I felt that, ultimately, he was my responsibility even though I could not care for him. Knowing whose hands I left him in was crucially important to me. I had no money and could only offer my services as a furniture maker as payment. Such a payment was a trifle compared to what the monks would give Thomas if they took him.

A monk walked towards us and seeing the bundle he asked what he could do for me. I told him the story, desperately trying not to break down. "I have nowhere to go. Any help you can give would be a gift from God."

"Are you Catholic?"

I answered honestly and told him I would gladly convert if it meant that they would help Thomas. I added that my other son, Johann, had been baptized as a Catholic.

"Has this baby been baptized?"

"*Nein*," I said with tears beginning to fill my eyes. I could not stand the thought of Thomas dying and being imprisoned in hell because we had not baptized him. "Please baptize him."

"Bring him here and I will baptize him now. Then we will talk."

The monk took Thomas to the baptismal font and the baptism was performed. In joy I hugged the monk who then introduced himself as Petr. I had to believe that God was acting through this monk. He promised to take Thomas to the hospital but could not promise that he would survive. Thomas was so thin and unresponsive. He asked me to bring my family the next day to be baptized in the Catholic Church and to see how Thomas was in the morning. The next day I brought Johann to the church and told Father Petr that my wife was too ill to get out of bed. I promised I would start attending Mass at the Catholic church in our village. Johann and I were baptized and we became Catholics. That evening I sat down by the Rega River and wept for myself, for Johann, for Thomas, and for Sophie.

I did start attending Mass, believing that God could certainly be found in any church that believed that Jesus was God's son and died for our sins. I prayed in German and tried not to think of all the things I had been taught about the papists. During the service I knelt and remembered as much as I could of Luther's teachings. I could feel myself slide into a hopeless lack of understanding of the whys of my life and wondering if God was really there. I did not know how I was going to get through the days. Day by day I tried to feel joyful in little things: Johann's eyes, a good bowl of soup, a new customer, the beauty of poetry. Eventually I was able to get through a day without crying in absolute fear that I would lose Sophie.

The hospital and the monks were able to keep Thomas alive. At home Sophie was fading away. She got out of bed twice a day to relieve herself, wash her face, and comb her hair. She barely ate. She no longer prayed. Worse, however, was that she stopped talking to or caring for Johann and she had completely forgotten that she had a baby named Thomas. I could not bring his birth up to her without her becoming agitated and thrashing around in her bed. She would scream, "*Nein, nein, nein. Ich habe keiner kinder!*" I have no children! Slowly her mind was becoming unraveled and there was nothing I could do. I cared for her the best I could but had no idea how to help her. Several of the women in Temeswar would visit us, mainly to see Johann and bring food, and they merely shook their heads. They told stories of other new mothers who became this way after a difficult birth. I did not have the courage to ask what had become of them. She lost weight, had sunken eyes with black circles, her hair was falling out, and she was unable to carry on any kind of conversation with me. She looked blankly out the single window and would sometimes appear to be talking to someone.

A few days after taking Thomas to the monks, I went to the bedroom to try to get Sophie to eat something. She did not stir when I called. I went over and kissed her gently on the forehead and realized with a sense of dread—and, to be honest, a sense of relief—that her suffering was over, that Sophie had died. Her inability to desire life had taken its toll. I cleaned her, combed her hair, and dressed her in her best dress. I told Johann that I was getting his mother ready for a trip. She was going alone but would certainly come back with something for him.

"I don't know when she will be back," I said. "She is happy, though, to be going. Johann, she has been so sick, and this is a wonderful day; she will be up and out of the house."

Johann continued eating and playing with his wooden horse, believing every word. I was inept at telling him the truth and felt sure this lie was better for him. All could be explained when he was older.

I went to Gretchen's house and told them that Sophie and Thomas had died. I wrapped a small bundle and put it in her arms, hoping that this would pass for Thomas. We built a coffin and placed Sophie in it. I went to see the monks in Temeswar, and they came to the house to say prayers and Biblical passages. They read from the Book of Job using my German Bible. Although it was Luther's translation, they agreed. "I know that my Redeemer liveth, and that He shall stand at the latter day upon the earth; and though after my skin worms destroy this body, yet in my flesh I see God and not another."

Although only Gretchen and her family and Johann and I were there, it seemed right that Sophie would be surrounded by those she most loved. Gretchen made up lunch. All of us just picked at the food and complimented Gretchen on everything. Johann ate everything that was placed in front of him. He was able through his wonderful nature to keep our minds off what had happened. I then left with the monks and the coffin to go to Temeswar to bury Sophie at the monastery. Their kindness and goodwill stayed with me throughout my life. I knew that religion was more than merely a church. At the deepest level it somehow did not matter if a person was Lutheran, Reformed, or Catholic. These good men and my friends were trying to give me courage.

Gretchen and her family became "adopted" parents of Johann. At dinnertime I would pick up Johann from their home, have dinner with him, bathe him, read to him, and get him to bed. In the mornings, we would have breakfast together and then go to the shop to set things up for the day. He would sweep the floors, dust the furniture, and help me with my "sums" for the ledger book. Little by little he learned the numbers and how to read small words. In the afternoons he would be with our friend Gretchen and her children. We told Johann that his mother had gone back to Germany, but after a while he did not ask about her anymore. He went on with his life, not knowing.

However, my despair was enormous. Losing Sophie and then Thomas. Life seemed to be turning inside out. I felt as if my skin had been flayed and left bare to the world to hurt and damage me. With no family around to help me bear the sorrow, I turned inward and found little succor. I tried not to let Johann see my sorrow, but by the end of the day I was wretched. I ate only because I needed to show Johann that my life was "normal." There was no Elysium, only a seething hell of sorrow unabated. As time passed, scabs did develop over the wounds, but they could be easily scratched off by the simplest things. Hearing someone sing, laughter, Johann playing on our bed, the smell of cooking were all simple but devastating reminders. I tried to think of these memories as important, in that they reminded me of the happiness I'd had and for which I was thankful; but this was not always possible. I gave her clothes away and put away her favorite things. I saved some things to give to Johann if he married and had children. In time I would relate the stories of his mother and how much we both had loved her. I wrote in my diary the things I wanted to tell Johann when he got older.

Stefan's notebook:

> *I must tell Johann about how Sophie would listen to me read poetry and how much she liked the one poem, believing it was about us.*
> *I will tell Johann about our trip down the Danube and how we met so many wonderful people who became our friends.*
> *Johann must know what a loving wife and mother Sophie was.*
> *I will tell him about how we met and the hardships we faced before we left for Hungary. I will not tell him about Sophie's father. He does not need to know what a brutal man he was. The wonderful home Sophie made for us. How she loved to meet with the women to gossip and weave wool for clothing, and the wonderful homemade bread she made; and, of course, those fattening desserts.*

Eventually, the kindness of the monk. The kindness and love
that Gretchen gave Johann.
Sophie's favorite poems.

The list went on and on, and in some way writing these things down did help me. Remembering the good kept my mind away from sorrow. I made up a story to accompany each object of hers that I would give Johann. The books of poetry would be given to him also.

I took him to Mass every Sunday at the Catholic church in our village. I prayed for Sophie's soul. Johann always knelt quietly beside me and repeated the words, not knowing it was his mother for whom we were praying. As he got older, I still could not bear to tell him the truth. I kept writing in the diary and thought that I should merely give it to him when he was old enough to read and ask questions. I doubt that he even knew who Sophie was. My life in many respects had ended, and I wondered what I had done in life to reap these miseries. But I thanked God for the friendships that were helping me through these ordeals.

The monk Petr continued to care for Thomas during all this time. There were enough monks that they could take turns with the duties of caring for a child. They loved telling him their favorite Bible stories, and often there were women who came to the church and were happy to have a chance to do something for Thomas. They did not know of his circumstances or how he came to be with them. I learned about his growth and well-being once a month when I visited the monks in the evening on Saturdays. Gretchen always took Johann on Saturday shopping trips in Temeswar. I would go along and tell them I needed to buy some supplies for the shop. As much as I hated not being able to claim Thomas as my own, I knew that this was better for him. He would not miss what he had never known. Ten fathers might be better than one. They gave him the last name of Stellar because he had brought a special light into their lives.

Johann loved to use his hands, and I often found him with a scrap of wood, carving out remarkable shapes and animals. They were roughly hewn, and he painted imaginative faces on them and painted the shapes in geometric designs. He had the beginnings of a menagerie of animals he kept in his room. He had named each one and would talk to them at night. He made others for our customers to give to their children as gifts. Although my wonderful Johann could not make up for the loss of Thomas, I was glad that I had Johann. My spirits eventually rose, but at moments I would still feel the sense of enormous loss. Questions that I could never answer. Even if they could be answered, they would make no sense to me. Loss was my companion, never far away.

Part Two

Thomas and The Violin

My life continued, days becoming months and months becoming years. My shop was doing well, allowing me to save money for Johann. I hoped that he would be able to continue schooling longer than I had and the money would be able to send him to university. He was bright and curious. Listening to all his questions, I remembered how curious I had been about the world. When I thought deeply about my life, I didn't regret the move, but I also thought that Sophie would be alive if we had not come to the Banat. But I also knew my love of Johann was a love that I would never had known without Sophie, so her death may have had meaning. There is nothing one can do to change the past, but I was determined to provide all I could for Johann's future.

One crisp, clear fall afternoon in 1770, a violinist appeared at the door of my shop. He introduced himself as Henry Eckert and informed us that he was providing entertainment in Temeswar's theater and was also attempting to set up a music shop to give music lessons. He gave us a sample of his playing, to Johann's and my delight. Henry was remarkably skillful on his violin and a gregarious, happy person. He played like a gypsy with fire and spirit. Henry stated that he was beginning to make friends and already had a few students from families who had brought instruments with them.

Henry had broken a peg on his violin and wondered if we could make another or repair his broken one. Johann with great assurance said to give him one day and he would have another ready for him. We both laughed at Johann, and Henry replied that such a small boy could not possibly carve a violin peg so quickly. I told Henry I would help Johann and that we could make a new peg.

To my surprise, Johann worked all day to make new peg from a small block of wood for the man. Of course, I also made one for him. When Henry returned, Johann showed his peg to him and refused payment; instead he wanted the man to play his violin for him. The music mesmerized Johann. He was speechless. The man, not knowing what to think of Johann's silence, turned to go.

Johann gently grabbed Henry's arm and asked to see the violin. "How are these made? And from where does this sound come?"

"Each violin has a soul embedded there by its maker. It is up to the performer to release the soul as he plays music."

Johann looked at Henry with questioning eyes, not understanding how a soul could live in a violin. Henry, seeing that Johann did not understand, continued his explanation.

"It is actually a wooden box with holes, an arm to hold it by, and strings running the length of the box and arm. When I pluck or bow the strings, they vibrate; the vibrations go into the box, come back out, and make sound. The magic that makes a great violin is something I know nothing of. There are makers in Italy and Germany who are famous for the beautiful sounds of their violins. I think you should learn to play so you understand how everything works together."

Henry smiled as related the information. He had been like this as a child, and he knew that Johann was not going to let another day pass if his father did not let him learn to play the violin. For the next several days, Johann begged to be taught how to play. As fortune would have it, the fiddler stopped by again and wanted to know if Johann still wanted to learn how to play. He would give Johann an old violin that he had found and begin to show him how to play, in return for some repair work on other musicians' instruments.

"I can learn to play the violin, Papa!"

I answered that I needed one more day to think about it.

That night I took Johann to hear Henry play at a local inn. Johann found himself a table as close as he could get to where the musicians were playing so he could watch and listen with no interference. He heard the *Verbunko* and the *Csárdás* and other folk music of Hungary. The dancing was so passionate, Johann's mind twirled. Some of the men pulled Johann into their dance. Luckily, he only fell twice. He had time of his life and could not sleep all night.

"Papa, how wonderful tonight was. I can't remember being happier. Music can really make life fun. I could play for both of us and we would be happy every day."

In the morning I agreed to the lessons. The lessons began the next day after the shop had closed and before Henry was working at the theater. Sometimes I took Johann and his violin to where Henry played. Johann played along, trying to match the fiddlers' fingering and bowing. Within a month Johann could play simple tunes in first position. His intonation was remarkable. Within the year, Henry allowed Johann to sit in with his friends and play. Johann observed everything.

Johann was now seven years old. Henry knew there was only so much he could teach him. Henry had become fond of Johann and believed he could help him become a fine violinist. Henry had been in the boys' choir at St. Stephen's Cathedral in Vienna between the years 1761 and 1766. When his voice broke, he had to leave the boys' choir and find a way to support himself. He made a meager living by being a street player. Like many boy choristers, he had been left to find his own way in the musical world. Some boys, when their voices broke, retained the beauty of sound they had as children and were able to stay in the choir as countertenors, tenors, or basses. Some families had enough money to continue their boys' music education, which allowed them to go to music schools. Most often these options were not available to the boys.

By 1769 Henry was tired of being poor and decided to travel down the Danube to Temeswar, which had started to be called the second Vienna. He found jobs as a performer quickly and found students easily. Almost everyone had a piano or some kind of musical instrument in his or her home. Henry was able to play at banquets, at functions for the wealthy, at weddings, and of course in the theater orchestra. The cathedral also had wonderful masses, which often included soloists and instrumentalists. Although he was not making much more money than he had in Vienna, food and a small room in Temeswar cost less than in Vienna.

The cathedral was also a home for some of Europe's greatest musicians and a showcase for their music. Herr Martin Demohl, the music director at the cathedral in Temeswar from 1768 to 1794, would often procure music from composers from Italy, France, and Germany and perform those pieces during services for which he had adequate performance resources. Having been trained in a European music school, he was capable of conducting the choir and instruments and thus providing exceptional music for the services at the cathedral. A rich musical tradition had already been established there by the time he was hired in 1768. Michael Haydn had written a Mass for the dedication of the cathedral in 1754, setting the standard for its musical endeavors. With the publishing house Artaria in Vienna, music of the European masters became more available. Besides the beauty of Temeswar, the musical culture of the town was rich and varied. Henry was happy and productive, and he had a new home.

On the large feast days, Johann and I went to hear the music in the cathedral in Temeswar. We heard Masses, Te Deums, and requiems with chorus, soloists, and orchestra. This music would stay with Johann for the rest of his life. The magnificence of the space, and the music resounding through the nave, took Johann's breath away and put him in another world. Often there were tears in his eyes and he sat as if frozen to the pew. Henry was always glad to see us and would invite us to meet his friends. There was always gossip about the music and musicians in Vienna and Salzburg. Occasionally Henry would hear about his friends still in Vienna.

The most famous and revered of Vienna's composers in the 1770s was Franz Joseph Haydn. Haydn had also been in the boys' choir at St. Stephen's in Vienna. Haydn, like Henry, had seen some lean years after he left St. Stephen's, but eventually was hired by Count Morzin as the count's musical director, or *Kapellmeister*. When the count fell into financial difficulties, Haydn was dismissed. His next employer was Prince Nikolaus Esterházy, who would be his employer for thirty years. Haydn's life would never be the same, and his reputation as Europe's greatest composer of symphonies was ensured, influencing composers for generations to come.

Haydn's orchestra at the Esterházy palace in Eisenstadt had sixteen players and it was a musical laboratory for Haydn. He could hear all of his compositions, try new ideas and approaches, get important criticism from the best musicians in the orchestra, and get paid. He claimed that because he was isolated from other composers and trends, he had to be original. Although the compositions were owned by the Esterházys, he eventually wrote music for publication, assuring a wider audience for his works.

Joseph Haydn and Esterhazy Palace

Henry had heard from his friends in Vienna that Haydn was a congenial man and easy to approach. With luck, Henry could obtain a meeting with

Haydn and let Johann audition to become a student of Haydn's. He wrote a few of his friends and asked if this was even possible. One of his friends wrote back that Haydn was always open to hearing new talent. He suggested that Henry write a letter to Haydn and place with it a letter of introduction from his friend. The back and forth of the letters between himself and his friends would certainly give Henry and Johann time for further study and practice. After a year, Henry believed it was time to approach me with his idea. He had already written Haydn and was waiting for a reply.

I was not prepared for this suggestion. My first reaction was "*Nein.*" My strong reaction caused Henry to step back. Johann had heard the conversation. He entered the room in which Henry and I were talking and at once started begging me to consider the idea.

"Papa, please! Why can't I? What an adventure for me! You know how much I love my violin, and to be able to play it better and to play it day and night would be . . . I don't know how to say it. A dream for me. Please, Papa!"

As the begging continued, I remembered Sophie begging me to return to her home in Germany and the Black Forest. Her heart had never been in the move. Now my son was asking me to let him move to Eisenstadt and fulfill his dream. Perhaps this was a way for me to honor her memory by giving her son his heart's desire as she had given me mine. I knew the pain this would cause me—another abandonment, another leaving. I was unable to claim Thomas, and now losing Johann would take another emotional toll.

"Let me have one day to think about this. What if this Haydn says no? Would Johann come back? To be so disappointed at such an age. My heart would break for him. Do you really believe he has a chance?"

"Herr Fritz, this boy has a gift with the violin. He is only a child and listen to how he sounds on my violin. Look at the joy on his face when he plays. People want to hear *him* play, not me. You cannot deny how wonderful this is. He must at least be given the chance. Please listen! Johann, play something for your father."

Johann picked up Henry's violin and tuned it. He placed the bow carefully and pulled it slowly over the string, making a beautiful crescendo, and began to play Bach's first violin part of the second movement of the *Suite in D major*. Although he had not learned all of it, I was astounded. The sound appeared to come from somewhere outside of the world. I had heard nothing like this. I had only heard Henry play the popular music at the inns and had no idea that this kind of music could exist. After listening to my son, I quietly said, "Come back tomorrow after I close shop and we will talk again."

I know that Henry saw the tears in my eyes, but he sensed that I would not be able to refuse Johann the opportunity if Haydn would take him on as a student. Henry knew enough about music and musical training to know that there were only a few people who could play with Johann's brilliance and intuitive musicality. When Johann and Henry walked through the door the next day, I felt tightness grab my heart. Knowing I would lose the third person in my life whom I loved gave me physical pain. I knew that life would never be the same without this love. I would be totally alone in a house to which I had brought a wife and where I had heard the cries of two children being born. I had also prepared my wife for burial here, and I might as well have buried Thomas with her. I would never really know the child, kiss him, or do any of the fatherly duties I had so imagined. My heart broke and there was no repair. This was a fracture that would never stop hurting and would never heal.

Over the next few days, Henry told Johann as much as he could about Haydn and the palace of the Esterházys called Esterháza. "I have been told that the palace grounds are an entire city. Gardens, stables, houses for the staff and servants, a room of mirrors, and the palace has one hundred and twenty-six rooms. The concert hall extends over three floors, has frescoes on the ceiling and walls. The walls in almost every room have gold overlay, and the rooms all have several chandeliers. If we are not careful, we will get lost just walking in the gardens."

Johann gasped as Henry related the stories he had heard. "What a life Haydn must have there! My mind cannot see what this will be like!"

"Yes, Johann," I said, "one can only imagine what it is like to work in a palace. I have heard it rivals Louis's Versailles. Imagine! In Hungary!"

Between my regular furniture business and some valuable commissions from the wealthier citizens of Temeswar, I had been able to save up money. I told Henry I would give him enough money for both of them to travel to Fertöd, Hungary, and enough for one week's lodging. During that week, Henry would surely be able to set up an audition for Johann.

It was late October 1772, Johann was eight, and the trip could not be delayed, because the weather would soon change and make travel very unpleasant. Before he and Henry left, Johann practiced as much as he could when he was not helping his father. He continued learning the Bach and learned two short pieces by Leopold Mozart, a bourrée and minuet.

Johann continued to learn as they traveled, including his note reading and harmony lessons. They played scales and exercises together. Although Henry had hated practicing these, Johann somehow made music out of them. At night they would stop in small towns and always found someone who was willing to feed and house them. When people overheard Johann play, they would stand outside the door in amazement. For entertainment Henry would play Hungarian music, which often led to a night at the local bar or inn. At the inns, Henry was able to learn all the news of the surrounding areas and often what was happening within the Empire.

Haydn had become Count Morzin's first vice *Kapellmeister* in 1761 and was promoted to head *Kapellmeister* in 1766. Between 1770 and 1780, Haydn alone wrote at least twenty symphonies as well as string quartets, operas, piano works, and numerous works using the baryton, a bowed string instrument similar to a cello, which was Prince Nikolaus's favorite instrument. Because Nikolaus began to love opera, an opera house was also built at Esterháza. Johann would be exposed to all manner of classical music. This would be an education in itself. Hearing and watching musicians play and sing would provide the basis for his immersion into the life of a musician. He would no longer learn in solitude but in an entire world of music.

Henry and Johann continued talking about what the Esterházy palace would be like. There would certainly be a room for orchestral concerts to take place, in which the décor was as beautiful as the music. The floors would have parquet flooring with beautiful designs, and there would be chandeliers, gilded walls, and beautiful paintings and art work. Henry enthralled Johann further by adding, "I am sure that are at least one hundred rooms. Can you imagine being able to hire your own orchestra merely to entertain the Prince? There are also rooms for operas—if you don't know what that is, you are in for a feast of singing, theater, orchestral music, and fun. I hope that you will be able to see and hear all the things that the Esterházys have. Maybe it was a good idea of mine to bring you here, because I will be able to experience all of this myself." On each leg of the journey, Henry would tell of the musical adventures he had in Vienna as a choir boy at St. Stephen's. With each story, Johann's eyes grew large and a thousand questions were asked.

Once they arrived, through perseverance, Henry was able to get Johann a moment with "Papa Haydn." They had to wait three days, but during these days they could explore the grounds and get to know the servants and the daily events of the palace. Johann was immediately liked by everyone. His politeness and willingness to help endeared him to the kitchen help who fed him and Henry. They also gave Henry and Johann a place to sleep in the storage room of the kitchen. The maids and servants loved hearing Johann practice and assured him that Papa Haydn could not help but love him.

Henry asked the servants if they knew of any kind of musical employment that was available at the palace for Johann or himself. One man told him that Haydn was always looking for copyists. "They aren't paid very much, so he often loses them. Perhaps you could be a copyist and earn your lessons that way." Johann wasn't sure what that was, but he would do anything to continue his studies. He asked what a copyist was. Henry told him it was a person who copied out Haydn's compositions into individual parts for the orchestra. It was demanding work because you could not make a mistake. "But you are smart, and who knows?"

When the day arrived, Johann and Henry put on their best clothes and tuned the violin, and Johann played through the Bach twice. He was as prepared as he could be. Henry believed that Haydn would hear the beauty of Johann's soul as well as the child's astounding ability. He had to admit that he didn't teach him the most essential thing about music—its ephemeral beauty; that music caused tears in the most hardhearted person, and combined with the soul of the performer, especially such a pure one as Johann's, was one of life's greatest gifts.

They entered through the main gate and were greeted by a guard who ushered them into the rehearsal room. The guard introduced them to Haydn, who rose to meet them and shake their hands. "So, I understand you have brought a boy of exceptional talents to play for me. I assume that he wants to take lessons and study music with me. Alright, let's hear him," Haydn said with warmth. He then returned to his writing desk, sat down, and turned so that he would face away from the child. Johann played some open fifths and tuned his violin slightly. Henry went to sit in a chair at the door to the room.

It seemed that Johann was unaware that he was to start, but he was deep in concentration. He took a breath, closed his eyes, and pulled his bow across the string, steadily and slowly emitting the beginning F-sharp. The sound was soft but not timid and had a fullness to it, keeping it from being overly bright. Through the four beats of the first measure, the note grew in intensity, and it sounded like a beautiful "oh" sung by a soprano. When the first note moved to the B, it was if the air itself was changed and for a moment a swirling satin ribbon could be seen. By the end of the second measure, Haydn had heard all he needed to know that this child was a gift. The remainder of the piece was one revelation after another. Somehow this small child understood the mysteries of the music. In its entirety the composition became one undulating phrase that strung together notes, each of which was placed perfectly. The repeat of the opening phrase became a whisper, a memory that became sweeter because it was a memory. The second section moved through the modulations as if they were new currents added to an already perfect stream. The rising, insistent section was delayed by the fall of a ninth that the child treated as a logical moment, allowing the melody to sweep up again to the highest note of C-natural that although only an embellishment became a new place of beauty, allowing the final moments to return gently as if to the beginning of the stream. Haydn remained silent for the duration of Johann's audition. After a few seconds he rose and turned to face the boy, who stood quietly with the violin still under his chin. Haydn's face had turned red with emotion. He walked to Johann. Softly he spoke.

"Johann, what do you know of this piece and who composed it?"

"Nothing, sir."

"Who taught you to play this?"

Henry was not being rude when he interrupted. He only wanted to make it clear that the only thing he taught Johann were the notes and how to read them. "Sir, I merely taught him the notes. The music that you heard is from the child himself. I beg of you to take him into your care and teach him. I believe that it will be well worth your time and the time of the world."

"Sir, I will do anything to repay you," Johann said. "I love the violin and this music that it makes. I only want to be surrounded by these sounds night and day."

"Well, let us see. How about if you and your friend—Henry, is it?—stay for a month, and I will know better what to do. Henry, you can work for me, I am sure I can find plenty around here for you to do. Johann, let us find you and Henry a place to stay and we will begin some lessons tomorrow. You indeed have a miraculous talent."

Haydn's day was extremely regular. Rising early, he dressed himself and then went to a table near his pianoforte and started composing. He would stop for meals and would stretch his legs. In the evenings he would attend rehearsal or go to the opera. By nature friendly and happy, he was loved by all and would always have time for friends in the evenings. Haydn agreed to meet Johann the next morning after he had spent two hours composing, right before breaking for lunch.

Johann was ushered in, and he quietly approached Haydn's working table. He took out his violin and stood still before the great man. Haydn put down his quill and moved his papers aside. He rose from his desk and asked Johann to put his violin back in its case for a while and accompany him. They walked to a large room with many books and pieces of music. Haydn took down a folio, which had the name *J. S. Bach* written on it. "This is the man who wrote the piece you played for me. He has gone out of style. Currently we like music that is more elegant, less complex, and it is meant to please everyone. It is simple and natural but always gallant. Bach died in 1750, and sadly so did the people's taste for his music. But I believe if they hear you play they may change their minds about some of his music. Take a look at some of his compositions and tell me what you see."

Johann took the pieces of paper and studied them. He turned to the second and third sheet and then back to the first. He was unsure what Haydn wanted him to see. He could read many of the notes but was unsure about so many of the other markings. "Sir, I do not know what you want me to say. I see many, many notes that seem to have patterns and designs to them if I look at them all at once. If I look at them as individual notes they are just like other pieces of music. The whole piece seems like a weaving of some sort. It is very beautiful and complex."

Haydn then showed him a folio of music marked with words he could not read. "There are fewer notes and more white spaces," Johann said. "It looks as if I could play it now."

"Johann, this is a simple way to show you the difference between Bach's music and the music that is popular today. As you can see, one is much more complex than the other. The one that looks simpler is an opera by Pergolesi, *La serva padrona*. It is a comic opera that people love. It is something that everyone can like and enjoy. It is about everyday life and everyday people. Like the Prince, people want fun entertainment, and comic opera is how they are entertained. We do many operas here at the palace. As you said, the lines in the Bach seem to weave together. What do you notice about the lines in the Pergolesi opera and how they relate to each other?"

Johann noticed that there appeared to be phrases that were of the same length and that the notes, if you lined them up and down the page, were also easier to comprehend together than Bach's.

"These differences do not make one better than the other. They are just different and people's tastes change. Now music like Pergolesi's is what they want to hear. It has a regular, structured feeling to it. It is like adding building blocks that are all the same size to create a building. I can tell that you really love the Bach you played for me. Play the piece again for me on the violin I have brought in, and then tell me what it is that you love so much."

Johann picked up the violin and tuned it. Placing it under his chin, he pulled the bow slowly over the F-sharp. The violin was better than the one he had played and learned on, and at first he was startled by the beautiful sound the violin emitted. He continued through the entirety of the piece, stopped, and held his bow over the strings. Johann took time thinking about what he loved in the piece. The beauty of the sounds from this violin only increased his love and admiration for the composition.

"When I play this piece, I feel as if the melody is being spun out as in the story of Rumpelstiltskin. My father told me this story when I was much younger. I couldn't imagine making gold from straw. But I think this is what Bach does. He takes notes and makes gold."

"Johann, that is a magnificent image. What else do you hear or feel when you play this?"

"I don't hear anything else, just these notes. I don't think about myself. It is like the music is somehow inside me and being released as I play. The entire world goes away. I also think there are more ways for me to play this piece and I am only doing it one way. Can you teach me another way?"

"Let's not think about that right now. There are so many beautiful pieces for you to learn, and learn to love. Here is a sonata written by an Italian, Porpora, whom I knew in Vienna. It was written in 1754, I imagine before you were born. The Italians have a great history of violin-making and writing for the violin. I especially like Porpora's compositions for voice. I think many of the great composers write for instruments as they would for the voice. They try to find what I call a singing melody. This is Sonata in C Major for two violins. Do you know what it means when I say C Major?"

"Yes, no sharps or flats and the third of the scale . . ."

"Play the C Major scale for me so we can talk about that third."

Johann did and they talked about the major scales and what makes a scale minor. Haydn played the first movement so Johann could hear it and watch the notes. He then asked Johann to play with him as much as he could. Not really amazed but happily pleased, Johann was able to get through the first movement without too many mistakes. They had to stop a few times for Haydn to show Johann bowing, phrasing, and wrong notes.

"Take this and practice it for a couple of days. The tempo is like walking at a very slow pace."

Haydn then walked slowly around the room as Johann played the opening again to show him what the word *adagio* meant in regards to tempo. "*Adagio* means slow." He also told him that the movements labeled *adagio* were to be the most expressive and heartfelt. "You don't need to worry about anything but the right notes. Put your own heart into it, as you do with the Bach. I will see you again in two days and hear what you have accomplished. Do you have questions?"

"No, sir. Thank you so much. I will work very hard. Do you have any work I can do for you?" He started to hand the violin back to Haydn.

"No, Johann, keep the violin for a while. It seems to suit you. As far as work goes, do you think you could gather all the music from the music stands in the music room from our performance last night? Put them all in the folder on the harpsichord. Then straighten up the room for tonight. Oh, there is a rehearsal tonight. You should come. Hearing music is a large part of a music education. Be there after dinner."

Haydn then left the room, leaving Johann in a daze. He thought: "I should have asked him more questions. I don't know what some of the marks mean on the page. I will only learn the notes as he told me."

That evening Johann eagerly went to the rehearsal. They were practicing a new symphony by Haydn. The opening four notes made Johann jump from his chair and knock it over. The musicians stopped abruptly and looked at him. Haydn declared, "Ah, exactly the reaction I was hoping for." Johann was to learn that this symphony was a kind of experiment Haydn was undertaking.

The next day, Haydn called on Johann to walk with him before sitting down to write. "Johann, what did you think about last night?"

Johann did not know where to start. "Sir, there is so much I thought, that the thoughts kept me awake all night. The opening notes, which would startle anyone thinking they were about to hear, as you say, music that was pleasant. And then, those trembling fast notes. My heart started beating faster. There also seemed to be large breaks and the music would change completely."

"Yes, those are called movements and they are meant to change character."

"I loved hearing all the instruments. I don't know the names of all of them."

The conversation continued with Johann giving Haydn a fresh and innocent view of his music. This was not the opinion of some jaded music critic who had an ax to grind, but an honest hearing. These conversations became crucially important to Haydn as a way to learn how his music was heard by an ear not colored by years of hearing, playing, or analyzing music. Johann, on the other hand, gained a musical education without being in a classroom.

Johann's progress on the violin soared by leaps and bounds. In a year, Henry was so amazed that he felt a bit jealous and intimidated. He decided to return to Temeswar and continue his teaching and playing there. It was certainly time to return. "Johann would not really miss me," he thought. "He will make friends with the musicians here quickly." Although Johann had written his father letters, Henry could now tell Stefan the stories of his son's advancement and how much Haydn loved him. In fact, Johann was almost a constant companion to Haydn. He was so well-mannered that no one really even noticed him. He was always there to do little things for Papa Haydn.

Johann wrote often to his father about the happenings at court, his lessons, and most of all his dreams for the future. "I hope that I will be able to play for all the courts in Europe. I know I can bring them joy, longing, sorrow, hope, and all the other human emotions when I play. I can make lives better. Also, it helps me not miss you so much, dear Papa."

By the time Johann was sixteen, he was able to play in the orchestra when extra players were needed. The men were kind to him, even though some were a bit jealous. They realized what an enormous talent he had. Because Johann was so kindhearted and considerate, he never really felt or observed their jealousy. Also, Haydn was sure that he never played favorites and Johann was treated no differently from the other musicians.

By 1780, Haydn knew that Johann was ready for the larger musical world. He had written a Te Deum for Empress Maria Theresa. She had commissioned it, and Prince Nikolaus had agreed to let Haydn compose it for her. In late summer Haydn took Johann to Vienna, where he could introduce him to the Empress, play for her privately, and play in the orchestra for the Te Deum. Haydn believed firmly that once people had heard Johann, he would find a patron—if not the Empress herself, then one of the others who would be at the concert. He would also take him for a short visit to Vienna, the musical center of Europe.

Johann was thrilled about the trip. He imagined so much happening that his thoughts kept him awake, and often during the day they kept him from practicing and from his work of copying parts as well as checking instrumental and vocal parts for mistakes. Even the most experienced of copiers would delete or repeat a measure, words, or articulation and dynamic markings. Tedious but important work, it also allowed great insight into the compositional processes of Haydn. Johann had never tried composition; he feared that it would be a dismal attempt after performing and hearing Haydn's compositions.

Johann traveled in the carriages of musicians and singers Haydn was taking with him. This allowed him to hear stories about the Empress. "She has a good voice, and I understand in private concerts Haydn has accompanied her." "She is a great lover of music and is a patron of some musicians." "I hear that it will be performed for the arrival of Lord Nelson." These and other conversations about people he had never met or heard of filled the days. The most important piece of information was talk about the child prodigy Mozart who was in Vienna. Although the musicians were situated in Hungary, news and gossip about musicians traveled far and wide.

Johann found his life turned around after his arrival in Vienna. The performance of Haydn's Te Deum was received with great *bravos,* and the Empress herself rose to kiss Haydn. Johann was able to procure an audience with Maria Theresa the next day.

"Your Majesty, my name is Johann Fritz and I am a student of Maestro Haydn. I would like to play for you *Variations on La Folia,* accompanied by Maestro Haydn and Herr Weigl on cello." Johann had done his own arrangement, taking elements of those composed by Marais, Corelli, Vivaldi, and Scarlatti. He had studied all to learn the technique of variation writing, improvisation, articulation, bowing, and ornamentation.

When he was done, Maria Theresa went over to Johann and asked him to come sit with her. Haydn and Weigl left, and Johann accompanied the Empress to a small sitting room.

"Johann, as a lover of music, I can say with certainty, your playing was remarkable, not just because of your virtuosity but because of the depth of feeling with which you imbue the music. Each variation was a new—let me see how to say this—a new world. Your lessons with Haydn have served you well, I assume."

In fact, Johann's performance had been extraordinary. One variation seemed to drop tears. Soft, like a whisper, it conveyed a loss that could not be spoken. The leaps were impeccably in tune and played with aplomb. The rests were filled with anticipation. Each variation seemed to flow effortlessly from the preceding one. The siciliano was not pastoral but rather like a lament. It was reminiscent of Bach's use of the siciliano in "Erbarme dich." Some variations appeared to carry words, as if the notes could create sentences and thoughts. The whole composition urged the listener on to the last variation. On the last variation, Haydn and Weigl had stopped playing and Johann became fire.

"He has been my guide through everything. He has become a teacher and father to me. I cannot repay him or thank him enough," Johann said to Maria Theresa.

"What are your aspirations, Johann?"

"More than anything in the world, I would like to share music with the world. I am not interested in the fame it would bring, but rather the joy of playing and seeing its effect on people. It is my language."

"Well, Johann, I can be of service to you in this if you promise to visit me often and play for me. There is an aria from this child-man Mozart from his opera *Il Re Pastore*, "L'amerò, sarò costante," that has come into my hands. It has a violin obligato. I would like you to learn it and perform it with me at my next concert here in the palace. To ensure that you have a place to live and practice I will procure a room for you at the *Michaelerhaus*. Porpora, a remarkable woman composer Marianna Martines, and the Dowager live there. This will put you in touch with people you will need to know and with whom to cultivate friendships. There are many private concerts here in Vienna where you can meet patrons and may even meet this young Mozart."

Johann was speechless but managed to stand and kiss the hand of Maria Theresa and mumble a thank you.

"You will need to stop mumbling and assert yourself, Johann, if you are going to make it in this circle of musicians. Doors will not open up by magic or because of your talent. Be assertive in life, as you are in your playing. Play for everyone, and everywhere. I am sure you will bring joy and astonishment to those who hear you."

By the next day, Johann had settled in. Haydn came to visit and said his goodbyes and left with a short blessing: "Work hard and remember what music is to you. God bless."

In a few weeks, after rehearsing with the Empress Maria Theresa, Johann and she gave a private concert of the aria and some other pieces by Mozart. Johann's violin matched the vocal quality of Maria Theresa with the uttermost sensitivity. It was as if two perfectly matched voices were answering each other with words of everlasting love. The everlasting quality was tied to the yearning the violin produced in its echo of the voice, especially in the cadenza. Johann had written his own cadenza to the aria. Neither "voice" outshone the other. They were united as in perfect love. There was a deep silence after the aria.

Johann's life became hectic and filled with anxiety for the next few months. It was wise of Haydn to have taught him all the major violin pieces so he could pull them out and perform them at short notice. He met all the important patrons, and they were willing to help him. He found himself in the circles of Vienna's greatest musicians, professional and amateur, and intellectuals. He often thought, "Am I worthy to be in the company of such people?" Reserved by nature, he talked only when spoken to directly. He realized he had much learning and reading to do in order to be an active part of such circles. He contacted Haydn and asked him to send more scores and a reading list that included philosophy, poetry, and music treatises. When he was not playing he was reading. Eventually he became more accustomed to participating in the conversations. He became known as a serious thinker whose opinion was not to be taken lightly.

One question that had settled into Johann's mind occurred after his performance of Mozart's "L'amerò, sarò costante." Was there a difference in the effects created by the music when the melody was sung and when it was played on the violin? The audience seemed moved without any notion of the text. How many times did they need to hear the text—or in fact, did they need to hear it at all? Yet he knew that in sacred music what inspired him was the singing of great religious texts set to wonderful music. It seemed that the words inspired the music. When he asked these questions one night, everyone had a different opinion. He concluded for the evening, saying, "Is it not sound, then, that we respond to? If a person doesn't speak German, how can he respond to a German text in the same way a German does? Yet he does."

As he walked home, he also was transfixed by the notion that he did not know what made a melody beautiful or even from where melody came. He only knew that he would rather play than think, and that in playing he understood great mysteries. But, alas, these mysteries could not be put into words.

In more discussions he began to understand that these questions were ancient and had never been answered. He listened to people discuss Plato's views on music, and even Mozart once spoke up and said his father had told him that Adam was imitating birds when he created music. "But what does it matter?" Mozart added. "We all know the power of music, and we should just carry on."

But Johann strove to understand the "why" of music.
It was from Beethoven that Johann would begin to learn the answer.

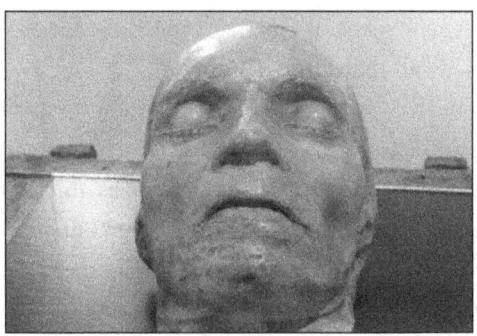

Beethoven's House, Front page of score to Fidelio,
Beethoven's death mask (personal photographs)

A new chapter Johann's life began in 1793 when he met and befriended the great composer Beethoven. Beethoven had left his home in Bonn for Vienna at the age of twenty-two, when he was invited to study with Haydn. Count Waldstein had given him letters of introduction to ensure that he would meet wealthy patrons. However, his studies with Haydn were tumultuous. Two more different personalities and approaches to music did not exist. Haydn had both feet in the Classical style, and Beethoven was leaping towards the Romantic. What Beethoven wanted and needed; Haydn was not able to give.

Beethoven took Vienna by storm and quickly took on the title of "Vienna's greatest pianist." Through a series of competitions, Beethoven was able to defeat the other pianists in the city. His improvisations were beyond comprehension; when he played his own compositions, women wept because of the emotions they evoked in them; and his compositions, whether for the piano, the symphony, or the string quartet, often introduced innovations, and many were declared unplayable. Beethoven had assimilated the models of Mozart and Haydn and was ready to forge beyond them. The major personal crisis he faced at the beginning of his creative powers was deafness.

In a letter, Beethoven wrote: "You will realize what a sad life I must now lead. Seeing that I am cut off from everything that is dear and precious to me . . . I must withdraw from everything and my best years will rapidly pass away without my being able to achieve all that my talent and strength has commanded me to do." With a sure and forceful belief in his talents, he did not give up. Deafness seemed to help him block out "old" sounds in order to create new ones. A new surge of creativity was unleashed as a great storm on an ocean, swallowing all that came before.

Johann heard Beethoven play his own piano compositions several times between the years 1798 and 1802. He left the performances in a state of wonder. He believed fervently that Beethoven was able to create in musical notes entire thoughts, a philosophy not only of art but about the meaning of life and art. Beethoven's music had opened a floodgate of personal emotion about life and death, happiness and sorrow, pathos and desire.

Haydn had introduced Johann to him in the year 1793 after one of Beethoven's concerts in the salon of Prince Lobkowitz. He played several of Bach's preludes and fugues, which was the highlight of the evening. Haydn told him how much Johann admired Bach and that Johann played Bach with exceptional beauty.

Beethoven remarked, "So, you are the violinist I have been hearing about from Haydn. You have made an impression upon him, especially the Bach you played for him. I love Bach." He then made a very good joke: "He [Bach] is not a brook but an ocean." The word *Bach* in German means creek or brook.

"Why don't you come to my house with Haydn and play for me tomorrow?" he added.

"Of course!"

The next day, Johann arrived at 10:00 a.m. Not knowing what his habits or composing times were, he knocked sharply at the door and heard nothing and feared that he was not there. Johann knocked again more loudly and called, "Herr Beethoven?"

"Come in!" he finally answered in a loud and irritated manner.

Johann did and feared that the meeting was to be a disaster. In front of me I found a disheveled man and a room in need of assistance. Beethoven seemed neither embarrassed nor willing to change either condition.

"Ah, Johann. I had forgotten you were coming. Please play the violin part from Bach's Suite in D, the second movement, that Haydn has raved so much about."

Johann didn't even take off my coat. As quickly as possible, he took the violin out of its case, tuned, took a deep breath, steadied my bow over the string, and commenced playing.

He waited a few moments after Johann finished, then came up to him and locked his dark eyes on his. "Well, that is something. Why don't you play something of mine and see what you do with that? Here is the violin part of a piano trio that I am working on. I think you can read it—with difficulty, I guess. I will play the piano, of course, and try to fill in the necessary cello parts. This one should give people food for thought!"

They played the first movement together. Although it was dark and brooding, there was also a sense of lyricism. The opening was started almost like a question and then turned into a flurry of notes. The piece moved quickly between harmonic centers. The piano part was very virtuosic, and it seemed as if the cello was going to receive an equal treatment with the violin and piano. At the end Johnn had many, many questions, and having no background in composition, he feared that the questions were silly. Beethoven, however, seemed engaged in what he was asking. When Johann asked him if he thought the music had a meaning, his eyes lit up and he answered with great force, "Yes".

"Do you sense that the opening themes are in an argument and trying find the truth? Music is a revelation. It reveals thoughts, passions, ideas, and—yes—my life. My music expresses what is in my mind and my soul, and it reaches out to you, inviting you into the discussion. Music can free us from the misery of life and offer us freedom." Then, to Johann's surprise, he sat down at his desk and started editing the score.

It was as if there was no one in the room with him. He was somewhere else and alone with his thoughts. Johann finally said goodbye. He spoke without looking up. "Come back next week and I will have more for you to play."

After a month or so Johann was asked to join him regularly. Sometimes he was there but too busy to see Johann, sometimes they met in the coffee house, and sometimes Beethoven forgot. However, he asked me to play the first violin part in the premiere of the three piano trios at Prince Lebowski's. "Haydn will be there, and I believe he will have things to say—as he usually does."

Haydn was there. "Herr Beethoven, what a wonderful evening of chamber music. The first two piano trios were top notch. The third was rather, well, how should I say this? I would hold off publishing it. I believe the public will not understand it and find it too difficult."

"Why, because it does not sound like you?" Beethoven answered with obvious irritation. "Why should I copy you and not find my own way? Find a different path, one that I dare say will be better?"

At this point Haydn turned to walk away, and Beethoven stormed out of the house. "He is just a jealous fool with no real imagination." He shouted loud enough for many to hear.

Johann did not follow him, believing that conversation with him would be impossible after this perceived affront. I did write a note expressing my enormous gratitude to him for allowing me to perform such inspired works with him.

Johann attended a performance of Beethoven's *Eroica* at the palace of Prince Lobkowitz in August of 1804. It was dedicated to the prince. Everyone had heard the story of how Beethoven, who originally dedicated the symphony to Napoleon, had violently scratched off the dedication on the title page when he heard that Napoleon had declared himself Emperor. Beethoven had in consternation loudly stated, "So he is no more than a common mortal! Now, too, he will tread underfoot all the rights of Man, indulge only his ambition; now he will think himself superior to all men, become a tyrant!"

Beethoven, during the two battles Napoleon waged against Vienna, sided with the Viennese, even setting the words of a patriotic poem "Ein grosses deutsches Volk sind wir" ("A great German people are we") to music. Beethoven did agree with the ideals of the French revolution, which were antimonarchical and democratic. He had compared Napoleon to the great consuls of ancient Rome; but *Emperor* was another name for a monarch and against all democratic ideals.

The reviews of Symphony No. 3 in E-flat were far from flattering. Many complained that it was too long, that it had no beauty, was untamed. Some, a minority, saw it as the model for high class music. In the journal *Der Freymüthige* in 1806 it was written: "If it does not please now, it is because the public is not cultured enough, artistically, to grasp all these lofty beauties; after a few thousand years have passed it will not fail of its effect." What I heard was a miracle.

One of Beethoven's favorite books was Homer's *Odyssey*. He loved the stories of the ancient Greek heroes who, through trials that brought them near death, became transformed. As Johann listened to the last movement, I heard a theme that he had used in his *Prometheus* ballet. In a moment, Johann understood that to Beethoven the hero was a person like Prometheus, who gave light, enlightenment, to the people. Before going home after the performance, Johann stopped at a café to talk with friends. They spent hours discussing the meaning of the symphony, and why Beethoven used a dance theme from his Prometheus ballet in the last movement. They finally concluded that the last movement had such joy and abandonment to it that it must represent some kind of transformation. The clue for me was the missing C-sharp in the last movement's theme. The theme was also so truncated. Johann said to his friends, "it isn't really a theme, it is only open fifths. It outlines the important notes of the original theme of movement one."

The second movement could only be called a funeral march. Johann suggested that since Beethoven believed the symphony was in the memory of a great man, the funeral must be for the man.

"Yes," chimed in one of the friends. "And as in the fourth movement, the C-sharp is missing, but he does give us a whole triad, not just fifths."

"But why?" was the big question.

Johann's student Marie, who had joined the group of friends, added that she felt the only movement that did harken back to the opening theme was movement three. "Why would he use the same material, altering it slightly in some movements, and leave it out in one?"

"My guess is that he is transforming it. Eventually only using the most essential elements. Stripping the theme, or maybe even a hero, of everything and leaving just the essence, the life force of the person," Johann added with some hesitation. The only way to know for sure was to ask Beethoven himself.

Days later Johann remembered conversations he had had with Beethoven. His beliefs that music did mean something, that it sought to be a "higher philosophy." Johann concluded that Beethoven felt that somehow music was like an epic, where the notes embodied the deeds of the great, the flow of thought, the dialectical process, the holy, and morality. If Johann was right about these concepts, then the *Eroica* was about the ideal of Hero. Not a single person, but the idea of great heroism. Johann began to realize that at the core of the symphony was also the life of Beethoven. The first movement was the hero in all his glory and that the C-sharp in the opening theme was a foreboding that something would destroy or weaken the hero. The funeral march was the outcome of some struggle or plight. But did it mean death? Could it not also be a realization that struggle is essential to test the resilience and mettle of the hero? Overcoming was essential to the actualization of the hero. What joy there would be, knowing that life will continue and that through the test one gains supremacy and a spiritual awakening. The symphony with its germ of a motive from Prometheus now became something miraculous. A revolution of its own, more powerful than anything Napoleon could achieve. Here was freedom, true freedom. Freedom to create, think, feel, and live.

Try as he might, Johann could not explain how this realization impacted him, but he felt that he now knew that notes were more than sound. His group of friends discussed his concept of the symphony for weeks. He bought a copy of the score and with my analytical skills attempted to go further into understanding these mysteries.

The time he was able to spend with Beethoven became less and less as the years passed. However, each meeting was of the greatest importance, even if all he did was listen to the conversations around him. His belief in the power of music to reach an understanding of the great mysteries never wavered. As his music grew more complex and harder to understand, Johann could sense the enormous struggle within this great man to deal with not only his physical suffering but also the injustices of the world, the loss of liberty, and how to achieve the ideals of the enlightenment. Although his music was clearly about the power of emotions, he also understood the importance of freedom. In reality he was imprisoned by deafness, as Florestan was, in his opera *Fidelio,* and as humanity was imprisoned by tyranny.

It was not until his ninth and last symphony, which was premiered in 1824, that he reached an answer. In one bold gesture he reaches out to all of us in the fourth movement, as the bass soloist sings "No more these sounds." Not just the sounds of the music but the sounds of tyranny. "Rather let us sing agreeably and joyfully." What strange words for the soloist to sing before the music of Schiller's "Ode to Joy." Beethoven interrupts the chaos of instrumental music that preceded the words, halting the music to say, "Rather than this, there should be this." Not chaos but harmony, simple song, and joy. Should we be divided by mere custom when there is such beauty and joy in the world for all of us? Certainly, above the stars is a loving Father. Put away war and conflict and live in peace and joy.

With a stroke of enormous brilliance and faith, Beethoven uses words when perhaps the sound is not enough. Words and music together, the human and the spiritual worlds are joined to present his argument and, like a bolt of lightning, reach out to all.

Johann had gladly agreed to play in the orchestra for the premiere. At the rehearsals, he almost stopped playing when the bass soloist intruded on the orchestra with the words "No more these sounds." There is no other way to describe the moment when he heard the powerful voice with an expansive interval of a fifth on the word *friends,* which he then held for what seemed an exorbitant time but to say that it was a command.

What followed was a simple folk tune, or maybe better a hymn. Beethoven then through orchestral sound and voices illuminated the world about a higher and more spiritual way to live in the world, as a free, moral person. Freedom to be. Freedom to live in peace. Freedom to love. Yes, he had liberated not only himself from suffering but the entire world.

Johann wept throughout the fourth movement and at times believed he was hearing what Beethoven must have heard from God in his deafness. Flights of angels, choruses of people, dancing, and people kissing. This became for Johann the greatest moment of my life. To be there with this man in a hall where everyone rose from their seats in honor of him and in agreement with his vision. This music invaded all his being and all my thoughts.

Johann visited Beethoven for the last time shortly after the premiere of his Ninth Symphony. His only desire was to tell him how much playing in the concert and hearing this music had meant to me. Beethoven looked so much older than the last time I had seen him. He was also weak, and I sensed he was suffering horribly from his abdominal issues. Johann did not stay long for fear of keeping him from something important or adding to his suffering by forcing him to talk with me through the arduous process of reading my written questions and thoughts, for by now he was completely deaf. He was glad to see Johann and thanked him for his fine insights about the Ninth. Johann thanked him profusely for the friendship and for sharing with him his ideas about life and music. He said, "I don't think I am dying yet! Save all those thoughts for when you visit me on my deathbed. I will need the cheering up." Johann apologized for making him think that is what I meant. He asked him what his next project was, and he stated that he had several ideas about his latest string quartet. His publisher had asked him to do another finale for his Op. 130. He had originally written a Grosse Fugue. I could not but think that Bach on his deathbed had written a fugue. Beethoven showed me the fugue, and as with everything else he had written, Johann was taken by its complexity.

"This is terribly difficult and demanding for the players," Johann said. "Were they able to carry it off?"

"Of course not. I might as well have had cattle playing the instruments," he replied.

They both laughed at the thought of cattle playing. The vision of cattle sitting in chairs and trying to hold the instruments was more than amusing, and he made noises of what he thought it would sound like.

With him now in good spirits, Johann took his departure. Kissed his hand, as if he were a king, and left. He walked home sullen and deep in thought, sure that this would be the last time he saw him.

Beethoven died on March 26, 1827. He was only fifty-six, but the severe illnesses he had suffered made him appear years older. Reports surfaced about his last days and what he had to endure. His abdomen was drained at least five times, becoming infected the first time. Thankfully, he eventually slipped into a coma. When they moved his wasted body, they saw horrendous bedsores. Both his sister-in-law and his close friend Hüttenbrenner were at his side. His last words were "Pity. Pity—too late." They were a response to learning his publisher had sent him twelve bottles of wine. Johann like to believe that God knew this great man had written all that was in his soul and he did not die before he was finished with his work.

PART THREE

Thomas

Drink beer for health!
—Hildegard of Bingen

The monks gave Thomas a new name, "Pomuk," after the patron saint of Temeswar. St. John of Nepomuk was the patron saint of secrets. The name was perfect for Thomas since he was a secret that the monks had agreed to keep. The story of the saint was one that everyone grew up knowing. St. John had refused to divulge the secret of the confessional when King Wenceslaus asked him to reveal his wife's confessions in order to learn if she had a lover. St. John was drowned, and legend had it that his tongue remained intact in his tomb for three centuries. So, Thomas was Pomuk and the monks kept the secret of Stefan's confession.

As quiet and serious as Johann was, Thomas was gregarious and lively. He never was in trouble, but he was mischievous. He loved hiding things from the monks—especially the older ones who tended to be forgetful—and stealing bread from the kitchen, was usually late for vespers (or any religious service), and was known to laugh during prayers because he was thinking of other things, such as the look on a monk's face when Thomas purposely sang too loudly in church.

Like Johann, Thomas was also on a journey of discovery. Thomas often followed the monk Sebastian on his duties with the sick. He would listen carefully as Sebastian explained what was wrong with the patient and what the monks' methods were to heal and help the patient once they had determined what was wrong. Often Thomas would hand bandages, pastes, and medicines to Sebastian, always asking what the medicines were, how they were made, and how they helped. As Thomas grew older, he was able to do certain procedures by himself. Thomas also found new ways of helping the patients. The most important aspect of his work was how he treated the people who were under his care. He talked to all the patients as if he knew them personally. With the children, he was their best friend or big brother. The monks noticed that the patients Thomas talked to and spent time with seemed to recover more quickly. They realized that time spent with the patients was as important as any medicine. This was especially true with those whom they considered beyond hope. The medicines that took away pain did not comfort the soul. Thomas had found a way to prepare these patients for death. The monks also found that when Thomas made the children laugh and smile, their pain seemed to diminish. He allowed the children to occasionally play jokes on him. They would pretend they were asleep when he came to change dressings or give them medicine, and they would hide the food they didn't like, and hide under the cot to avoid the older, less friendly monks. The simple act of reading and telling stories helped their aching bodies to relax and helped them go to sleep.

As time went on, it became known that Pomuk was a gifted and gentle healer. He had a gentleness and a kind of confidence that made the patients believe everything was fine and would be fine. He began preparing medicines for the patients and was amazed at the effects, good and bad, that they had on people. One of the monks who worked in the pharmacy gave Pomuk a book by a famous German nun, Hildegard von Bingen, who was a healer. It was amazing how things found in nature could cure certain ailments. He studied her book *Physica* arduously and learned about the healing properties of plants, trees, rocks, foods, and animals. There were plants he had never heard of and a world of ideas he had never envisioned. He tried a few of her medicines, of course with the permission of the monks. Field mint was for discharges of the eye, fennel for digestion and melancholy, valerian for pleurisy, and ivy cooked in water and placed on the thigh and navel of a woman would help with heavy menstrual flow. Pomuk had to ask the monks about many of the illnesses and medical issues that Hildegard talked about in the book. He would often follow the doctors and monks and give these treatments to the patients. Even if they did not heal the patient, the patients felt better. More and more, Pomuk began to believe that these simple medicines were helping. He believed that the time he took with patients, talking and visiting, also helped. Pomuk started his own garden of herbs at the monastery to use on his rounds and share with the monks.

The monks encouraged Pomuk to write down the remedies he used and to include the simple things he did to relieve some of the pain and suffering. Pomuk gladly did this and organized a book that was like Hildegard's. He found that the patients with whom he had built friendships seemed to heal faster than those who were unfriendly or distant. He also observed that those dying were helped greatly by the spiritual support of the monks and merely the presence of another person who held their hands.

Father Petr decided that Pomuk should take his gifts and his love of healing seriously and study with an apothecary. Temeswar had one that was established in 1735. According to Habsburg law, one had to study with an apothecary for five years before opening one's own store. It was possible that Pomuk could also become a lay doctor or resident healer.

At sixteen, Pomuk went off to study with the pharmacist at "The Black Eagle." Thomas was thrilled to be learning about healing and the arts of medicine. He had become well known for his garden of herbs, and mothers often came to him when their children were sick. He supplied his herbs, stones, and gems to the pharmacist, Wolfgang Herder.

Herr Herder was delighted with Thomas's book of "cures," and the two of them set off to provide people with Thomas's discoveries. Thomas was encouraged to learn more about remedies that could be supplied at the pharmacy. In the evenings he read as much as he could of Hildegard's book. He experimented on himself and Herr Herder. Of course, there were failures, but many of his concoctions were excellent. He found that he could make herbal teas that helped with stuffy noses, digestion problems, inflammations, and aches and pains. Steaming the herbs in the sick room also gave comfort and broke up congestion. He made many different kinds of salves, and of course there were the mixtures with horrible odors, which—no matter how well they would have worked—no one would buy. Clearing the store of their scents was another issue, for which mint, lavender, and sage worked the best. Women came in and would ooh and aah over how wonderful the store smelled, and Pomuk began using herbs in homemade soaps and creating mists that the women used on themselves or in their homes. Many asked if he had mists to attract men, keep away bugs, help children sleep, and even help men stop drinking. For attracting men and helping them stop drinking, he assured the women that he had no cure; but he found that cinnamon could keep some bugs away, and velarium could help with children who didn't want to go to sleep.

Pomuk also provided another service to the village. After the store had closed for the day, on his way home he would stop by the women's homes and deliver their medicine. They of course always invited him in, and he would have delicious dinners and desserts with them. He was the women's favorite "son." If only they were younger and they could marry him! they often exclaimed, or, if only their sons had turned out like Pomuk!

Thomas cut a fine figure. He was tall, well built, with beautiful wavy hair and shining brown eyes. Walking down the street, he always greeted everyone with a "good day" or "how are you," and he meant it. He stopped for chats to catch up with everyone and all the news of the day. Straight-backed and confident, no one would know that he carried with him the silent sorrow of abandonment. He wondered daily about why his mother and father had left him. The love of the monks was vast, but he knew that other children had the love of parents, which was different. Thomas had asked a few times, and the monks said they knew nothing of his past, only that they had found him at their door. They assured him that many loving mothers had done the same when they knew their circumstances prevented them from keeping the child. He wanted to shout: "Like what?" Resigned and sad, he eventually stopped asking questions. He knew kindness in his life, and maybe that was more than enough. As he worked in the village, he saw beaten children and wives, men dying from alcohol, and syphilis. Kindness was as necessary as love. Love did not stop the beatings or the drinking.

Pomuk was too busy learning and healing to court girls, though many girls tried to gain his favor. There were always simple, homemade presents left at the store for him, often with forward invitations to come to dinner or visit the bar. Pomuk always refused politely. He knew that he would find the right wife on his own. For the present, he was enjoying life and had all that he wanted.

My life after Sophie's death was solitary, but I soon settled into a routine. Although I was never really happy, I was content. I could not be with my sons, but I did know they were good people. I had friends who always raised my spirits, and my shop seemed to be always busy. Gretchen helped me with my laundry and baking, but I found cooking enjoyable. I would often have Gretchen's family over for a Sunday dinner of ham, potatoes, and vegetables. Her children were wonderful and most of the time not fighting. They often helped in my garden with weeding, as long as I supervised to make sure it was weeds they pulled. Gretchen would leave bread, butter, and jam for breakfasts. Sausage and cheese were always available at the store.

I often encountered a young woman at the meat store. One day, we talked about which cut of meat was better for goulash and which was best for roasting. Of course, like a thrifty woman, she also told me what to do with leftovers if I bought a roast. I chose the roast. She then helped me pick out the best spices and vegetables. One afternoon we continued talking as we left the store. Her name was Katrina. I asked her if she would like to have a glass of wine or a cup of coffee with me. I hoped that since she had seen me several times, she would not be too shy but say yes. She did.

We walked down the street to a shop that made the best Red Forest Cake outside of my mother's kitchen. Conversation was slow. When I asked her if she liked poetry and who was her favorite poet, her face brightened, and she smiled. Her whole mien changed, and then our conversation became so animated that people turned to look. One man who was in earshot chortled, "Who would think that discussing poets and poetry would be this stimulating?" I turned and asked invitingly if he wanted to join in the conversation.

"*Nein*, but thank you for asking. You know there are two small bookstores in Temeswar. Why not visit them and build a library of poetry for yourselves?" Of course, we took him up on his idea, and the next day I closed my shop and the two of us took a day's outing to Temeswar. We had enough money between us for each of us to buy one book of poetry. We found a book of poems by Herder, called *Stimmen der Völker in Liedern* (the voice of the folk in songs). It seemed perfect. Poems of the voice of the people. Igniting my interest in poetry again was a godsend. I found myself happy when I read the poems, and having someone to read them with me was wonderful. I had forgotten how much I loved reading words and the way poets put them together. I was always amazed how the words took on different meanings when used by poets. Simple, common words took on connotations I had never thought possible. A path became a way into the future or the past, a bloom was a young girl, a mountain was a cathedral.

Katrina and I often met on Sundays for lunch. Gretchen was glad to see that I had made a new friend, and I am sure she hoped that it would develop into a romance. Katrina would pack a basket with homemade bread, sausages, fruits, and wine. We would sit under the beautiful trees that had grown up around my house. In my mind, under the trees, looking at the landscape of farms and houses, we became part of the poetry.

Our favorite poem was Herder's German translation of "The Erl-King's Daughter." Dark and evil, it reminded me of some of the folk stories I grew up with. Katrina would read the lines spoken by the daughter. I tried my best to be dramatic and read like an actor, but I think I failed miserably. With defiance I recited the words "No, I will not dance with you," and horror struck on the last line:

"*Da lag Herr Oluf, und er war tot. Aber der Tanz geht so leicht durch den Hain.*"

There lay Herr Oluf, and he was dead. But the dance, ever so lightly through the grove, went on.

Katrina laughed and said I sounded like an old man with a terrible cold.

We had a common interest in poetry. Unlike Sophie, Katrina's interest was intellectual. I found this comforting. She would be able to understand my sorrows in life.

One evening I invited her to my house for dinner. She thought my request strange, since she really didn't believe that men cooked. I told her it would be nothing special, I only thought she would enjoy having me work, rather than her doing all the cooking and cleaning. This was also a very novel and unusual thought for her. She seemed skeptical but agreed. I had picked some flowers and put them in a vase, put a tablecloth on the table with napkins, and tried to make the house look as if a woman could live there. After dinner I asked her to marry me.

Katrina's mother and father were thrilled that their daughter had found a man to marry. She thought herself plain and was therefore quiet and did little to attract attention. I, however, found her beautiful. Her leg had been broken when a cow she was milking bolted suddenly and struck her. She would always walk with a limp that made her slow, and therefore she did not go out often. I did not notice it nearly as much as she; I was glad I had met someone with whom to share my time. She was easy to talk to, loved poetry, and did not mind my bouts of silence. Physically, she could not have been more different from Sophie. She was tall and sturdy with unruly blond hair and pale blue eyes. Her face was oval and long. Her lips were full and very seductive. She was very beautiful, but even though I told her so, she did not believe me.

We married in a quiet ceremony in May of 1783 with only her parents attending. She had made a lovely new dress for herself, and I bought a new suit and shoes. She kept house and fed me, and as time went on, we learned to love each other.

On a cold day in November 1783, my friend Gretchen and her daughters, Helga and Rosina, entered the pharmacy where Thomas was an apprentice. Gretchen now had three children, and her youngest, Jacob, had spent the night coughing. She wanted some herbs for the sore throats that were vexing the family. When she started to pay, she took a long, hard look at Pomuk.

"*Mein Gott!* You look exactly like Herr Fritz when he was your age. I would swear he was you. You gave my heart a jump."

That evening, she came to my house and told me what an uncanny resemblance the apprentice Pomuk had to me. Katrina added that she had seen a very strong resemblance also. When she was in the hospital as a teenager with her broken leg, it was Thomas who helped her heal during her hospital stay. Over the next week, Gretchen could not shake the thought of the resemblance between Pomuk and myself.

"I never did see Thomas in the coffin, he was wrapped too tightly," I said.

"Do you have relatives, Stefan, who have moved to the Banat?"

Katrina went to the pharmacy herself and was also shocked at the likeness. "There is such a resemblance that he must be related to you somehow. He even has your manner of speaking."

Eventually I went with them to the pharmacy to see for myself. I did not talk to Thomas but was taken aback by the resemblance. Gretchen and Katrina told their friends to go and see the young man who was Stefan's doppelganger. The questions continued, and I was eventually worn down.

Slowly I revealed the whole truth about Thomas, who was now known to everyone as Pomuk. Afraid to reveal the truth too quickly to Pomuk, I asked the advice of the monks. I knew that the meeting would need to be soon because the women would not be able to keep the secret. The monks agreed that they would act as intermediaries and promised to begin to tell Pomuk of his past. Eventually they would invite me into their conversations.

The meeting with my son was enormously emotional. Guilt and happiness mixed within me. Words seemed hard to form and thoughts raced through my head. I understood that this young man needed to hear the whole story and to see that what I had done was an act of love. I explained that I had realized he needed more than I could provide, and that my sense of loss was enormous. I told him I would love nothing more than to begin anew with him. He could set the pace and the boundaries. He rose slowly from the chair in which he was sitting and walked toward me. I rose to meet him. He stretched out his arms and embraced me. Overcome with relief and love, I sank into his arms and sobbed.

"My dearest Thomas. I have prayed for this moment. Your loss has been a burden that at times was almost impossible for me to bear. Let me look at you!" I broke away from the hug and held him at arm's length.

We talked the entire night. I told him stories of his mother and our journey to the Banat region. He was thrilled to know he had a brother who was a wunderkind. It saddened him that I had had to part with Johann but agreed that with a talent such as Johann's I had done the right thing. We talked of maybe going to Vienna to visit Johann and hear him play. I suggested that Johann might like to return home for a visit and said I would write and ask him to visit and meet his brother and my new wife. Thomas agreed to help me write the letter so I would include information that Thomas felt was important for Johann to know about him. I had no idea how Johann would react, but I knew he must be told.

24 October 1784

My dearest Johann,

It is with joy and trepidation that I write this letter. I am sure that the news will surprise you, but you have a brother, Thomas, who was born a year after you. He is alive and has returned to our home. Your mother did not return to Germany after his birth but died from complications of childbirth. I was unable to care for both you and your brother, so I found a home for him with monks in Temeswar. They have nurtured him, educated him, and raised him to be a wonderful young man. He is a pharmacist. So, I have two very accomplished sons of whom I am very proud.

Thomas wants you to know that he is overwhelmed with the idea of having a big brother. He wants to meet you and reunite the family. I hope you can find a way to visit us and share all the love of a reunited family. I have also remarried, a wonderful woman by the name of Katrina. She takes good care of me and has provided us with a warm and loving home.

There are so many feelings that I have right now that I am unsure how to put them down on paper. Of course, any questions you have I will answer with an open heart. I have told him your story about the violin and your travels. I have given him your letters to me to read so he can know more about you and the events of the world you have seen.

I look forward to your letter filled with questions.

Your loving father

Stefan

1 November 1784

Dearest Father,

I was quite taken aback by your letter. Not from anger but from surprise and of course some fear. Of course I want to meet my brother. Please tell me all you can about him before my visit. Also, could you have him write to me a letter, not long, but rather one that tells me of the things he most wants me to know about him. I will do the same and send it to you to give to him.

Things are, as always, busy and wonderful in Vienna. I meet all the famous musicians and am getting very well known as a performer and a teacher. Each month I have new students. I have a female student, Marie, whom I have become very fond of. I do not believe she knows how I feel about her. I hope that eventually I can ask her to marry me. Her parents are wealthy patrons of music in the city, and I have played private concerts in their house. They have asked me to dinner several times and I believe they think I would be a good match for Maria.

How is Henry doing? I think of him often and hope to see him when I visit. I want to thank him again for his guidance and the doors he opened for me. Maybe we both can play together for fun at the inn in Temeswar or at the theater.

I will write when I know for sure when I can visit. I look forward to the letters from you and Thomas.

With great love

Johann

It was a family reunion of enormous proportions. Johann had married and would bring his wife. Two new wives and a lost brother!

When Johann and his wife arrived, we spent many nights talking till morning. Johann learned that two of my brothers and their families had moved to Schowe and that I would be joining them once they found a house there or in a neighboring village. Thomas planned to be there also, when he finished his apprenticeship, and was preparing to open up his own shop, Pomuk Pharmacy. Thomas and Johann also learned of the sad fate of their mother. I gave both of them the things I had saved of hers and let them read the notebook full of stories about her. Johann learned about his mother's love of poetry and that Katrina and I also shared this love. He promised to send books of the most recent poets.

"Send? You can't be going back?" we all said almost simultaneously.

"Yes, Father. That is where Marie I have a life and a home."

Stunned as we were, Johann began to tell about his life and work and we slowly understood that Vienna was Johann's home now. Although Temeswar was a growing town with the beginnings of a great musical culture, Johann would not be able to find the work he needed to give a good life to Marie, his wife. Marie's desire was to stay close to her family. I remembered Sophie begging me not to leave Germany, and I was immediately swayed by Marie's earnest desire to stay close to family.

After a week and a day full of tears from all of us, Johann and Marie packed and returned to Vienna.

On the journey back to Vienna from visiting the family in the Banat, the sun eventually began to shine and Johann found myself thinking of the next concert and the music he was preparing. The depressing thoughts of leaving father and home made Marie quiet and contemplative. Eventually they began to talk of our friends and upcoming outings.

When they returned, Johann's life of performing and teaching continued, and within a year Marie and Johann had begun a family, with the arrival of a girl named Charlotte. She cooed from day one, and Johann believed she was trying to mimic the sounds of the violin. Her whole demeanor changed whenever she heard music coming from the studio. Marie and Johann were in no hurry to encourage her to be a musician. The opportunities for women were so limited. She could become a singer, but that would mean weeks and months of traveling to opera houses all over Europe. For most women the adventures of a singing career and the excitement from these could not sustain an entire life. Soon the desire for husband and family took over. Also, the machinations and jealousies that I had seen over the years amongst singers attempting to gain the title of Prima Donna were enough to make me never give Charlotte lessons or encourage her. For the meantime, it was enough to listen to her beautiful coos.

Marie's father was thirty-five when she was born. He was an officer in the Imperial Army of Austria. Her mother was the daughter of a university professor. Her home was comfortable and loving. She had no brothers or sisters, and to say that she was doted on would be an understatement. She was educated by both parents, Otto and Gertrude Wolff, making her education a mixture of beauty, philosophy, and discipline. Johann became an addition to the family and found that their love of each other, and eventually of him, filled a void. Johann again had had a family. Otto and Gertrude became his parents and Marie a loving wife. In many ways she was Johann's intellectual equal. Her abilities on the violin were good, but her curiosity about life matched his and they often had heated discussions between family members but always in the interest of learning and truth.

Marie's father had been one of the first graduates of Theresianum Knight Academy, founded in 1746. As stated by Empress Maria Theresa of Austria, her desire was to create "generals with a fatherland." The school motto was *Armis et lettres* and therefore it cultivated a devotion to learning and knowledge of war. Herr Wolff rose to the rank of colonel and was known for embodying all the virtues of his profession: love of military, discipline, punctuality, respect for superiors, and unconditional obedience. Marie's mother, Gertrude, loved music, coffee, planning good meals, hosting musical events and parties, conversation, reading, and of course buying beautiful clothes. Gertrude had been pleased when Marie began taking violin lessons from me. She rapidly improved and seemed to love playing. Never did they have to ask her to practice, and she loved playing for important visitors.

Johann went to Marie's house for her lessons. She was a true Viennese beauty. Blonde hair and blue eyes, petite, lively, and well mannered. He loved visiting and would often stay for coffee and dessert. It was during these conversations that he was introduced to the philosophy of Johann Herder on nationalism, the folk, and music. Gertrude, an avid reader, had been reading Herder.

"If I have understood Herder—I should talk with my father also—each nation is different and has developed its own language, music, and costumes, and we find the roots of our . . . oh, what should I use . . . national character in our folk music and poetry," she stated confidently, ready to engage in a lively conversation.

"Mama, do you think he means to say that someone like Beethoven does not express the German soul?"

"Marie, perhaps Beethoven's music is—" Johann began to suggest but was politely interrupted.

"But, Johann and Mama, Beethoven is German. He thinks and writes in German. He talks German, eats German food, etcetera and etcetera. How can his music not be German? He did not study in Italy, France, or England, so what he knows about music is from Germany and his own soul," Marie continued in her defense of the Germanness of Beethoven.

"He admired Napoleon," Johann added in a controversial and goading tone.

"Yes, but when he showed his desire to swallow up Austria and Vienna, I think he saw the true man and the true nature of the French," Marie added.

Marie was becoming very interested in the direction the discussion was going. Her eyes flashed and her cheeks reddened. Both of us adored the music and person of Beethoven. We believed that Beethoven's music was about the human spirit, no matter whose spirit. His music aroused emotions in people. Could sadness, joy, tenderness, love be different for each nation? We all agreed that the music of the Italians and French sounded different from Beethoven's, but that was part of the beauty of all music. Beethoven had studied scores from many different composers and taken what he needed.

The debate went on politely until dinner, at which time I excused myself. I bowed to the ladies and headed home. I was very agitated, intellectually, by our conversation. Could one nation's culture be better than another's, was one language better than another, were people envious of others' cultures and achievements? At this point I felt I had come upon a reason for some of the petty arguments I often heard among musicians and friends. Envy.

Marie and I married in the spring of 1786, before our summer visit to my family in the Banat. On our return we learned that her father and mother had given us a house where we could live and I could have a studio for practice and teaching. Marie and I had three beautiful children, Charlotte, Stefan, and Michael. The boys took music lessons, but music did not "take" in them. What they loved was soldiering with their grandfather. He bought them metal soldiers and they would reenact battles, especially those against the Turks and the French. The boys would go on to pursue careers in the military, and Charlotte would wed, have children, and live a life of culture and learning.

Otto Wolff had a large library. I was able to read many of the works of Goethe, and I sent volumes home to Father, knowing that he would love his poetry. Marie and I would spend evenings with her family reading Goethe's poems, and of course each one of us was on a different side when we discussed their meaning. I believe that I began to see what a nationality was. I was proud that Beethoven and Goethe were German and that they were loved by so many people. Bach, Haydn, and Mozart were all a part of our culture.

I had never thought of Germany being a nation or that Austria was a part of Germany. I knew that Austria and Germany shared a common language and that Germany was made up of many states with their own monarchies. I could begin to see that a united Germany would be something to be proud of. A people united by language, art, and customs. This unification would help to guard us from the Turks and from the French.

During the siege of Vienna in 1805, Beethoven's *Fidelio* was premiered. We did not attend because of the overwhelming presence of French troops in Vienna. We heard that revisions were made following a disastrous premiere, and the opera was then received better by the public. However, it was not until 1814 that it finally met with general approval. Marie and I attended the performance at the Kärntnertortheater.

We talked very little on our way home. I am sure that both of us were lost in our own thoughts about the opera. The people around us in the theater were all sharing their opinions and thoughts, most of which were positive. The length of the opera and the first act seemed to be where most of the criticism fell. The real core of the opera was not the love interest of Marcelline falling in love with the disguised Leonora but the courage of Leonora in her heroic endeavor to save her husband from execution. One could not but see the ideals of the Enlightenment in saving humankind from tyranny by self-sacrifice; however, there were two musical numbers that were sublime. The otherworldliness of the music, the words, and the scene itself heightened my awareness of the suffering of Beethoven himself and the suffering of people, because the music promised such hope.

At the beginning of Act II, the prisoners, by an act of kindness, were brought up from their dank and miserable cells to spend a moment in the sunlight. "*O welche Lust,*" oh, such light, they sang as they slowly ascended and their eyes were able to see in the brightness. Surely this was divine light, God descending to the poor and wretched. The music was one long, slow rising arc as the prisoners ascended, but also a musical depiction of a magnificent sunrise. Slow rising chords gave way to gently flowing sixteenth notes, like a gentle breeze, and the voices of the men's chorus rose one at a time until all were singing. Not angels, but humans understanding the release from suffering.

The other piece that affected me most was the first act quartet where the four soloists, each singing of his or her own thoughts and feelings, repeated in turn the opening phrase in imitation. Their words were different, but they sang the same music. Did it matter that their thoughts and feelings were different, that they each wanted different things? No, they were humans. Although separate and different, they were the same. The only way this concept could be communicated was through music.

Marie shared her thoughts when we arrived home. She was moved by the love of Leonora for Florestan. So great was her love that Leonora shielded Florestan with her own body when he was about to be stabbed. "And then she says she did nothing. Nothing, Johann. I have never seen a woman act this way. Is she merely a woman or is she an Athena?"

"Would you not do the same for me and our children, Marie?" I asked.

"May I never be put to the test. I hope to God I would be able to. I believe that I love you all as much as she loved Florestan, but what if she had failed, and then both of them would be dead? But that is not what Beethoven wanted. He wanted a hero. Can't a woman be a hero?" she asked impudently.

Our conversation lasted until early morning. Who and what were the characters meant to represent? Did the music tell us anything about them? I concluded they were mere human beings who were called upon do great deeds. Marie was not convinced.

I finally had time to read many of the works of Herder on music and his notions of Germanness and national character. He wrote with great passion on what he believed was the tragic fate of the German nation: Germany had become "a slave and a wet nurse." If I understood his argument, it is by returning to our folk songs and our stories of the past that we will ignite, in our souls, and become great. Our feelings and senses, which are the greatest part of our being, are inspired by the simple and profound music of the people. Song, for Herder, was enormously different from the other arts. The difference, of course, was that there is singing. Which, if I follow his argument, lies in the "melodic path" or *Weise*, as he called it. Each song has a spirit that can touch us. This spirit is not artifice. It remains true to the content. This is why we cannot adopt the music of another country. The German language it essential to this spirit; language is tied to the melody and how it is formed. I cannot tell you how many times I read certain passages, attempting to understand.

Some of the songs of Schubert immediately came to mind. Were these not in the spirit of folk song that Herder was talking about? His *Erlkönig*, with the text by Goethe, was taken from the Nordic poem "The Erl-King's Daughter," a folk legend. I pondered these ideas and found myself agreeing more and more with them. At dinner Marie and the children would discuss them with me. At night we would sing Beethoven's settings of folk songs and read folk stories. I hoped that I was instilling a sense of heritage in the children and also steeping them in German culture.

It was not long after my final visit to Beethoven that I caught a very bad cold. It quickly turned into pneumonia. Our doctor comes every day, but no matter what he does, I am not getting better. Marie is beside herself. She makes soup, she cleans the bedding every day, she bathes my forehead; but the fever will not stay down. In a month, I have become worse, and I can barely breathe or sit up in bed. The children visit me once a day, but even they cannot raise my spirits. I know that I will die. When I reflect on my life, I realize what a remarkable journey I have been on. A son of poor farmers, who by luck had a violin placed in his hands. A journey to a palace, meeting the Empress Maria Theresa, playing for Haydn and Beethoven, and being able to could count these men as friends. I have witnessed the defeat of Napoleon, lived through a siege, married a beautiful and loving woman, and had three children. Death does not scare me; I only wish I could live another life of such blessings.

CHAPTER TWELVE

The Third Colonists

S tefan narrates

Katrina and I were to see the last group of colonists from Germany arrive in the Banat between 1782 and 1787. Joseph II had declared in the Edict of Tolerance in 1781 that Protestants were now able to be colonists. Fourteen villages were formed, and about three thousand families moved into the southeastern area of the Banat. A home, garden, fields, and tools were given to each family.

Two of my brothers, with their wives and children, had decided to join me. I had written them in 1786 telling them about my new wife and the adventures of Johann and Thomas. When they heard that we were doing well and our village was growing every year despite hardships such as drought and flooding, they decided to come and start a new life as I had done. Life for them had not gotten easier in Germany,

To aid in our transition to being with my family, I told Thomas that I was originally Lutheran but had hidden this fact to be a part of the colonization of the Banat. Also, and more importantly, that I willingly was baptized in the Catholic Church to save his life. He was also baptized into the Catholic faith at the same time. I said I would understand if he did not want to move with us to the village to which my brothers were headed, but I hoped that desire for family would convince him to move with us. The people in the surrounding villages would need a pharmacist, and he would certainly be welcome. He would finish his pharmacy apprenticeship in 1788 and could then move to Torschau and set up a small business near where my brothers would be living.

We could become a family and enjoy all the things that come with family: love, understanding, aid, support, etc. I was not naïve enough to not realize that things like jealousy, anger, and resentment also come along with family. All I could think about was being surrounded by a large family again.

"Father, after the sacrifices you made to give me life, I can in no way return enough goodness to you," Thomas replied after a moment of silence. "Let us make a family together. I will think about becoming Lutheran. As of now, the fact that we are together is all that is important."

I was forty-two when my brothers and their families arrived. A total of fifty-nine people traveled down the Danube to Schowe. After spending the winter in the neighboring village of Torschau, on May 26, 1786, they moved into Schowe. My brother Joseph was forty-four. His wife, Eva, was forty, and their two boys, Klaus and Dietrich, were eighteen and twenty respectively. My other brother, Georg, was thirty-eight, and his wife, Anna, was thirty-six. Anna had lost several children because of miscarriages, but one daughter survived and was eight. Her name was Maria. Eventually Klaus, Dietrich, and Maria would marry, there would be grandchildren, and our relatives would populate the small village of Schowe.

Each of my brothers received a house, and Katrina and I lived with them until we were able to procure our own house. I was hoping that Thomas would marry quickly and have his own place to live. The village was between the Danube and Theiss rivers. It was beautiful farmland and I felt this could be home. Not merely a physical home but also the spiritual home I sought. I might be able to put behind me the miseries of the first years. I had kept these deep inside me for so long. Over the course of the next few weeks when I told them all that had happened, my family members were glad they had come and that I again had family. They even understood my conversion to Catholicism and were glad I was returning to the Lutheran faith.

The land was flat, had rich, black soil, and only needed to be cultivated. As I had previously experienced, there was much work to be done, but all of us were used to hard work and began the process of planting our crops and settling into a home. The hard work was something from which none of us shied. We had deep connections to the earth and felt that the earth needed us as much as we needed the earth for our survival. The earth, whether it was our native soil or not, was what provided us with life, food, and a sense of obligation. If we took care of the earth, she would take care of us.

Thomas, Katrina, and I found a house in Torschau in 1788 that had been abandoned by a family who decided to immigrate to Russia. It was perfect for the three of us, and I was able to build, with help of several villagers, a shop for myself. Thomas found a house that he wanted to turn into a pharmacy, where he would plant the garden he was going to grow his herbs in. He could eventually move into the house by himself. I could not be more pleased with the arrangements. Thomas would have a house to eventually move a new wife into, and Katrina and I might be able to start a family. Thomas was given several important essentials from Mr. Herder for his pharmacy. Mr. Herder was sad to see Thomas go but glad to know that he would be starting up in a new village with his family.

By the early 1800s the two villages had wheat and hemp growing, gardens planted, clean houses, and growing populations. Thomas married Rosina, Gretchen's daughter, in 1790, and they had three beautiful girls: Hilde in 1792, Isolde in 1794, and Annika in 1796. I was an *opa*! Amazingly, I was also a new father. Katrina gave birth to my third son in 1791; we named him Martin. The children played together day and night, and often Martin thought that I also was his *Opa*, his grandfather. No matter, I loved them all and my life was once again filled with joy.

Each year our villages grew. We built schools, shops, restaurants; we had everything we needed. Our houses were painted, porches swept, gardens tilled and hoed, rooms cleaned, meals prepared. We had great pride in how our villages began to grow into towns known for their order and cleanliness. Young married couples walked in processions to the church on the main street. Children played in sunlight and in the meadow. When it rained they played on the porches and helped their mothers in the house, which of course was done with much complaining. As the children grew, there was school and homework. The boys, as most boys will, got into trouble at school and in catechism class. The boys made fun of the girls, whose feelings were often hurt and they went home crying. The mothers would go out to the street to talk about the happenings at school and discipline the offenders. Although the girls could also cause trouble, such as by putting vinegar in the boys' water, they never seemed to get disciplined. Many of the girls were also of enormous help to their mothers since many families had as many as six children. Everyone shared in the chores and worked in the fields.

Summer evenings were spent on porches, where the daily gossip and news could be shared. Winter nights we sat by the fire mending clothes and tools. We read newspaper reports of what was happening in Temeswar, Austria, and Germany, and at the bars we discussed the world. The world was changing around us, and we were like a pocket of life separated from the outside. We had rights and privileges that we never would have dreamed possible. Although in a foreign land, we were happy Germans. We made friends with the neighboring peoples and lived in peace with them.

Hardships also were many. As with all farming, the weather could be unpredictable. There were droughts, and floods ruined entire crops. There were illnesses, diseases, and unexpected deaths. But this was part of the double-sided coin of life. I had been through so much that I understood that life would become meaningless without hardship. Our joys would not be as perfect as we experienced them if they were not surrounded by sadness. My brother's daughter, Maria, married and started a family. One of her children as killed in an accident at my brother's flour mill. Believing she could ride the huge wheel, she was caught in the gears and killed. Her mother and father then lived in a silence that the whole town felt. We never talked of her or what had happened. It took my brother days to return to work. The child was always in our hearts, and we shared their sorrow as much as we could. We were all glad they had other children who needed care and love. But the loss was enormous to all of us.

Our family was not excluded from other hardships. My nephew Dietrich was a troublemaker and was continually having to be disciplined. As a teen-ager he found a group of boys whose escapades got worse as they got older. He got a young girl pregnant and they had to marry. Their marriage was not loving or healthy, and after returning home from the pub he was known to beat his "lazy wife" savagely. She eventually moved back with her family, and her father threatened death if Dietrich came around. He was constantly in need of money and was known to frequent the loose women of the village. He eventually contracted syphilis. He died a miserable death, alone and crazed. My brother and his wife brought him to their house the last days of his life. They kept him comfortable and suffered with his rantings. We all were relieved when he died. His life was a reminder to all of us of what happens when God is not kept close and held in your heart. The path to perdition was only a curve in the road of a good life.

But there were also wonderful, joyous events in our lives. We had music in the house. Henry was still a close friend. He brought his violin over for parties and played at all the family weddings. One of my brothers played the bass, and when he found other men who played instruments, he started a band. They played for the pure joy it brought them, and of course dancing and drink were loved by all.

Thomas had a wonderful wife in Rosina, and I had a loving daughter-in-law. She helped daily at the pharmacy, learning his trade. The move away from her family was hard, but they visited her family every Sunday for church and dinner afterwards. Thomas and Rosina were married in the Lutheran church and became members there. Thomas sang in the choir of men and boys. He had obviously inherited his mother's voice.

My nephew Klaus married and he became an apprentice at Thomas's pharmacy. He continued to work on his father's farm as much as he could, but he loved seeing what Thomas was able to do for the people, and to be honest, the hard work of a farmer did not appeal to him. Klaus and his wife had three children, two boys and a girl. Their boys would take over the family farm.

In the Spring of 1807, I noticed a large lump under my arm. It was sore and grew larger very quickly. I showed it to Thomas. After much examination of the spot and other areas of my body, he said, "Father, I think this is what doctors call cancer. I will look up what is being done to rid the body of this, but I am afraid that many people die because of this. It appears that you are developing lumps in other parts of your body also." I went back to Thomas's pharmacy the following day. He had numerous books laid out in front of him, and we sat down together to read what he had found.

"Some doctors are cutting out the tumors. But, Father, this is very painful, and many get infections from the surgery, and most often the lumps keep on reappearing. I have looked at all the herbal books I have, and there are things I can do to help with the pain caused by the swelling, and changes in diet have been known to help. I think I would advise against removing the tumor. I think the herbal and dietary methods will not heal you, but they can make your life better. What do you want me to do?"

After reading the materials with him, I decided that he was right and that what was most important at my age was to have good days. I have had many good days using the treatments Thomas recommended, but after four months there is not much more he can do. We both know *I* will die within a month. I spend my days reading with Katrina, playing on the porch with the children, drinking beer, eating soup, and talking with friends. Johann has sent me books by Goethe and I especially like the poems. My favorite is "Über allen Gipfeln." Its promises of rest give me comfort and courage. Its images of the woods also finding rest harken back to the evenings in the Black Forest when I was a child. My soul and homeland will become one in an evening soon.

"Over Every Mountain Top"
Over the trees a peace comes. The woodland is still and quiet throughout, barely a breath is heard. The birds are quiet on the bough. Only wait, soon you also will have rest.

PART TWO

There was little change in the daily lives in the villages of the Banat. Thomas, Rosina, and his daughters worked daily at the pharmacy. There was the planting of herbs, the drying of them, the mixing and measuring of medicines, the ordering of medicines, keeping the books, managing the store, greeting the shoppers, cleaning the store, plus all the other chores in running a house. At least four villages procured their medicinal needs from our store. We were able to hear all the news from the Banat, Austria, and Hungary. The gossip was plentiful too. Who was dating whom, what crops were doing well, how the grape and wine vintages were, and all the births and deaths. We seemed to have more news than the newspapers—good and bad.

Thomas' oldest daughter, Hilde, married the Lutheran minister in Torschau, Pastor Paul Schmidt; Isolde married a local farmer, Adam Schnabel; and the youngest, Annika, married Dr. Joseph Knapp and became a midwife. As the wife of a Lutheran minister, Hilde kept records for the villages of Torschau and Schowe. She was the librarian for our small music collection as well as books. Hilde also started writing pamphlets about the medicinal purposes of herbs and flowers and a cultural history of our villages. The pamphlets were available for free at the pharmacy and at the church. Like me, she believed that sometimes simple home remedies were the best and most effective. The pamphlets were written like cookbooks with recipes to follow. For example, the recipe for a simple cough medicine read:

> One ounce of red clover blossoms
> One pint boiling water
> One cup honey
> Boil the blossoms and strain

Add the honey and bottle
One teaspoon twice daily

She included only herbs and oils that could readily be found, such as mints, lavender, cream of tartar, turkey rhubarb, basil, sage, rosemary, tarragon, and chamomile. She listed them in alphabetical order and explained what each herb would heal or help cure. She also included drawings of the herbs, as she said, "to make the pamphlet beautiful to the eye." Using the herbs in teas was the simplest and often the most helpful for ailments such as insomnia, nerves, and headache. She also found that heating flat stones and placing them on sore muscles relieved some of the pain. Oils could be used on dry skin and chaffing as well as blisters. She relied heavily on the Hildegarde book that I had been given by the monks and my own mixtures that I had developed. Hilde was known throughout several villages. After the doctor had seen a member of a family, Hilde would visit the family to make sure they were following his orders and to bring them food and drink. She had learned from me that kindness went a long way in healing the sick. She would leave additional herbal medicines and always spend time in prayer with the patients and their families. Even after the patients were well, many families would ask her to return to make sure they were really well.

Annika had met her husband, Joseph Knapp, at our pharmacy. He was the doctor for three of the nearby villages. Having taken over from his father, he was already well known by many of the people. As a boy he had often accompanied his father on visits, and he seemed like a family member to many. Constantly busy, he was thrilled when he married Annika because she would be able to help him with cleaning the instruments, keeping his medical records organized, and greeting his patients. She often went with him to visit people who could not get to the office because they were too ill or had had a major accident on the farm or in their shop. The most common injury was the loss of a limb. and Annika helped with keeping the injured person still, applying the tourniquet, and washing and bandaging wounds. She also learned how to sew up minor cuts and flush out wounds.

When Annika had children, she learned from her husband the best and healthiest ways to give birth. Because women in the Banat were used to hard work in the fields, they were strong and mostly healthy. Some women went into labor in the fields, then cleaned up the best they could, wrapped the babies to their bodies, breastfed them, and went back to work that day or the next. However, there were real dangers. Breech births were common, as were excessive bleeding, pelvises that were too narrow, and infections. No matter how many babies Annika helped deliver, the hardest for her were those stillborn and those with birth defects. Often the birth defects were so massive that the child had no hope of living. There was no preparation for these events, and they broke the hearts of many families, including our own. Annika also knew the power of kindness and would often stay to help the mother clean the infant and prepare the child for burial. Annika knew that if the mothers did not participate in these preparations they often would not accept the deaths. I had told her about the problems my mother had after my birth and how many women suffered from this kind of malady after giving birth. Annika would tell the father to come and get her if he felt that his wife was not getting out of bed and attending to the baby and the household enough. She developed teas and a schedule for the woman to follow, and spent time talking with her. Laughing, she found, was an enormous help. If she could get the mother to laugh at silly stories or events going on in the villages, she often was able to help her turn a corner. She also helped the mother around the house and with caring for the other children. I wondered how she was able to have four children of her own and raise them too.

Annika found that her work with mothers and their infants helped her with the horrible ordeals her sister Isolde faced. Isolde had heartbreak after heartbreak with her pregnancies. She miscarried twice, had one stillbirth, and then a child who was slow. He was slow to talk, walk, read, and understand and retain instructions. But this child gave joy to all who came into contact with him. He was named Lukas. Isolde and her husband, Adam Schnabel, felt it was fitting since the story of Anna and Simeon is found in the Gospel of Luke. Like Anna and Simeon they had been blessed after many years with a child. Although there was sorrow, there was joy that she had given birth to a living baby.

Lukas was a calm, happy child. No one realized at first that he was what people called slow. "Oh, he will walk, he is just taking his time." "The words will come when he is ready." These were comments that all the women of the village gave as advice to Isolde.

Hilde related to Annika a conversation she had had with Isolde asking her if she thought that something was wrong with Lukas. Isolde with noticeable anxiety in her voice said, "He is so behind other children his age. He seems to get lost in his own thoughts and does not readily engage with the other children."

"I will have Joe make a visit and spend some time with Lukas," Annika replied. "He seems physically fine, and he grows like a weed. Maybe the women are right. He has his own pace. Women often know more than doctors since they are with children constantly."

Joe and Annika visited Isolde and Lukas often and spent most of the afternoon with them. Joe did notice that Lukas did not respond to things most children did. He didn't play for long periods of time, losing attention, and often wanted to sit on his mother's lap. He also noticed that Lukas was still in diapers when most children his age were able to go to the bathroom. He told Isolde that he would consult some doctors in Vienna who worked with children to see if they had insights.

Joseph finally had a long talk with Isolde, saying that she needed to understand that Lukas would live a long and happy life. "The doctors told me that children who are mentally slow can be productive adults and live good lives. He will struggle in school and may be made fun of, but these are things that most children have to deal with. You always have Rosina and the family to help. Keeping him away from harmful people and things will be the hardest trial. Children like Lukas often are gullible because they have a hard time knowing what is wrong and right."

Hearing the doctor's report Isolde started to cry, and through sobs said that after finally having a child, it was devastating to be told that her baby was anything but perfect. Joseph told her she should be glad he was a happy, loving child, and with the wonderful home they were providing, Lukas would become a wonderful young man.

For a month, every time Isolde looked at Lukas, she would run to him, hold him, and cry. Sadly, Adam wanted little to do with Lukas. Joe had seen many men who were not able to be good fathers, but Adam seemed embarrassed that Lukas was different. Rosina made sure Adam always came to our house with Isolde and Lukas. We tried to engage Adam to do things with Lukas. We had picnics and went for walks. In winter we made cider and had Adam and Lukas work on mashing the apples and straining them. They would make a snowman together and make bird feeders out of pinecones. However, once back at home Adam shied away again from Lukas.

Isolde and Rosina devoted their lives to Lukas. Rosina would bring Lukas to the store and teach him about the herbs, and he would help plant them. This gave Isolde time at home to manage her own house and to help Adam on the farm. Isolde was patient and dutifully tried teaching Lukas his numbers and to read in German and Hungarian.

The Fritz family grew and prospered. We were Germans who had been blessed in a foreign country. Although our villages were small, we had a communal sense. Almost everyone in the village would show up for weddings and other holidays, and we supported each other physically and spiritually in times of sorrow. Paul helped everyone to see that God was always there and that although we might worship him in different ways, we were all Christians. Also, when hard times fell on a family, Paul made us realize that this was a part of God's plan and that we could not see or understand the plan. These were very enlightened thoughts, and most Lutherans did not agree with him. We kept many of his ideas and thoughts within our four walls.

Joe had friends who had visited England. Thye told us that a book by John Paget had been published in London and was about his journey in the Banat. It was a wonderful report of how many people lived their daily lives in the Banat and how a friend of his from Scotland was envious. He sent Joe a paragraph from the book for our enjoyment. We all read it and bragged about our good life:

> It is, in fact, impossible to imagine those who live by the labour of their hands, enjoying more of the material good things of the world than they do. In addition to the richest land in the country, the Banat peasant has many privileges peculiar to himself, conferred when it was an object to attract settlers from other districts, and these he still preserves. Among other things he is free from the "long journeys," the "hunting," the "spinning," the "chopping and carrying of wood," and from the tithe of fruit and vegetables. He has, moreover, free rights of fishing, of

cutting reeds, and feeding his pigs, and gathering sticks
in his master's forests, many of which, though trifling in
themselves, give to the sober and industrious peasant, a
great opportunity to improve his position. But, more than
all, he has the liberty to redeem half his days of labour, at
the rate of ten kreutzers, or five pence per day, an advantage of which he never fails to avail himself.
—excerpt from *Hungary and Transylvania* by John Paget
(London 1839)

As idyllic as this may have sounded, the life here was hard. There was little
money and it always seemed only to live from hand to mouth. Everyone had
to work, and children after the eighth grade stopped school to work in the
fields and stores, take apprenticeships, help their mothers raise the children
and do daily chores, care for the aging grandparents, and this list could go on.
However, the Germans who had moved to the Banat had their own land and
were in charge of their own lives. Eventually the Banat became the breadbasket of Europe.

Singing was a wonderful pastime and a way to spend wonderful Saturday
evenings. Thomas joined a men's choir made up of men from Jarek, Torschau,
Sekitsch, and Schowe. Our director was a teacher from Sekitsch by the name
of Michael Klein. Thomas had never heard many of the songs from Germany.
Having been raised and educated in the monastery, he knew the music for
Mass and holy days, how to read Latin and German, and how to care for the
sick. Music opened up his German heritage and also the Lutheran love of
music. He loved the hymns and chorales and their settings by Bach. We often
started the evening with Luther's hymn "A Mighty Fortress is Our God."
As the man sitting next to him said one evening, "Sing Luther's hymns is
a good way to clear out the throat and they are a good theology." It was
music like this that gave the early settlers courage and comfort. The texts of
many of the Lenten hymns showed Thomas a completely different way of
understanding Jesus. This Jesus was more personal, and His sacrifice was each
sinner. It was a personal act of love and one had to accept personally. It was
through the experience of singing Lutheran hymns that turned Thomas to
the Lutheran faith.

The best time of year for singing was of course Christmas. After Advent, German Christmas songs rang out from the churches and homes. The men's choir even sang a performance of carols in all four of the villages, after which the women served spiced wine, cookies, hot chocolate, apple cider, and hundreds of German pastries. Thomas was glad they sang first thing, because none of us would have been able to take a breath or stand in a straight line after the Christmas celebration.

Thomas had gone from being an adopted child of monks to a respected pharmacist with three beautiful girls and grandchildren. The family had books and music, a life that had both festive moments and ones of deep despair. As was often quoted in church, "To everything there is a season."

CHAPTER FOURTEEN

Vienna

*You sacred art, how in many dark hours, when in life's
tumultuous cycle I have been flung, you have kindled my heart
to the warmth of love and taken me to a better world.*
—Franz Schober

Although Charlotte, the daughter of Johann and Marie, was adequate at the piano, she was a very fine singer and was always buying sheet music to sing at home. She took voice lessons only to gratify herself, not to perform on stage. Her mother was very encouraging and would often have her perform for friends after dinner. It was at one of these evening "performances" that she met her husband, jurist Hans Müller. They married in 1809 and her father played the violin at the church. He played several Bach pieces and gave the ceremony a true sense of holiness.

After a short honeymoon in the Alps, Charlotte and Hans moved into his apartment, which was near to his office. She of course, had to redecorate. She wanted a home that was warm and inviting but not ostentatious. People should not be put ill at ease in a person's home and feel that there is a competition to have the best and most expensive things. Charlotte did buy some art by recent German artists and sculptors. The colors of yellow and grey were chosen for the living and dining areas and blue and white for the bedroom. These colors were clean and bright and gave a sense of openness. The tall windows were decorated with silk curtains and are plain so as not to distract from the few pieces of art. Italian marble tables were acquired for the living room and, when asked, she was proud to say that the marble had come from Carrara. Their china and silver were very simple so as not to clash with flower arrangements for special dinners. Hans had bought a beautiful grand piano that he moved into a vacant bedroom, which he made into a music room that contained her sheet music and books. Since he had his own study, he thought Charlotte would like a room that was only for her. f

In 1811 Charlotte gave birth to the love and joys of my life, twins. We named them Johann Heinrich after my father and Elsa after Hans's mother, a mixture of both families. Charlotte was glad that her mother could come over and help me with the daily routine of feeding, bathing, and cleaning, and the endless laundry. It seemed felt that her days were filled with only the demands of the children and was glad when Hans came home so they could talk. The evening was when she could go to her music room and sing, taking the cares of the day away in the melodies she sang. The twins were healthy and active and they grew quickly. Doted on by the grandparents, they wanted for nothing. Their weekly outings always meant ice cream, candy, and of course the new toy. As the children began to talk, they immediately learned to say "Grandma, please could I have" or "Grandpa, could you get me," and it seemed as if their wishes were our parents' commands.

1814 was the year of the Vienna Congress. It felt as if the whole of Europe was in Vienna for the year. Delegations ate at our restaurants, bought our clothing, attended concerts, and entertained. It was a fabulous time with parties and dances, new dresses, and evening concerts and operas. Charlotte met some of the most important people in Europe, and there was an air of peace and security throughout the city. Vienna and Europe were ready to enjoy life and prosperity.

Hans spent weeks reading the reports, attempting to understand what legal implications there would be with the proposals once they were signed. Many evenings their house was filled with Hans's fellow lawyers all debating the issues, the treaties, the alliances, and most of all if this would lead to world peace after more than twenty years of war. Many wondered what the fall of Napoleon would do to those liberal ideas of freedom and equality. Others felt that a return to law and order was best for the world and that certain freedoms would lead to uprisings and chaos in the streets. Prince Metternich certainly was on the side of limited freedom and law and order.

Metternich was the host of the Congress, so his voice was often the strongest. What he wanted most was the restoration of the monarchy. He claimed that the chaos France brought to Europe was the result of their liberal views of democracy. Surely nationalism would lead to revolutions with each ethnic group wanting their own nation and their own government. What would Hungary do? There must be obedience to political authority, and reform must come gradually.

Hans feared that Napoleon and the horror of the French Revolution would ensure that the governments would refuse any kind of moderate change in regards to individual rights. "I am not against law and order, the balance of power, and a legitimate government. We should not open the doors to those ideas that led to Napoleon. However, should not those of us who own land and have ties to the nobility in some way have a say in the government? Of course, the monarchy should rule, but don't you think that a constitution would provide some means of protecting speech and thought?"

"Yes, speech and thought! Isn't that what sparked revolution in France? *Liberté! Equalité! Fraternité!* These ideas are French, not Austrian. I also fear the goings-on at German universities, the harborers of liberalism," one of the men shouted, standing up.

"I am not talking of liberalism run amok. Let's be sensible and look at what the outcome of radical conservatism could lead to." Hans replied gesturing for him to sit.

"But this is what the law should do. It should guard against those who would bring down government." Another quest added with a tone of reconciliation.

Amidst all of these thrilling discussions Charlotte developed a desire to learn about world happenings. All she had known were the raising of children, entertaining duties for all the visitors we had, making sure that Hans's needs were met, and of course the daily running of the household. And of course, she had music.

One of Hans's friends informed Charlotte about some splendid home concerts called *Schubertiades* that he had attended. He knew of our family history regarding music and wondered if I would like to attend one with him. She had heard of Schubert and the beautiful songs he was writing, so she quickly agreed.

Hans and Charlotte were to go it was at the house of my Hans's friend and fellow jurist Eduard von Bauernfeld. Her father, Johann, also agreed to go. It was a delightful evening of music to be shared by the family. Charlotte's father had heard of Schubert and knew that Beethoven thought highly of him. The baritone Johann Vogl would be singing, with Schubert at the piano. The program was to be a Goethe evening. Johann was thrilled because he knew his father, Stefan, loved the poetry of Goethe. "If only he were alive to hear this evening of the most beautiful settings of Goethe," he said. "I must admit that I like them better than Beethoven's. Schubert must have some unique comprehension of the poems. He is able to get to the core of the poem, understanding the meaning of each line and word of the poem. I know I am not being clear, but wait. I do hope you get to hear his setting of *Der Erlkönig*. Your grandfather and his second wife would read the poem dramatically when they first met each other. Hearing this for the first time, I understood what Herder meant when he talked about the music and poetry of the folk."

Franz Schubert.

Just as Johann finished reminiscing, they arrived at the house. Many people were already there and taking their seats. Luckily, they were able to get seats close to the piano, on the left, where Charlotte could watch Schubert play. As the room filled, some people sat around the back of the piano and others stood. It was an informal setting, and we were glad there was to be no artifice. Vogl, who was much taller than Schubert, sat next to him. The beautiful chandelier was dim enough not to give a harsh light to the room, creating a very warm and intimate atmosphere. Vogl then introduced the first song: "Nur wer die Sehnsucht kennt".

> Only he who knows longing knows what I suffer. Alone
> and cut off from all joy, I gaze up to the firmament towards
> the other side. Ah, he who knows me is far away. I am
> dizzy and my heart burns. Only he who knows longing
> knows what I suffer.

Charlotte was transfixed during the performance. When Johann asked her later that night what she thought of the Mignon song, she answered gave a complete and accurate description of the song, "I cannot believe there is anything more beautiful. The melody is so simple, as was the accompaniment. The opening line of text was repeated twice, reaching an understated melodic climax on the word *Sehnsucht*. There was nothing overwrought. In its simplicity it was direct and profound, perfectly matching the text. After the word *allein* (alone) the melody rose steadily to the words *seh ich ans Firmament nach jener Seite* (I gaze up to the firmament towards the other side). Then the accompaniment prepared us for the inner turmoil by changing from a triplet motion to sextuplets and triplets. Then two bars prepared the return of the original melody, which Vogl performed at a piano dynamic, and then a swell to and accent on *kennt* (knows) and a melodic descent into a pianissimo. Using the simplest of musical means, Schubert captured every idea, emotion, and word. Each section led organically into the next, creating a moment of deep sorrow, a sorrow that without art cannot be expressed."

Once started she could not stop talking about the piece and its performance. Although the song had not been published, Charlotte could see the manuscript from where she sat. It was as if she had memorized it.

"Yes, there are people who know this yearning. I was carried into Mignon's soul, and I could truly feel and understand her longing and sorrow. It was the music that transported me into the inner life of this mysterious girl, Mignon. The words alone would not have had the same effect. Schubert had taken the text and through melody and accompaniment created a whole third realm of existence. I felt that music had the power to allow me to feel empathy for my fellow man in a way I had never experienced before. Putting this into words is almost impossible."

I am not sure I even heard the next song, and I know I did not move.

We did get to hear *Der Erlkönig* and all three stated that they did not know music could create such horror. Schubert without hesitation had launched into a frenzy of repeated forte chords. Never does the emotional and musical intensity stop in song. There were shifts to the major mode and arpeggiation of the chords, thinning the texture, but the sense of horror permeated each measure. The four characters had different vocal ranges and slightly different accompaniment figures, and Vogl was masterful in changing his vocal quality for each of them. The child was sung almost in a falsetto, the father in a lower, somber tone, and the Erl-King had the quality of trickery to it. He was cajoling and enticing, and only when he seized the child was his true character revealed. When Vogl spoke the words *und bist du nicht willig, so brauch ich Gewalt* (and if you are not willing, I will use violence), he almost shouted, causing several in the audience to gasp. At this point there was an accelerando as the father spurred his horse onward to find safety for the boy. But as the horse slowed to a halt, we became aware that the child was indeed dead. The final words, *in seinen Armen das Kind war tot* (in his arms the child was dead), had no accompaniment and were whispered, which by a negation of sound made them real. The song ended with two chords.

The audience was deeply moved. Johann could not believe that Schubert had written this when he was eighteen. Charlotte told Johann that, in the words of St. Paul, she had barely put away childish things at eighteen and her was Schubert writing this masterpiece! This was an evening they would never forget.

Charlotte and Johann heard through gossip that Schubert's personality had changed and that he was becoming thoughtless and even rude at times. There was much speculation on why this was. Many believed he had contracted syphilis, and this was causing the changes. Indeed, he had contracted the horrible disease, and in the next years he was to suffer terribly, yet he never stopped composing. Charlotte and Hans attended Schubert's Benefit Concert on March 26, 1828. As always, the music was sublime. It occurred a year to the day since the death of Beethoven, whom Schubert worshipped.

Auf dem Strom, a piece for voice, piano, and French horn, contained fragments of Beethoven's *Eroica*. All who loved Schubert and Beethoven knew the statement that Schubert had made: "Who can do anything after Beethoven?" When Beethoven was alive, Schubert surely must have felt that he lived in the great man's shadow. Yet his death had profoundly moved Schubert; he was one of Beethoven's torchbearers, and all could see the depth of his suffering on his face.

Johann had taken Charlotte to the premieres of Beethoven's *Eroica* and the Ninth Symphony because to him they represented the German spirit. She and her father would often discuss Herder and talk about how Beethoven's music was what the German people were capable of creating and how the Germans lived. A powerful and spiritual people. Although Schubert's music may not have had the overwhelming power of Beethoven's, it went to the heart, and it brought forward the inner being of Vienna, its eloquence and lyricism. Schubert plummeted into the soul and understood the nature of humanity with all its brightness and darkness. When Schubert quoted Beethoven in *Auf dem Strom* it was an enormous tribute. Although Schubert might have felt inadequate to take up the mantle of Beethoven, his contribution to music was great and important. After Schubert, song would never be the same.

Charlotte tried to keep in touch with people who knew Schubert to learn how his health was. She was distraught when she learned that Schubert had died on November 19, only eight months after the benefit. Thirty-one years old! In his last days he was often delirious, sang unceasingly, and was reading *The Last of the Mohicans*. Schubert's obituary was written by his father:

> Yesterday afternoon, at three o'clock on Wednesday, my
> beloved son Franz Schubert, artist and composer, died after
> a short illness, and having received the Holy Sacraments
> of the Church. He died at the age of thirty-two (sic). We
> beg to announce to our dear friends and neighbors that
> the body of the deceased will be taken on the 21st of
> this month, at half-past two in the afternoon, from the
> house standing No. 694 in the new street on the Neuen-
> Wieden, to be buried near the bishop's stall in the parish

church of St Josef in Margarethen, where the holy rites
will be administered." Vienna, November 20, 1828. Franz
Schubert, schoolteacher in the Rossau.

After the funeral, friends gathered together to mourn and remember
the life of this great man. It was there that Charlotte learned that when his
brother visited the evening before his death, Schubert begged to be taken to
his own room and bed and not to be left "here in the corner under the earth."
His brother was unable to convince him that he was in his room and bed.
Schubert replied, "No . . . Beethoven does not lie here."

In the last year of his life, Schubert wrote a song cycle which he called a
group of "horrifying songs." He performed them himself sometime in 1828
for his closest friends at Schober's. Their darkness and gloomy nature took
all by surprise. His friends did not know how to react to them. "His voice
was full of emotion," someone noted, when he said they would grow fond
of them over time and claimed that "they have cost me more effort than any
of my other songs." Oh, if only I could have been there to hear them. I had
to wait twelve years until Vogl gave a performance of them. Knowing the
closeness of death, Schubert was perhaps saying "*Gute Nacht,*" good night, to
the world itself and asking who would play his songs after his death: "*Willst
zu meinen Liedern Deine Leier drehn?*" Will you turn your lyre to my songs?
When Charlotte finally heard them, she fwas unable to think of anything else
for an entire week. Some claimed he had died of typhus, but most agreed
it was the last stages of syphilis that finally took him. In any case, he had
understood suffering and the nearness of death more than any of us in the
room. Such beauty mixed with sadness. Although Schubert, the man, was
gone, his music would continue to be played and sung in our homes and in
the concert halls of Vienna, and therefore he would not die.

Johann Heinrich, the son of Hans and Charlotte, was to be known as
Henry so as not to be confused with his father. He followed in his father's
footsteps and studied to be a jurist. He attended the University of Berlin, and
after completing his courses he took the examination. This arduous event

consisted of seven hours on legal theory, a written essay on the conduct of a trial, and several written legal opinions on various cases. Henry's performance was stellar, and he was asked to join the law faculty. Both parents I were thrilled.

Henry met Karl Fritz, a relative from the Banat, in 1847. They were both attending a lecture on Kant. Afterwards they literally ran into each other at a coffee house. Karl was backing up and nudged Henry's elbow spilling Karl's cup of coffee over both of them. They went to the restroom to put cold water on the developing stains on their shirts. "Why don't you join me at a table?" Asked Henry. "We can talk about the lecture."

They found a table in a fairly quiet corner. There was much talk about what they had heard about Kant. Karl eagerly started the conversation. "I do think that motivation is important in judging whether a person is good or bad. But the minute I say that I find a dozen objections to that principle."

"Yes" said Henry. "I am a lawyer, and many cases are tried on the motivation of the person. Was a person killed because a man was protecting his wife and child is much different than killing a person who is about to stab you".

"But whose law are we to follow? Man's or God's?" Karl asked. "Aren't most civil laws based on . . .". His sentence was interrupted when Karl Marx arrived at their table. He was going to meet Karl after the lecture to discuss it. Karl stood up and introduced Karl Marx to his relative Henry. Both Marx and Karl were attending the university and were in a class together.

To say that the conversation from that point on was lively, would be an understatement. There was no rancor, and all opinions were taken seriously. Marx believed that Kant was not taking into account where the person was born, his parents, and the economic and social conditions that had shaped the individual.

Henry became very interested in how upbringing and environment were fundamental in the formation of morals. Would his family see 'right and wrong' differently than people born and raised in Vienna? Henry wrote home about his meetings with Karl and wanted to know more about his family in the Banat.

Karl had related that he did not know much since his grandfather, Johann Fritz, the famous violinist, had never really shared much. Johann had left the Banat for Vienna at such an early age he had few memories and had only returned to visit the family once. He told Karl that the family were farmers and merchants, of simple stock, and good hearted. More than distance seemed to separate the family once Johann had moved to Vienna.

The earth seemed to move in 1848. Hans's fears of the iron fist of Metternich had come to fruition. People had doubts that the peace so welcomed in 1814 would remain. What would the ramifications of spreading hunger, the impact of industrialization on artisans, rising nationalism, and the inability of the monarchy to deal with any of these crises have on the Empire. Anger was building in the rhetoric of thinkers and journalists and this anger would become rage. In March, Vienna was again at war, but this time between students and the troops of the king.

PART THREE

1848. The Year of Revolutions

Karl Fritz was thirty when the Hungarian Revolution began. Martin, his father, had decided to move the family to Novi Sad in 1920. Martin had become extremely adept and creative in cabinetmaking, a family craft, and wanted to open his own shop. Martin branched out into furniture of all kinds and his shop was becoming too small for his work and ideas in the Banat. He had become well known in the region for his elegant designs, and he believed that the wealthier citizens in Novi Sad would appreciate his skill—and he was right. People from Temeswar, Buda, and Pest, who came to Novi Sad for trade, also began buying cabinets and furniture he had built. As the years went on, Martin was pleased with his work and how his family lives had improved.

When Karl was little, he and his friends played in the alleys between the stores, and often got day-old bread and overripe produce from the vendors on the street to take home. They also played in the church cemeteries and were run off by the priests and ministers. One time they had to polish all the chancel ware as punishment for the sacrilege of desecrating the cemetery by making tracks in the wet soil. When went home with my hands blackened, he was also punished by his father. He had to kneel on hard beans in the corner of the kitchen. He would eventually cry because of the pain, and then was sent to my room to think about his sins. However, most of the time, life was wonderful. He was carefree and unaware of the enormous changes that were to occur in the world.

As he grew up he began to appreciate Novi Sad and that it had to offer. There were fabric stores, pottery stores, places to buy books, restaurants, bakeries, artists and poets, newspapers. The streets were wide, and carts with horses traveled freely down them; the buildings were well painted; the houses had wonderful gardens; and there were items to buy from all over the world. The Danube bordered the city, and there was a military fortress along one of the banks, the Petrovaradin. A whole education was at arm's reach. He could easily travel to Temeswar, where there were a library and theater. Art, literature, theater, and music that he had never seen or heard were available for the taking. He learned some Hungarian and was learning Serbian. Both languages would benefit his father's business because he could converse with more customers. Being able to read and write in more than one language also gave him access to more books.

The Lutheran school Karl attended was vigorous, and the teachers urged me to continue his studies at university. His hopes were to attend a university in Germany where he could study law or medicine. In preparation he started to study Latin and often did Latin exercises with the pastor of their church, who was glad to have someone eager to learn and read books he had used when in seminary. The pastor also had wonderful books of poetry and a book of stories by the Grimm Brothers. Karl loved these stories and would tell them to the family at night. His mother was genuinely afraid of them, making Karl and his father laugh. They were truly terrifying, and many nights Karl could not close my eyes, thinking of all the horrible deaths and creatures that were chronicled in the stories. His favorite was "The Juniper Tree" because of its happy ending. Father and son are reunited, and the wicked stepmother is punished. This seemed just to him; though horrible things had happened, there was goodness at the end. Karl wanted life to be like this.

It was in Novi Sad that that he was introduced to Jews and their religion. At the beginning of the eighteenth century, there were only three Jewish families in the city. However, by 1830 Novi Sad had some forty Jewish families. It appeared to Karl that they were active in all areas of life in Novi Sad but they lived together in a tight-knit community. They spoke German or Hungarian and socialized only with one another. They had their own schools and city leaders. As a young child Karl knew very little about the hatred of the Christians for the Jews. This was to change when he met the love of his life.

He met Hannah when he delivered an order of two chairs to her family's house in the Jewish district of Novi Sad. She was the most beautiful girl he had ever seen. He was thirteen and she was twelve. Waiting for her father to come to the door to accept the order, Karl and Hannah struck up a conversation about music. He told her that his Uncle Johann was a well-known violinist in Vienna and that he had known and worked with Haydn and Mozart. Although Karl did not really know him, the stories of his life were told over and over again in his household. Hannah was enthralled. She was an excellent pianist, and, like most people of the time, her favorite composer was Beethoven. She introduced me to her parents, and they offered me coffee and a pastry. He did not have time since my father was expecting me at the shop but, he promised he would stop by the next day when he had more time.

When Karl arrived at their house the next day, they went into the music room where a marvelous array of Hungarian pastries and coffee was set out. Hannah's parents asked her to play a Beethoven sonata. When she was done, Karl enthusiastically stood and applauded loudly. She was marvelous. Hannah begged him to tell some Beethoven stories, a request he gladly agreed to.

After about an hour, Karl excused himself to go home. "I am sure that I have overstayed my welcome. Thank you for the wonderful food and Hannah, I could listen to you all day." Hannah's faced reddened. Karl shook her father's hand and thanked him again. Hannah invited me to come again, with her parents' permission, the following week. They agreed and Karl was thrilled.

On my way back hope Karl thought about his visit. He was impressed by their generosity and their intellect. Their home was filled with books, art, and music. He had never been in such an affluent home.

Karl went to their house often after his initial visits. The parents could see that he was an honest and sincere young man and at the time they did not seem concerned that he wasn't Jewish; he was a friend of Hannah's. Over the next few years, Karl became more relaxed during the visits. Sometimes he went merely to talk with her father and borrow some of his books. He knew so much about art, literature, and philosophy. Outside of his teachers, Karl knew no one with such a vast education. Herr Rosenstein was a medical doctor, but his university training had also given him a broad education in philosophy and literature. Frau Rosenstein would often joke that if she had been willing to wait until Herr Rosenstein had finished his studies to marry him, she would have been sixty. They let me borrow books, and I found that Herr Rosenstein was enamored of my questions and took time to answer them. My favorite writers were Goethe, Schiller, and Kant. We all thought that Beethoven's setting of Schiller's "Ode to Joy" was a masterpiece. We had fun attempting to sing some of the parts. We would usually end up laughing so hard that all attempts to keep time or any kind of order were failures.

And most importantly, there was Hannah and her beautiful playing. She was improving by leaps and bounds and was eventually admitted to the music conservatory. And eventually Karl realized he was in love with Hannah.

Karl had never known a Jewish person before and had only heard whispering when the Jews were mentioned at home. Karl's home village, Torschau, was mostly Lutheran. Karl knew girls who worked for Jewish families as maids, but there was never any mingling or contact in a social setting. Slowly Karl began to ask my father some questions.

His immediate response was that I should have nothing to do with the Jews beyond business. When asked why, he only shook his head and said to obey and not question him any further about the issue. "They are not like us, even if they speak our language. They are greedy and charge interest on loans, keeping people owing and never able to get ahead economically. Martin Luther hated the Jews. When they would not accept his teachings and convert, he called them *Judensau,* Jewish pigs. They are unclean and we should have no contact with them. We should burn their houses, synagogues, forbid their rabbis to teach. Just stay away and don't dirty yourself by being near them."

Karl could not believe this, but then again, he knew nothing about them or their faith. But surely this was not what I had witnessed at Hannah's house—unless they were devils who were trying to deceive me. Martin Luther had written often about his personal visits with the devil, so Karl knew there were devils in the world and could take many forms. He was at a loss; he knew that Hannah and her family were good people. He could not reconcile both views, one personal the other religious.

Hannah and her father, Herr Rosenstein, came into his father's store. They were looking for a new cabinet for the china Herr Rosenstein had bought for his wife on their anniversary. I blushed. He didn't want his father to know how much time he was spending at Hannah's house and what his true feelings were for Hannah.

"My family so loved the small table you built for our library that I thought I would not look any farther than your store. Do you have something that would match it?"

His father saw Karl blushing and knew immediately that he knew the beautiful Hannah and that she was the reason for my questions.

"Yes, right over here."

Karl's father and Herr Rosenstein went to the other room to look at the curio. Hannah stayed behind to talk with Karl.

"I have learned a new Beethoven sonata and would love for you to come over to hear it. I thought I would have a few of my friends over also. I would like you to meet them."

Karl was unsure how to answer. He was afraid his father would come in hear the conversation and know that he was visiting the Rosenstein's. There would then be an argument at home.

My father and Herr Rosenstein returned to the counter to discuss payment and delivery of the curio. "Hannah asked her father to invite me to their house to hear more about Beethoven and play the piano for me." My father looked at me and then at Herr Rosenstein.

"Has my son been to your house?"

"Yes, we invited him in when he delivered the table and since then he has often visited us. What a wonderful young man your son is. It would be our pleasure to have him come to hear Hannah play the new Beethoven sonata she has learned. That is unless you have some objection."

Karl's father, not wanting to alienate a good customer, reluctantly agreed. "I am sure he could stop in for a short visit when he delivers the curio."

Karl could feel his father's agitation over being deceived and then having to agree to another visit. However, Hannah, in all her naïveté, clapped her hands and gave her father a quick hug, which made him blush. All she saw in Karl was a person with similar interests and who was there to listen to her talk about her day, her dreams, and her desires.

After they left, Karl's father said that after dinner they needed to have a conversation. Karl feared that his father's anger would end my visits to the Rosenstein's. I had resigned myself to the fact that Hannah would never agree to date me, but I hoped we could be friends. That night after dinner Karl's father asked him what he thought he was doing. "There will be nothing but sorrow if you continue with this 'friendship'. You have fallen in love with the girl."

Karl tried to tell his father he was wrong and that they were only friends.

Karl's father laughed, "Is there another friend of yours who makes you blush when they come into the room?"

Karl knew his father was right, but he could not imagine not seeing Hannah. Karl tried to tell his father that the main reason for going to the Rosenstein's was to talk with the father and read some of the book Herr Rosenstein had in his library. "Herr Rosenstein is teaching me things that I don't learn in school. We both want me to go to university and Herr Rosenstein knows what is necessary to get accepted. I would have a real chance of matriculating."

"Do you think you are learning enough to get a scholarship at a university?"

"Papa, I want to go to university, and I will work very hard to gain admission. I don't believe I was meant to be a farmer, and I know I don't have your talents. As I read more books, I find myself wanting to read more. I want to make you proud and provide for you and Mama when you get older. My teachers believe that it is very possible that I will get a scholarship."

Reluctantly Karl's father agreed to let Karl visit but he wanted a report on what he had learned after each visit. Karl was to go to their house only once a month. Karl was willing to agree to any stipulation his father put on his visits. He agreed and hugged his father.

Warmly his father returned the hug. "You are such a dear son. I hope that your dreams come true. But life has a way of placing stumbling blocks and sorrows in our way. Your great-grandfather's life was so hard. We should go and visit relatives in the Banat and hear stories and take some of our earnings to them. I have heard there have been some heavy snows and flooding in the

Banat, which has made harvesting crops almost impossible. I am sure my family could use some extra money. Besides, I miss my parents and we should visit them."

Karl was thrilled, he did not remember much of his original home. All h knew of his family were stories that his parents told. He knew that his father was the first son of my grandfather's second marriage. The sons of the first marriage were Johann and Thomas. Karl of course had heard about the famous Uncle Johann and that he was living in Vienna and that Uncle Thomas was a pharmacist in Torschau. Plans were made to visit the next week. His father wrote and heard back almost immediately. They would love our visit.

Since our visit was to be close to Easter, they decided to stay through the Easter celebration. The painting of Easter eggs and waking up to find them hidden throughout the house by the *Osterhase*, the Easter Hare, would be a memory always cherished. The village leaders had decided to hide Easter eggs throughout the village, giving all the children a delightful day and hopefully wearing them out.

After a morning in church, they walked home for a fabulous Easter meal of chicken dumpling soup, potatoes, vegetables, salad, and of course an assortment of cakes and candy. After our meal my thoughts centered on our Good Friday service, in which we heard the Passion Story. Karl wondered how Hannah would respond to the story of the suffering of Christ. She had told him they were waiting for the Savior and that they believed Jesus could not be God; no one could equal God or be God, even though we are all created in the image of God. That it is not possible that Jesus is God. They would never find agreement on this issue. It seemed to Karl that without Jesus, who could be saved? Karl wrestled with these thoughts during their time in the Banat but was afraid to discuss it with anyone in the family.

The villages of Torschau and Schowe were beautiful and peaceful. The trees and flowers were blossoming, fields were being tilled and planted, women were cleaning out their houses, airing clothing and linens, young girls were making spring and summer dresses, and children were running through the streets. Two things struck me: the seeming poverty of the people and a sense that there were some tensions within the village. There were conversations among the adults about tensions between the ethnic groups. "The

Hungarians want us to speak and learn in Hungarian, and if we are living in Hungary we should speak like Hungarians." "They want us to change our names into Hungarian. I fear that we will have to leave and give up all that we have worked for." These comments were expressed over and over. What Karl believed about the world was quickly changing. It appeared to Karl that the people I knew were willing to fight to have their own countries and their own identities, and the Germans were caught in the middle. Karl saw that we would eventually have to take sides. But with whom to side was going to be an enormous question. Karl did not know Germany. Although his entire spoke German, ate German food, worshipped in German, were educated in German, and understood my ancestry to be German, all I knew was Hungary and the Hungarians. The conversations usually centered on these issues:

"Are we not Germans? Our homeland is Germany. Yes, we are living here, but that does not mean we should become Hungarians in language and customs."

"The Jews speak both Hungarian and German. But that is because they have no homeland. All of them are foreigners."

"Ach, the Jews! What a people. Dirty as pigs."

"What are the Serbians up to? I hear talk that they want a separate country. That means Vojvodina will exist in another country. Once German, then Hungarian, and now Serbian."

These conversations, with their inherent distrust and even hatred, often lasted into the night. The more the people drank, the more hateful and bitter the conversations became. Even though Karl's father was better off and had so much to be thankful for, he entered the conversations with vigor. It seemed as if Karl's father had not shed his old life and its beliefs and ways. I didn't recognize the man who emerged.

Karl's grandfather's brothers, who had left Germany as adults, felt that they were being discriminated against. "They know we are hard workers. They want the fruits of our labors but want to give us no rights. We are like serfs here. I fear the Serbian youths who constantly are taunting my sons and their children. This all will break into fights. Who will defend us?"

In the urban areas, such as Novi Sad, there was a push toward Magyarization. Many people had changed their names to be Hungarian.

Surviving economically and socially was more important than remaining culturally German.

Karl was too young to care about all these politics and hatreds. He cared about getting into a university and Hannah. Karl's grades were excellent and all the time he spent with Herr Rosenstein had helped with this entrance exams. He was not only accept but was awarded a scholarship.

In 1836 Karl, along with Karl Marx, enrolled at the University of Berlin. Being a university student and meeting Karl Marx put Karl's life on a trajectory that would make him question all that I had been taught in school and at home. His life and the lives of my family members would never be the same.

Karl was enrolled in a course taught by Eduard Gans. He had begun to have doubts about entering the fields of medicine and law and decided he needed to enlarge my base of knowledge. He missed the conversations with Herr Rosenstein and felt that some of the courses were dull. He believed he would find what he wanted to do certainly within a year, and the courses, such as the one taught by Gans, were necessary as foundational courses. Gans had taken over teaching Hegel's course on political philosophy. Gans had attended lectures by Hegel and was also a jurist. Karl thought might learn how philosophy could be applied to the law. Ihe hoped that in understanding the world, philosophy, history, and religion he would be able to comprehend the differences he had seen in the multiethnic society in which he lived. With a broader education he concluded that he would be able to be a solicitor to all the people in Novi Sad.

The conversations he had heard when visiting his relatives also made him realize that he knew little about politics and its effect on people's lives. Although it was peaceful and quiet in the village where he was born, underneath everything was the people's uncertainty about their future. Who would dictate so many of the things that make up an ordinary life: taxes, their schools and churches, the commodities they needed, tools of their trades? Whoever was in political office and made the laws, held the villagers' fates in their hands. The people had no voice. These concerns were of utmost importance, since it seemed to Karl his relatives were poor and existed from hand to mouth. If the harvest was bad, they had to hope they had stored enough from the good harvests. There was no money left over for simple pleasures. I did not want their lives but knew of no way to help them. Karl's father had even occasionally sent money to his family, but I felt that it was never enough.

There was a young man in the lecture hall who sat in front of Karl. He never missed class and took many notes. He had dark eyes, curly black hair that hit his shirt or coat collar, and a beard and mustache. There was an intensity and energy to him that was magnetic. After class he often gathered with a group of students to discuss the lecture. The discussions were animated, and the fellow student, whose name was Karl Marx, often dominated the discussion.

After class one day, Karl followed him and his group of friends to a café. Karl asked if he could join them and Marx answer was a resounding yes. "Of course, the more we can help people understand the philosophy of Hegel, the more our world will advance into freedom," he said enthusiastically. What kind of freedom he meant, Karl had no idea and he wasn't even sure he knew what "freedom" meant.

The discussion was far reaching, and all struggled with what Hegel meant by "freedom." Marx kept on interrupting his friends, asking subtle questions that began to undermine Hegel's philosophy. (Marx eventually would move away from Hegel's philosophy and demonstrate that there are people who can never be free because they are constrained by others who control their ability to reach their potential and be productive.)

Eventually this led to questions about the different classes in a society. How the rich want to keep those who are poor from ever getting rich by controlling their wages and gaining profits from their labor so the rich can get richer. Karl thought of his father and asked the naïve question of who was keeping his father from reaching his potential when Karl could see that his father controlled what he made and how much he charged for it, and that as a family they were gaining more money that allowed his father to become more productive. If his father had more money he could hire more workers, buy more supplies, enlarge his store, and advertise throughout the region.

"My friend, do you not see how your father is being deceived into believing that he is in control of what he is producing? I assume he has workers he must pay, which means that part of his profit is reduced to pay the workers. He cannot pay them what they want because then he would not have a large gain. He must price his products based on what he pays for the materials he uses. If there is a surplus of materials and their price is low, he can make more profit, but if there is a shortage of materials and he must pay more for them, he will make less. And who controls how much the prices go up for goods? Not him, he is at the mercy of the market and the state. This is a vicious circle from which he cannot break free. Thus, he has no freedom."

At this point everyone starting talking at once.

"Why does the state control the prices and not the people who need the materials?"

"We can all see that farmers are at the mercy of nature, yet they are not able to control prices so that they can live."

"Will people ever tire of this circle? Will the people—who are at the mercy of the rich, who use their profits not to pay the workers but to get richer—do something to gain their freedom? They cannot quit their jobs. They do not have the money to go to school and enter the wealth-producing professions—"

"Like us?" interrupted Marx.

Again, it seemed like chaos. Karl feared that they would be expelled from the café, but they just continued arguing and drinking. When Karl returned home early in the morning, he could not sleep. When it was time for class, he eagerly left my meager room and went to class to continue hid learning.

By the end of the semester, much to his father's chagrin, Karl had decided to read in philosophy. His father could not understand Karl's choice, since it would not lead to any kind of gainful employment or career. Karl told him he wanted to teach at the university level, but his father only kept silent. Karl had written several letters telling him of my friends and the exciting evenings at the café. Karl Marx had given him a copy of an essay he had written a year earlier for his gymnasium. There was a passage Karl shared with Father because it reflected most closely why Karl had chosen a different path:

> We must therefore seriously examine whether we have
> really been inspired in our choice of a profession, whether
> an inner voice approves it, or whether this inspiration is
> a delusion, and what we took to be a call from the Deity
> was self-deception. But how can we recognize this except
> by tracing the source of the inspiration itself? If we have

chosen the position in life in which we can most of all work for mankind, no burdens can bow us down, because they are sacrifices for the benefit of all; then we shall experience no petty, limited, selfish joy, but our happiness will belong to millions, our deeds will live on quietly but perpetually at work, and over our ashes will be shed the hot tears of noble people.

His father wrote back that he felt all of this was noble but very naïve. 'How are words going to make life better for you or for anyone?' was the general sentiment of his letter. Basically, his father was telling Karl that he was young and being filled with silly ideas by his friends. He could not understand how Karl believed that it was exactly the words of people like Karl Marx that were going to change the world. But Karl was sure that if he could continue his work in philosophy, he would find a way to put the words into action. At one of their evening gatherings, Marx had said very seriously that the purpose of philosophy was to change the world. He knew that action on those words was necessary.

After graduation Karl came back to Novi Sad and told my parents he was going to be a journalist to inform the people of the Banat and Vojvodina of the events that were happening in Germany and Austria. He believed that enormous changes were in the making and if he spread Karl Marx's ideas to the people they would join together and demand changes from the government. His parents were upset and believed Karl was endangering himself.

"We must change the world in order for people to live good and productive lives. How can they be satisfied with earning barely enough to put food on the table? We have been lucky. Surely you have heard how the peasants are suffering because of poor harvests? And with the potato famine in Ireland there is not enough food, and prices are rising and making what is available almost impossible to afford."

"Yes, Karl, but calm heads and reason must prevail. Of course, we care about what is happening—"

"But what are you doing? Do you realize that you will be out of business in the near future because of industrialization? Industries can make what you make more cheaply, and that is what people will buy."

"No, they will always want high quality."

"Yes, the rich, but the poor need furniture also. The artisans are suffering because their goods—"

Karl's mother interrupted sharply and told both to stop. "Please, Karl, you come home and we have to listen again to these ideas of yours. I don't know who this Marx is, but like all young rabble-rousers his ideas will go away and people will go on as before."

"You want our families to go on as before in those villages? Industry will take them over, no matter how good they are as farmers. There is an economic crisis and we all will feel its results. There is open hostility in Berlin by workers who are against the owners of factories and mills who are refusing to pay wages that allow their workers to live a good life. We have a chance to allow people to choose their own futures. You are lucky that your work has allowed you to move and gain capital, but your future is in danger because you do not own the means of production."

Karl's father slammed down his fist with such force that he put a crack in the table and his mother started to cry. Karl left.

He went to see how Hannah was doing. He feared that she had forgotten him, but she hadn't.

"Of course I remember you. I thought you had forgotten me, once your letters stopped. I must admit I was very sad."

"Hannah, I have met the most inspiring people, the most important of whom is a man called Karl Marx. I fear that he will soon be censored. His thoughts and ideas are emboldening people to speak out, no matter what their class, to gain freedom for all. Listen to some of the notes I took during our meetings. At his gymnasium graduation he gave a speech, "Reflections of a Young Man." He wants only the good for all men and not just the rich and noble. This is what he said: 'History calls those men the greatest who have ennobled themselves by working for the common good; experience acclaims as happiest the man who has made the greatest number of people happy.'"

Taking only a moment to sit down Karl continued, "And in a critique of the philosopher Hegel, he wrote: 'All forms of the state have democracy for their truth, and for that reason are false to the extent that they are not a democracy.'

"This is a good man trying to do good. Here, look at an essay he wrote just this year called 'The Wages of Labor.' Take it and share it with your parents and we can all talk."

"That will be wonderful." Hannah said as she smiled warmly at Karl as she took the essay from him to read. " I will bring some of my friends from the music school. They will be interested, I know. Sometime next week would be good."

They set a date. Karl worried about her "friends," hoping that one of them was not a boyfriend. Karl did meet the boyfriend. He was a cellist she often accompanied for programs in Novi Sad. He was ten years older than Hannah, but Karl could tell they were both enamored of each other. He was Jewish so Karl was sure her parents would have no objection to him. But as our meetings developed and grew, I could see that he was not interested in the ideas of Karl Marx or other writers who were called the Young Hungarians. He began to drift away and so did Hannah's interest in him. Karl could see her looking at him, and he knew there was something between them that could not be denied.

Many of her friends were very interested, as they too saw the world through different lenses than their parents. They also had poorer relatives around Novi Sad and saw how their lives were getting worse. We discussed the possibility of printing our own pamphlets resembling those created by Lajos Kossuth, in which he avoided censorship by saying they were correspondences. They decided include music reviews, poetry, and editorials that gave information about the communist movement in Berlin. Karl would provide the information from Berlin and Vienna. He was certain that I could also get newspapers from Vienna and Berlin. Several copies of the *Rheinische Zeitung* were in his suitcase when he returned, and they provided much inspiration and talking points. The friends all agreed that the first step that must be taken was to create a free press. Without a free press, no ideas or opposing views could be circulated. The old order would continue. They all agreed they were responsible for the writing and its distribution in Novi Sad and other villages in the Banat and Vojvodina, as well as, if possible, meeting with interested people who agreed with our views.

By 1847 the group of friends had over two hundred subscriptions in Novi Sad, and more young people, writers, and liberal thinkers attended our meetings. They moved the location of the meetings to a basement room of the synagogue. Residents from the villages often appeared and took an active part in our endeavors. Besides freedom of the press, they talked endlessly about how Hungary would gain its independence from Austria. Many Germans believed that Hungary should no longer be a part of the Austrian Empire.

They started each meeting reading recent poetry written by Hungarians, and Hannah often played music by Franz Liszt. Karl's favorite poem had become Vörösmarty's "Appeal": "Oh, Magyar, keep immovably your native country's trust, for it has borne you, and at death will consecrate your dust!"

They were all reading the poetry by Sandor Petőfi and János Arany who inspired in them a devotion to Hungary and its native language. We had no doubts that Hungary would become a sovereign nation with its own government, language, music, and most importantly freedom. Also important was reading the latest writings of Kossuth. For many of them he was the voice of Hungary, an orator of enormous intellect and power. Each of his sentences seemed a world. His call was heard by many.

When my father learned about our meetings and what our political leanings were, he said I was stupid. "Do you have any idea what you are doing? Your talking will lead to a revolution. All talk in Europe is revolution, revolution, revolution. This will not stop with a free press. Besides, we are not Hungarians."

"Father, all we know is Hungary. I was out of place when we visited our relatives. I don't dress like them, I don't think like them, they are prejudiced and may I add old fashioned."

"What! You would not have the life you have if they had not sacrificed everything to come here. Your life is due to their hard work and, yes, deaths. I don't know you. Is this what an education does, turn you from your family and country?"

"Father, we will lead the way in the world. Freedom and liberty for all men—"

"Get out, Karl, you can no longer live here. These ideas are clouding your mind. How will you find your way through this fog of delusion? Find your own place with those friends who have nothing else to do but go to meetings, drink wine and coffee, and plot the end of the world."

I left. I decided to move to Pest. I told Hannah that I would write often and inform her of all the events.

~

It was February 1848, and the French had overthrown King Louis Philippe and created the Second Republic. Of great interest was the creation of national workshops to provide work for the unemployed. The reforms also included the end of the death penalty, a ten-hour work day in Paris, and the end of slavery in the empire. These gave hope to all of us. Austria, too, was soon to see a revolution that, like the French, involved bloodshed.

Austria was only 25 percent German at the time. Its ethnic minority groups were all vying for independence. In Pest, Kossuth promoted gradual reforms. He was a nationalist and wanted Hungary to no longer be subjugated politically and economically to Austria. On March 13 a revolution began in Vienna. Kossuth's speech at the Hungarian Parliament lit the fire. He attacked Metternich's oppressive methods.

I wrote to Hannah of Kossuth's speech on March 3 at the Diet of Pressburg. This Assembly presented to the Emperor reforms for Hungary.

> March 3
> Dear Hannah,
> I heard the most glorious words today: "Yes, on us there falls the
> heavy curse of a suffocating smoke. From the charnel house of the
> Viennese system a polluted air is blowing over us, paralyzing our
> nerves and stifling our spirit." Kossuth spoke with elegance and
> fire. There was an enormous audience to hear him. He called for
> us to "raise our policy to the level of events." He demanded the
> replacement of Vienna's absozlutist government by a constitu-
> tion, the sharing of domestic tax, and the freeing of all serfs with
> compensation to their owners. He concluded by demanding, "If
> we disperse from the Diet without delivering to the people what
> they so rightfully and justifiably expect of the legislature, who
> will dare shoulder the responsibility for what ensues?" As you can
> imagine, we all felt ready to march to Vienna and protest and, like

the French, invite a revolution. However, this was not the means
by which Kossuth believed we should achieve the goals. Unlike the
French, he wanted no blood to be spilt. Many students and young
people began meeting and started to draft points that we wanted
the government to address. It was at one of these meetings that I
met the most amazing poet, Sandor Petöfi. He came to Pressburg to
hear Kossuth and ask people to join his group in Pest. As you can
imagine, I said yes and joined his following. We meet at Pilvax Café
and I am reminded of the evening I spent with Marx. I will keep
you posted on all our decisions and actions.
With affection,
Karl

March 15
Dear Hannah,
We have heard that there was an uprising in Berlin. Certainly
people are ready to engage in work that overthrows absolutist
governments run by monarchies and officials who have never
heard the voice of the people and what dire conditions many are
living under. We have also learned that on March 14 in a debating
session, Kossuth pleaded with the nobles to act wisely and keep the
reins "in our hands, because then we can continue in advance along
a constitutional path, but once the reins are jerked from our grasp,
God alone knows what the consequences will be." We know that
in Vienna the students are in the streets. Things have moved at a
frightening pace there. After the students presented a resolution to
the court on March 12, they marched with citizens to the House
of Estates for the opening of the Lower Austria Legislation. On
the thirteenth, troops were sent and demanded that the insurgents
disperse. The troops fired and there were injuries and deaths. We
have not received news of how many, but we were horrified that,
like the French, the Viennese would have to deal with the blood of
their citizens on their hands. The soldiers were ordered to withdraw,
and by evening Metternich resigned. The next day, protesters
demanded freedom of the press, the abolition of censorship, and

the writing of a new constitution. The world we know will be changed by tomorrow!

Affectionately,

Karl

On March 15 one hundred and fifty members of the Hungarian Diet, or assembly, entered Vienna. The events in Vienna had galvanized them to make sure the Austrian constitution would not include Hungary. Their demands included freedom of the press, trial by jury, equality of religion, and a system of national education.

The day before in Pest, Petőfi and our group, the March Youth, drew up a list of ten points we believed had to be present in any reform of the government. Top on the list was freedom of the press and the ending of censorship. Everyone in our group understood that advancement in any area of life was dependent upon the free exchange of ideas and a voice in government.

March 17

Dear Hannah,

On the 15th we marched to Landerer and Heckenast press to demand our points be printed for distribution. Petőfi has written a national song, which we recited. I must admit that tears form when I hear it.

> Rise, Magyar! is the country's call!
> The time has come, say one and all:
> Shall we be slaves, shall we be free?
> This is the question, now agree!
> For by the Magyar's God above
> We truly swear,
> We truly swear the tyrant's yoke
> No more to bear!

We all had such courage and hope. By the time we reached the National Museum, where the city council was meeting, there were five thousand of us! The mayor accepted and signed the ten points.

Petöfi has shared with us what he wrote in his diary the next day: "Today Hungarian freedom has been born because the chains have fallen from the press." By the sixteenth we saw banners that read "Long live freedom of the press."

Affectionately,

Karl

I was tired, dirty and had no money. I wanted to stay with the March Youth but I also felt an obligation to Hannah. I knew that we were in love, and we had to decide how to handle that which we knew neither of our parents would accept. The hardships that awaited us I would never have been able to foresee. My heart was bursting with love and the hope of a better life. I had bought a copy of Marx's *Communist Manifesto* in Pest to take home with me and share with Hannah.

CHAPTER SIXTEEN

Novi Sad

I am for my beloved, and my beloved is for me.
—Song of Songs 2:16 The New Oxford Annotated Bible, 1991

Hannah narrates

Karl's letters filled me not only with a longing for him but also with a desire to be a part of these momentous happenings. I always believed that life, for a woman, could be more than husband, house, and children. The events would lead to a new world for so many people. I could feel such hope but also fear for the resistance that awaited the reforms. I was not naïve enough to think that power would give up power. There is courage in numbers, but I saw that the numbers were few. I so wanted to be in Pest with him.

My letters did not contain any hints about my feelings for him but thanked him for all the news and expressed my excitement for what he was a part of. I told our group of friends what was happening and about the uprisings in Vienna, Berlin, and Pressburg. We printed leaflets letting people know of these events and what Kossuth was presenting before the Diet. Everyone was interested in the Opposition Part, which Petöfi headed, and Karl's reactions. My parents were also becoming involved, at temple, in the political happenings in Hungary and Berlin, from where they were receiving materials about Karl Marx. They understood that all of this could mean freedom for the Jews. They would not have to choose between their religion and their nation.

Perhaps it was youth that directed my actions and thoughts, but I could not imagine sitting back and waiting for events to take place. All of us in our group took on some task to spread the ideas of liberalism and the need for drastic change. Most of us were students, musicians, artists, writers, or poets. Eventually some more youth from middle-class families joined us. At the heart of all this for us was a chance for betterment, a way to seize the world and make it ours.

The first night that Karl was home, he came to my house and we talked all night with my friends and my parents. The news we were hearing from the South Banat, where Karl's extended family was living, was not good. The Serbians were committing more and more acts of violence against the Germans and other ethnic groups. We had heated debates over issues of race and nation and what it meant to be free. Karl told us about the living conditions of his family. Most were poor farmers, peasants really, who took pride in their hard work and agricultural abilities. There homes were clean and well kept. Some of his family members were doing well. They had a very successful pharmacy, one had become a midwife and was married to a doctor, another was a famous violinist, and Karl's father seemed very successful. But they seemed to be the exception. Their neighbors were Serbs with whom they did not associate. There were also several Jewish families; some of the women in his family did housekeeping and laundry for them. Karl was unsure what his family's fate would be if Serbia became an independent nation. "Why shouldn't the Serbs have their own independent nation?" he said. "They have a common language, customs—"

"Yes," my father broke in, "so why are we all learning Hungarian? We are Jewish and have our own language of Hebrew, or Yiddish, yet we think of ourselves as Hungarians. A nation is much more than language and customs. We had a nation—"

"Yes, but if we went back it would be Palestine. Wouldn't we have to live within the nation of Palestine? Would we be able to live as Jews in peace? Would there be temples?"

"We could find out, but you have good points. However, do we all not see what is happening? We are having a debate on nationalism and not the twelve points that were written when Karl was in Pest. We are mixing autonomy with individual rights and freedoms."

"But with a nation and a constitution, we will make sure that these rights are enshrined not just in our hearts but in our lives."

"Karl Marx has understood this. He claims we must take our rights. Demand them. Does it matter which nation or government is in power? It is up to the people to unite and do what is in their best interests."

"How can we do this if the guns and troops belong to the government? We must be able to arm ourselves. There has been bloodshed all over Europe. Look what has happened in Berlin! On March 18 four thousand people stood up to fourteen thousand troops with cannons."

"Go on with the story."

"The next day the King had to watch a parade, with his head bared, and see the mangled bodies of those that had been killed. The people made a point. They stood up against tyranny. Petőfi's poem. We have all learned the opening, but listen to the end.

> Our name will be noble once more,
> Worthy of our past, our great lore.
> Centuries besmirched our good name—
> Time to cleanse us of their deep shame!
> To the God of the Magyars we
> Truly swear,
> Truly swear, that we shall not live enslaved. No,
> Not ever!
> Over revered burial hills
> Grandchildren will fall on their knees
> And, citing our names in prayer,
> They will bless us all forever.
> To the God of the Magyars we
> Truly swear,
> Truly swear, that we shall not live enslaved. No,
> Not ever!

"People do not want to serve under a government and king who is not one of them. They want to be proud of their heritage. I think people now are willing to go to their deaths to achieve this."

"I want to return to the Serbian problem," Karl shouted. "The reason is part of my family lives amongst them in the Vojvodina and I have heard that there have been raids against the Germans and beatings of Germans. They may live in the same province, but they are segregated. Things there have been stable, since both Serb and German are peasants and trying to live as best they can. Hungary is trying to make them all Hungarian, and the Serbs refuse to assimilate. This will cause a civil war, and my family will be caught in the middle. How will Kossuth handle the Serbs when they make their demands, which they certainly will?"

"I agree, the sword will eventually have to decide, not words."

"I received news that tensions are growing between Hungary and Serbia as we speak. Listen to what Jalačić delivered in March to the Serbian people at his installation as Viceroy. I will quote directly so I will not be misunderstood. These are his words as taken down by a member of the Opposition Party: 'I am obliged to tell and warn you that with regard to our relations with Hungary we stand!' but then he goes on to say that these are mere words. 'But in the unhappy case that the Hungarians continue to wander aimlessly and to act not as brothers to us and our people in Hungary but as oppressors, let them know . . . that we are ready with the sword in hand!' I have heard that Kossuth told a delegation of Serbians that the sword it will be."

Voices got louder, wine flowed, tempers flared, but the friends all agreed that in order for life to be better, reforms must be achieved. Some wanted to talk about Berlin, others Karl Marx, others Kossuth, and still others wanted to know what those of us who were ethnic Germans felt, since we were probably going to get caught in the middle.

Eventually everyone left. A friend offered Karl a place to stay. He and Karl were the last to leave, and Karl took Hannah's hand. At the door he placed a gentle kiss on her lips. Hannah stood like a statue and regretted that she had not held him and kissed him back. There would be another time, she hoped.

The next day, Karl came to her house. "I must find a job, Hannah. I cannot go home, and I was wondering if you knew of anyone that needed work done. You know I will do anything. Maybe my father was right, education has not been able to feed me."

She said she would ask her father if he knew anyone that needed help. She turned to find her father. In a few minutes Hannah came back. "He suggested that you apply to be a teacher at Jovan Jovanović Zmal high school. It is growing, father had heard that new teachers were being hired and that the teaching was done in German." Karl had obtained high marks at the University of Berlin. He applied the next day and was given an interview the following day. When he gave the administration and patrons the list of courses, lectures, and professors with whom he had studied, they agreed that they would take him. The salary was meager but enough for room and board.

Karl enjoyed his teaching and the students. He formed a reading group with the older students, and they met after classes. They read recent Hungarian literature and poetry. They also read Goethe's *Faust* with them to help their German and to introduce them to perhaps the greatest German writer of their time.

The group of liberal friends continued to meet once a week and reported all the news they had heard. Hannah's parents continued to be involved Hungarian politics at temple and were always eager to hear the news also. Hannah noticed that after his sessions with his students, Karl was often very quiet. After one of the meetings gatherings, Hannah asked him if everything was going well with his students.

"They are wonderful, and they are more challenging than I ever thought they would be. Our discussions on Faust have given me much food for thought. We spent two hours on wondering why Faust was ready to end his life so easily. One student suggested that all he needed was a good woman; he believed that had certainly helped Martin Luther. Another suggested it was because he couldn't see that his students were any better off after studying with him. But what exactly did they want to know? I finally asked them. They all looked at me, hoping I would tell them what it was they wanted to know. But I didn't. They pushed me even further, asking what I thought I was teaching them. I couldn't answer. The lines still resonate in my mind: *Und sehe, dass wir nichts wissen können! Das will mir schier das Herz verbrennen.* (And I see, that nothing can be known! That burns me to the bone.) They so wanted me to give them all the answers to life and happiness. None of them felt any pity for Faust. They could see that he would grab at anything to find happiness, and that was the wrong way to live life. I finally answered that, yes, love, food on the table, work, and faith were perhaps greater than knowledge. I almost quit my job that evening. I see now why our reforms are important. If people cannot have those simple things, then what hope do they have?"

Hannah did not know how to answer Karl. After a long silence she said, "Karl, you are helping them think and find their own happiness."

"Hannah, I want those things also. I want you, a home with you, children with you, and a life with you. Do you think this is possible? A Jew and a Lutheran?"

He didn't wait for me to answer. He drew Hannah close, and his warm mouth enclosed hers. Hannah's heart actually hurt, and she felt dizzy. She had read about this feeling in books but never believed these feelings could be true. The other young men she had kissed had never made her feel this way. She then kissed him with such abandon and her kisses were returned with equal vigor. Karl abruptly got up and said, "We must stop, Hannah. This will only lead to sorrow and disaster for both of us. We must talk about our feelings and decide for ourselves what we should do. Come with me tonight to my room and let us find our way."

The night passed too quickly. Their lovemaking was like a hunger that could not be filled. She knew that she could not go back to her family, but she loved them and felt she had to tell them of the choices that they had made that night. The next day was Sabbath and she knew they would be worried when she did not return home. Karl and Hannah wrote letters to them explaining their plans and hoped they would understand how it was love that led them to the decisions they were making. In her soul she knew they wouldn't, and she also knew I could never return home. Both Karl and I were now without family. They were the family, and the only family for a long time that time. Their plan was to return to the villages where Karl's family was from. He said there was a village named Jarek where he believed he could find a job teaching. There would certainly be work there, and he felt that his family would speak well of him. He was not sure if they knew that his father had kicked him out of his home.

"They may refuse to have anything to do with us," he said. "But we won't know until we arrive. I will see if there is place for us to stay. But the most important issue is your conversion to Protestantism. We should meet with a minister tomorrow and set a wedding date."

Hannah agreed but felt like she was cutting out half of her heart. Karl would never know what this would cost her. She hoped that her love for him would be enough for half a heart. That night after Karl fell asleep and Hannah cried and prayed that God would find comfort her. Surely God would understand decisions that were made from love, but she felt she was deceiving myself.

They met at the Reformed church in Novi Sad and talked at length with the minister there. He had concerns, of course, but was eager to see me convert. "One less Jew" was certainly what he thought. He married us that evening after he questioned Karl about his faith. He was Lutheran and at least not Catholic. Hannah could not understand why there would be such divisions within one faith. They told him that they would be leaving as soon as possible for Jarek to start a new life where no one knew that she was Jewish. Again, Hannah was so naïve and clouded by love that she could not imagine the hardships that would develop.

Karl left his job, telling the school that there were family problems he needed to attend to in Vojvodina. They agreed and even gave him his pay early to help. He did not tell them of Hannah or his marriage.

Hannah learned that her parents had received their letters the following week as we were preparing to leave. Friends from our circle came to Karl's room and told them how devastated her parents were. My mother would not get out of bed for two days and my father did nothing but sit in his chair. They did not eat, nor did they leave the house. They visited their rabbi, which our friends said gave them some comfort. He told them to remember the story of Ruth.

Time moved quickly in the world and in my life. In October there was an uprising in Vienna that proved deadly. Events seemed to spiral out of control as both Hungary and Austria prepared for armed confrontation. After the commander-in-chief was assassinated by a crowd, Kossuth became Hungary's leader. Austria had a new monarch, Francis Joseph, who worked to pacify Hungary. In October at St. Stephen's Square, Austria's minister of war was lynched by a crowd, supported by Hungarians, as Austrian troops were preparing to leave for Hungary. Croatia shelled Austria the same month, and by October 31 stormed the city square. Karl Marx went to Vienna to encourage a workers' revolt. Hungary and Austria were fighting, and civil war broke out in Hungary. Austria prevailed, because Russia agreed to help Austria, and Hungary was put under martial law. There was also fighting between Hungarians and Serbs in Vojvodina. And Hannah was pregnant.

July 1849 the Austrian army was outside of Novi Sad. Hannah begged Karl to allow her to return to the city to get her parents out and away from danger. He would not let her go alone. Hannah was due in August, but Karl finally gave in to her and they both set off to retrieve them. They arrived at her house on July 10. It was such a bittersweet reunion. The emotions Hannah felt ranged from fear to happiness to sadness to guilt. They finally convinced them that they needed to get out of Novi Sad, and that they would help them. "You can live with us and see the birth of your first grandchild." This convinced the parent to leave. Karl and Hannah helped them pack. They were ready to leave when the Austrian army opened cannon fire on the city of Petrovaradin, where the Hungarian troops are fortressed. Karl went ahead to make sure they could find a clear road. Quietly so only Hannah could hear, Karl said, "Even if we find a way out there will be no way back."

"You go on ahead, Karl. Find a way out for us. We will hide and pray that we will survive. But with no way out. . . . Please just find a safe road and come back for us!" There was fear and panic in Hannah's voice. Her parents were hold on to her pulling her to an area that had not been hit by the bombs.

Chapter Seventeen

Vojvodina

Slumber now, you weary eyes, fall softly and blessed.
—Bach Cantata BWV 82 "Ich habe genung"

In 1849 the Hungarians bombed Novi Sad, virtually destroying the city and leaving fewer than seven thousand people of the original twenty thousand citizens. Karl Fritz had moved back to Vojvodina after losing his parents, his wife, and his unborn child during the shelling of Novi Sad, he was a broken man. He had also lost friends in the war against Austria and Russia. Paul and Hilde Schmidt took him in and tried to nourish him physically and spiritually.

Karl had gone back to Novi Sad to search for Hannah. He found her holding her parents under a large pile of rubble and was unable to move them from underneath. He tried for a day and at nightfall collapsed. A few people who had survived the bombing tried to help, but at night, when there was no light to see by, they begged him to stop. That Hungary would have destroyed an entire city shattered his beliefs about the revolution. For all of Kossuth's powerful rhetoric, all that it laid in its path was death and destruction, and the hopes of other ethnic groups were thrown in that path.

The city smelled of smoke, blood, and decay. Those who had survived were roaming the streets looking for loved ones and attempting to salvage what they could from the rubble. Karl's account was detailed and etched in his mind. He was never going to forget the sights.

"Hilde, I swear it looked like what I imagine Sodom and Gomorrah to have been. Mothers looking for children, children looking for parents. The horrible smell of smoke. I could smell blood and from the amount running in the streets I knew that thousands had died. I cannot imagine what the smell was like in a few days, with all the decaying people and animals. Occasionally someone would find an arm or leg hidden in the rubble and try to free the body only to find the limb was not attached to anything. The person would scream in horror but not let go of the limb. They had found a part of a loved one. I felt the most anguish for the children who would sit near a door of their house, the only thing left standing, and wait for their parents to come home. They often had a favorite toy with them, which they clung to and would not let go of. Many cried in pain or grief, I don't know. People fainted from grief or sat like statutes unable to move. I had a hard time finding Hannah's house because there were no landmarks I could recognize. I also think the shock of seeing nothing on her street kept me from finding it. There were one or two buildings on the opposite side of her street that were standing, and the people who lived in them were attempting to help the best they could. It was as if the only things that people were capable of doing were standing like statues, crying, or removing rubble. I will never forget this." Karl told his account often halting to take a drink of water or to stop himself from breaking down. Paul and Hilde did not interrupt him, they sat and listen to the horror unfold.

Paul and Hilde lived in the village of Torschau. When Karl arrived there it was a beautiful fall day, and the contrast between the beauty of the day and the horror of what he had left was enormous. Instead of children running to find their parents and homes, children were playing in the meadows and yards and laughing rather than crying. The air was filled with the smells of kitchens, baking, and jarring preserves. The old men were sitting on porches, smoking and sipping wine or beer while talking as if the events of the world had not reached them or were unimportant to them. The trees were an assortment of bright yellow, orange, and red. Children helped by raking the leaves but found they could not resist jumping on the piles. Carts carried hay and hemp to the mills, horses and buggies took people to other villages for visits and shopping, and there were sounds of music from some houses as children practiced their lessons.

Paul and Hilde had tried to stay out of the political atmosphere as much as possible. They believed that the Church was the way to help people, by giving them a promise for a better life in the world to come and giving them strength to bear their hardships because God is with them. Hilde did not know if this belief in the long run was right. Even though Hungarian had become the official language for government, education, and religion, Paul, the pastor of the Lutheran church in Torschau, still held some services in German. The Hungarians wanted complete assimilation; and wanted to take away the Germanness of our villages. They hoped that this would gain greater independence from Austria. If people did not assimilate, they would be denied education beyond the village school and remain at the level of peasants. Only people like Hilde's sister Annika, who married a doctor or who had inherited a thriving business, had any kind of social status. To Hilde it seemed that the idyllic nature of our homes was darkened by government control of all areas of our lives.

Many families in the church began to immigrate to America and Canada to find jobs and send money back to their relatives. It was the fathers and older sons that left to get jobs. This broke up families, and the money sent home was never enough. Some stayed, some came back. Life never got easier, and the conflicts never stopped. There was a deep longing in the separated families, and often the children did not know why they were left behind.

Karl began coming to church and made friends. He eventually found his own place to live and started working in a store that sold fresh produce. Hilde saw that he was also friends with many of the Serbians who came to the store to find German products that could not be found anywhere else. Although I never listened to their conversations, when he and his friends sat on the porch, I felt that he was very sympathetic with the Serbs who remained under the control of Hungary and found that more restrictions on political and civil right ensued. Karl's time with the nationalistic movements had given him insights into why people wanted to create their own sovereign nations based on language, heritage, religion, and customs. The feelings between the foreigners in another land and the local people were often ones of distrust and hatred.

After the year of revolution, Vojvodina became a district of Hungary with its headquarters in Ödenburg on the border of Austria. Nothing had been settled, and people felt like Germans out of place and unwanted. They were not Serbs, Hungarians, Romanians, or Croatians. In the small village of Schowe in 1820 the population of 2,136 consisted of 1,436 Serbians and 653 Germans. Tensions between the Serbs and the German seemed certain.

The Banat became an autonomous region under the Austrian crown and they ruled harshly. By 1860 the area administered by a governor, or voivodeship, was abolished. And then in 1867 Austria returned the province of Vojvodina to Hungary. The only way to survive was to ignore all the changes. We worked, worshiped, cared for our homes and children, lived and died.

Paul and Hilde had one son, Frederick. He was born in 1821. He was close enough to Karl's age to become friends with him. The relationship helped Karl return to family and loving relationships. Frederick became a confidant.

Hilde's father Martin had died in 1846. Hilde was glad he missed all the chaos of the revolutions. Hilde and her two sisters took over his pharmacy, hiring others to help when the demands of their families and work were too much. This helped Isolde and her son, Lukas, greatly. The customers were generally kind to Lukas. Some children made fun of him, but Lukas even as an adult did not understand their comments or jokes when he passed them on the street. The children who made fun had their ears boxed. The pharmacy gave Isolde had a place to go and take her mind off caring for Lukas. Hilde had the church for refuge.

She loved helping Paul with his visitations and bringing homemade gifts to new families and babies, and with funerals. Often Paul would read to her his sermons on Saturday night for comments. Hilde would often go to church during the week to find peace and quiet. She often took a lunch to Paul and told him all the gossip she had heard that day at the pharmacy.

As in all churches, there were problems of our parishioners. Men who drank too much and hit their wives and children; there were sudden deaths; infidelity; harvests that were poor, leaving people hungry; disasters such as floods and fires. But there were happy times that the whole village celebrated. Christmas, Easter, weddings, baptisms, harvest celebrations, *Kirchweih* parades that celebrated the anniversary of the church, and the evening celebration after a full day of butchering pigs.

Frederick married in 1849. He and his wife, Anna, had two boys, Hans born in 1851 and Josef in 1855. I was thrilled that they did not want to venture far from home and willingly helped Paul and me in the church. When old enough, Hans went to seminary and Josef opened a small bookstore that sold my books on herbal remedies, books on music, literature, and poetry, as well as newspapers, tobacco, pipes, and other sundries. It also became a meeting place for young people who could sit, read, and discuss the issues of the day. Hans became a Lutheran pastor and took a parish in a nearby village.

Josef married in 1875, and Hilde and Paul were blessed to see the birth and baptism of his son, Klaus. Hilde took ill the week after the baptism. She was not able to get out of bed for over a week, the fever was relentless. Paul had died a year earlier. On the day Hilde died she told her son Frederick that she was happy. "I knew that God would not keep us apart."

CHAPTER EIGHTEEN

Karl's New Life

After my return to Vojvodina, Karl searched for an abyss in which my darkness would find a home. Karl wanted to fall into it and be consumed. The darkness seemed more alluring to him. Karl's life continued but, in most respects, he was not living. Eating, sleeping, drinking, and tedious conversations did not constitute a life. Hilde and Paul helped Karl enormously, but it took years for him to realize that the darkness he so wanted to vanish into did not exist. He settled into the life of a small village and did not dream of revolutions, nation building, freedom, or changing the world. His bookstore kept me busy and provided books to read.

Going to church also helped. There he could see people living their lives. They had suffered tragedies and somehow were able to find happiness again. They had lost children and parents, wives and husbands, but knowing that you had to move forward beyond these events eventually seemed to produce an armor. Maybe a better word would be *resilience*, an ability to see beyond and find the joys that can heal physical and mental wounds.

It was at a Sunday church service that Karl met a woman. A beautiful woman by the name of Magdalena. She had long ash-blond hair and green eyes with long lashes that could be seen often because she always seemed to be looking down. With her head and eyes glancing downward she almost seemed shy, but as Karl watched her he realized she did not want to see life. She wore plain clothing, but the voluptuousness of her hips and breasts was obvious. Paul told him that she worked as a maid for a Jewish family. This one fact gave him courage to talk with her after church services. He eventually related that he had been good friends with a Jewish family in Novi Sad. Karl found ways to see Magdalena on the street and often to walk with her.

The more they talked, he realized there were people in our village who did not hate the Jews and understood the good in them.

"I really don't talk much about the family I work for," she confided. "I never know what other people's views are. There are a few of us who do household work, laundry and such, but we often differ on what we think of the Jews. I have found them to be generous and kind. They give me extra money at Christmastime for me to buy presents for my family."

I nodded my head in agreement with her assessment. "The family I knew often invited me over for dessert. The girl I knew played the piano, and I especially loved to hear her play Beethoven."

"It is hard to mingle, though. There are so many differences in our customs and beliefs. What little I've learned has intrigued me. Maybe we could meet, and you could tell me about the family you knew?" Magdalena comment was innocent, but Karl was unwilling to talk any more.

"Oh, it was just to hear music. I never spent much time with them talking about their beliefs and such."

Not wanted to end the conversation Karl continued. "But we could find a time just to talk about my time in Novi Sad during the revolutions," Karl hoped she would be open to meeting with him in a more formal fashion. Walks did tend to keep them from having any in-depth conversations.

"You were there during that horrible time? I heard the city was shelled and will have to be completely rebuilt." She had a look of interest and deep concern.

Afraid of letting her in too deep into his life he lied and said, "Yes, that's true, but I was not there when it happened. I luckily got out a few weeks beforehand. My mother and father didn't leave, however, and they were killed. I went back to find them and was unable to locate them. Please let us talk about other things. I don't want to dredge up these memories."

Magdalena crimsoned and said she understood.

"But Novi Sad was beautiful, and I would love to tell you things about my adventures there and in Budapest," Karl said. She agreed immediately that they should continue the conversation and asked Karl over to her parents' house for dinner the following Sunday.

After several Sunday dinners, Karl wanted to know if she had even been married. There had been only a few friendly kisses and hugs, but Karl felt that she was a good person and hoped with time they would have a loving relationship and perhaps marriage. Karl asked her why she had never married. "You are really very beautiful, and I can't image that you haven't had many young men swarming around you," I said with a smile.

She blushed and related the story of her former boyfriend. "I never was very outgoing, and his death was so terrible. I didn't want to be with anyone for a couple of years, and then the young men gave up trying to ask me out. One can only say no so many times."

"I'm glad you didn't say no to me. I hope we can continue to see each other." I then asked her if she would like to go for a walk and admire the beautiful flowers and trees along the main street.

They courted for several months, and when he finally asked her to marry me, she laughed and said, "I thought you'd never ask."

Ihe quickly retorted, "I was afraid of your famous 'no.'"

Magdalena was younger than Karl by ten years, but neither minded. Paul officiated at the service. I was very nervous and felt that I had been dishonest with her about my past. Paul advised me to tell her slowly and always with great love. I also asked Hilde what she thought about the way to approach my past with Magdalena.

"The past is the past, and you loved her," she answered. "Start with that, and don't tell everything at once. Know what is important: the marriage and the child. The rest will fall into place." Honest and profound advice, which I followed.

We had two children: a boy, Philip, in 1851, and a girl, Elisabeth, in 1853. Karl then learned how old he really was. They wore me out completely. Eventually Elisabeth helped at the bookstore and Philip helped his grandparents on the farm.

Karl enjoyed my uncomplicated life and shied away from anything dealing with politics and debates. When overhearing discussions in the bookstore, he would not allow himself to be drawn into them. Since his bookstore carried books in both German and Serbian, he was able to keep up with new currents in literature. But even novels contained political and social issues.

Over the first months of their marriage, Karl slowly began to tell Magdalena of my past. He told her that for a short time he had been a teacher in Novi Sad. "My real adventure, however, was my stay in Budapest, where

I became friends with men involved in the Hungarian revolution." It was as if Karl had told her he's been to the moon. She could not comprehend that he had been a part of something so dangerous and so, in her words, exciting and meaningful.

"A journalist!" She choked on the words in disbelief.

"Yes. I wanted the people in Novi Sad to see what was happening in their world. They needed to be aware of the growing nationalism and rise of ethnic desires for autonomy. I believed that Hungary was right. Being young and full of energy and ideas, I reveled in the atmosphere. Now I look back and shake my head in wonder that I was a part of it all."

"Tell me about it—all of it!" As she threw out these words, not in anger but in an awareness that I had a past she could not comprehend, Karl realized that the time to tell her everything was approaching. He began by telling her how I met Karl Marx in Berlin when he was at university.

"At university! Karl Marx—the Karl Marx that people talk about? The communists? What interest would he hold for you?" She was not shocked but concerned that I would align myself with such a person. Karl told her what attracted him to Marx and what a wonderful writer he was.

"He fervently believed that he was helping people. They did not need to be living in poverty. Industry did not need to own them. When I was with him, I could see a better world. My parents could not understand, and we eventually had a fight, and they threw me out."

Their conversation lasted for hours, and Karl could see a new world opening for Magdalena. There was a world she knew nothing about, and famous people were real. Magdalena had so many questions. It was as if she had become a child in school.

One day Karl brought home a copy of Goethe's *Faust*. After dinner he commenced reading it and remembered how much he loved it and also how hard it was for his students, who struggled with it and yet began to appreciate it. The story of Gretchen still haunted him. How she was mistreated and left alone to die in a prison. For what reason? A crime, a sin? No, love betrayed. Karl turned to the last chapter of the play and began to read.

> *Bin ich noch so jung, so jung!*
> *Und soll schon steren!*

Schön war ich auch, und das war mein Verderben.
I am still young, so young!
And I should already die.

I was beautiful also, and that was my downfall.

These words struck him, and he physically collapsed as if in pain. He could not prevent the flood of tears. He had not cried like this since my return to Vojvodina.

Magdalena came over to him quietly asking what was wrong. He read her the words and then said, "I still have much to tell you. Come sit with me and I will begin."

After several hours she embraced me with passion and said, "You have loved deeply and fervently Karl. I am so sorry that you had to love only to lose this love. But this tells me the worth of your love and how lucky I am to have gained your love. Keep her in your heart as a reminder of what love is. Ours is a different kind of love and perhaps wiser. I love you, Karl."

Karl looked at her with wonder and with a love that was deep and filled with a longing that he had not felt since Hannah. Yes, he could love again, and he had found a love that was not inferior but that gave him completion. He was whole again and able to find the beauty and goodness in the world around him. This love was a gift of immeasurable quality and one that he believed he did not deserve.

Magdalena kept a beautiful garden next to the house. Flowers, herbs, some vegetables, and a plum tree. They had grapevines growing on the fence, and a lilac bush. The scent in the evening permeated the house. The streets in the village were tree-lined, and as the seasons turned, they made the village look like a painting. The people always kept their houses painted and their porches swept. The children had a beautiful meadow to play in and for the most part stayed out of mischief.

Philip and Elizabeth thrived in this environment of carefree days; their only sorrow was having to go to school and study. They learned easily and had inquisitive minds. The bookstore became a garden of delights. Rainy days were spent learning the names of authors and books, learning the order in which they were kept and which ones had the best pictures and photos. They did chores at home and in the store, to be able to purchase books they wanted. Their tastes were eclectic and sometimes beyond their ability. However, Magdalena and Karl would read to them at night. There were thousands of questions. Education in the schools did not encourage questions, so there were often too many for them to answer all at once. Karl was never sure how this learning at home affected their schooling. Sometimes they would come home with more questions because their teachers had taught them something different from what they were learning at home. Karl told them it was important that they learn different opinions and answers. It was up to them to attempt to understand what the truth was for themselves, but they must always be polite and not argue in anger when someone disagreed with them. Karl had learned that in 1848. Anger was not the way to change the world or people's opinions. Anger led to hatred and hatred to violence.

Magdalena would bring leftover baked goods and desserts to the store for me to share with the customers. Thus, the store became a favorite meeting place for afternoon coffee. People would bring a pot of coffee to share while they talked. Because Karl spoke Serbian and had Serbian books, many Serbians would visit and talk with the other ethnic groups. It seemed to Karl that we were a diverse group who had learned to live with each other. There were Jews, Muslims, Orthodox, Catholics, Lutherans, Reformed, Germans, Croatians, Romanians, Hungarians, and Serbians all living within a few miles of each other. There was some intermarriage, but most married within their own religion and ethnic group. My hope was that our tiny area would be an example of how different peoples could live together.

CHAPTER EIGHTEEN

Berlin

A maiden or a little wife
—Mozart, sung by Papageno in *The Magic Flute*

Michael Müller loved to tell the story of how his father first heard, (Gertrude) his mother sing and immediately fell in love with her. It was the at a performance of Beethoven's *Mass in C Major* and she was the soprano soloist. He was not able to see her because his seat was in the nave. What he heard, though, was enough. He always told me that it was her voice that he really fell in love with, because it couldn't be her cooking or housekeeping. Her soprano voice had a warmth to it that almost made it sound like a mezzo-soprano. But she was able to sing up to a high E-flat with ease. Like all of us, she loved the music of Beethoven, and she was often called upon to be the soprano soloist for his *Missa Solemnis* and the Ninth Symphony. The story goes that after the performance my father found his way to the choir loft and immediately introduced himself and asked her to dinner that night. She accepted. It was a month after their first dinner that he asked her to marry him, and she accepted.

After marriage Gertrude gave lessons to several young women and continued to sing in small concerts around Berlin. She was known for her lieder interpretation. Even at smaller venues she attracted a large group of admirers. Some composers would come to hear their works performed by her. When I got older, I would often go to these concerts in the homes of famous people. The concerts and the people I met gave me a musical education that was unequaled. I heard conversations between my mother and composers about how the works were composed and their different interpretations. The people I met also opened up a world of ideas and backgrounds.

Michael's first real memory of his mother is of her singing was when he was sad. She sang a German folksong, which made him even sadder. It was the German folksong"Da unten im Tale," ("Down Under the Valley"). The sadness of unreturned love, although I had never experienced it at the age of five, felt true. He would sing the Brahms setting of it many times later in his life and always remembered her full, deep voice. He was sad that she never heard me sing professionally. It was his firm belief that the times she sang to him reached deep into his soul and our voices found each other.

Michael was allowed into his mother's music room whenever he wanted and could play the piano and sing as loud as he wanted to. He loved looking through her music and would pretend he could read the music and sing with great passion. As he got older he was able to read the lyrics, and he made up my own melodies according to what I thought was the correct musical sentiment for them.

Michael had inherited my great-grandfather Johann Fritz's violin and was given lessons on it as soon as he was able, he loved playing. Even as a child he was impressed by the stories he heard about great-grandfather and his adventures with Haydn and Beethoven. Knowing these gave him a sense of pride and ambition. He wondered if he would be able to write music like Beethoven. Could he lead a life like his great-grandfather? Could he be a professional, travel, and meet the great musicians of the day? But his musical ability did not lie with the violin; the melodies of the violin found his way into his singing voice.

His family moved to Berlin, where his father joined a law firm and eventually became a judge. His mother continued to give lessons and sing. Although Berlin was markedly different from Vienna, he soon found it to be an exciting and vibrant city. He loved the Brandenburg Gate with its goddess of victory riding above in a chariot pulled by four horses. He imagined the Prussian army defeating Napoleon and returning this icon to its place of grandeur in 1814. Napoleon had stolen it. Michael's father told him that

Napoleon wanted trophies from everything he conquered, and this was the most impressive statue in the city. He also learned that the Iron Cross had been added to symbolize the Prussian defeat. The people of Berlin had such pride in their city, culture, and homeland.

Michael's father took me to Humboldt University where he had studied and told him that many famous men had graduated from his alma mater. "Who, Father? Did you go to school with any of them?" I asked, hoping that I would hear some good stories from my father's past.

"I did not go to school with Karl Marx, but he was one of the most famous and believed that we needed a revolution to overturn capitalism. He actually served in the Prussian army for a year. I haven't kept up with him. His ideas seemed so inane to me, asking the proletariat to rise up," his father replied as if bored. He went on to ask what I had been reading and said he hoped I was behaving in school.

"Yes, Papa. I really like reading and hearing the poetry we study. Mama is reading me some of the poems of Goethe and Schiller." Michael hoped his father would ask him about his music lessons, but it was apparent that father had more important things on his mind.

Michael's introduction to great German poetry had an important impact on his musical education. It helped him to free his speaking voice and develop emotions that his singing voice could create. His mother encouraged him to create "open tones" when he read. His mother had him read to her, and often she would surprise me with the sounds she could make. Schubert's *Erlkönig* was one of Michael's favorites, even as a child.

He would act it out, riding on a stone horse in the backyard and yelling as the child cried out in pain. When his grandmother, Charlotte, was alive, she would laugh he as tried to be all the characters. He would intuitively use all this "training" when he sang the song in his first real lesson on it. He told my teacher that my grandmother had heard Vogl sing it. The teacher was impressed and asked what she remembered of the performance. He told him she was frightened even as an adult.

"You must seek to do this also in your performance without relying on theatrics. Do it with you voice alone," he said. This was his first real lesson. I was told to use hand and body gestures sparingly. If the voice did not tell the story, then my body certainly would not.

When Michael graduated from the gymnasium, he was accepted into the Berlin Conservatory. Training with his mother and grandmother had been so wonderful that his voice teacher at the conservatory said that all he needed was to receive coaching and to learn as much music as he could. Michael gave his first professional concert at the age of nineteen in 1864, a program of his grandmother's favorite lieder by Beethoven and Schubert.

There was an opera director at the recital. He had wandered in, having heard about the program the night before. He felt the recital would be good to clear his head of all the trials and tribulations that seemed to be endless at the opera house. Afterwards he introduced himself and told Michael that the Königliches Opernhaus was in dire straits. The baritone who was singing Papageno in Mozart's *Die Zauberflöte* (*The Magic Flute*) had taken ill and would not be able to sing for the next performance the following week.

"Can you learn it in one week?" he asked.

"Yes, I already know much of it by heart. My mother and I would sing the opera together when I was a child. I can come to the opera house tomorrow morning and sing it for you," Michael replied with an excitement that I could not hide.

The next morning, they met on the main stage and he sang the entire opera through for him.

"You are perfect! Young, full of energy, you know how to bring life to Papageno, and have a wonderful sense of the humor in this role. We will start staging for you this afternoon. Tonight you can work with the whole cast," the conductor said as he shook Michael's hand. "Let us work on the dialogue now," he added as he opened the score to Papageno's first line, "*Wer ich bin?*" Who am I?

Michael knew who he was, but the reality of the moment had not sunk in. At the conclusion of the staging rehearsal, he lingered after everyone else had left except for the stage manager. He wanted to take everything in and remember this moment. The merlot-colored stage curtain, the orchestra pit with the music stands, the conductor's podium, the mahogany wood chairs beautifully covered with cloth that matched the curtain, the curved balconies, the chandeliers, and the props all placed properly on tables in the wings. He had not been given a dressing room yet, and of course could not wait to see his costume and wig. How would they transform him into a bird-man?

He laughed and thought how proud his grandmother would be. The next evening was in costume, so he did not have to wait long to see. The feathers were real, and the colors of my suit, to which they were attached, were reds, yellows, greens, and blues. Michael had become a male bird with the most exotic colors. His hat looked like Robin Hood's and had one enormous feather. The bird cage, made of wood, was strapped on to his back and had a net attached to it. The shoes were like ballet slippers, and lederhosen completed the look.

After his first performance, when the curtains parted for him to take my bow, the audience rose to its feet. They knew Michael had learned the role within a few days' notice and were showing their appreciation. He went to the café next door with his fellow cast members and all celebrated his success. Their warmth and generosity were wonderful, and he learned that true artistry doesn't come from snobbery but in the comradeship of other artists. Just as singing requires an accompanist who understands the forging of like minds, so the success of opera demands a comradeship, each serving the music that is being sung.

The role of Papageno was one that he would perform many times, and he never tired of this life-loving character and his humor. He traveled to opera houses in all of Europe performing opera and lieder recitals. To be alive and singing when Wagner was composing was a singer's dream and he was hired to perform Gunther in *Die Götterdämmerung* at Bayreuth and sang several Wagnerian roles after that in houses throughout Europe.

Each time he returned to Berlin to visit family, he was amazed at the changes. It was a thriving, growing city. Michael heard that when Mark Twain visited from America, he called Berlin the Chicago of Europe. Since 1871 it had been Germany's capital. Government offices, a railroad system that made Berlin the hub of Europe, electric trolleys, and stores selling everything imaginable had sprung up everywhere. Cafés lit entirely by electricity seemed to make life one of speed and anxiety. Michael's father was seventy-nine when I saw him for the last time in 1890. He refused to venture out of the house, saying that it was too hard on his nerves. Michael's mother, however, loved everything that Berlin had to offer. His father feared they would go bankrupt if he allowed her out every day to shop. She bought art, linens, clothing, books, and music. Michael loved reading through all the new music scores she bought. They often spent the evening with her accompanying me on the piano as I sang.

The two of them went to cafés together and they met the artists and composers in Berlin. Of course, Michael was also introduced to all the available women in Berlin. At forty-four he was not sure how many women would find him viable as a husband. The amount of travel might be of interest to some, but if the woman wanted a family, it would mean he would be gone, leaving her to tend to the children and the house.

He met Clara. She wanted a family and did not mind being alone since she was an only child and her parents often left her alone with her grandmother when they traveled in Europe. She found she liked her grandmother better than her parents. She understood what the difference between being alone and being lonely was.

His mother was thrilled at the possibility of grandchildren and wanted them to start a family immediately. His father only hoped he would not have to leave the house.

Michael and Clara married after a short courtship of a month and within a year had a child they named Wolfgang. They both loved Mozart and were sure that Michael's renditions of Papageno and the opera would please little Wolfie. They took him to a production of *Die Zauberflöte* in Berlin when he was three. He loved it and would sing "Pa" from the duet between Papageno and Papagena. Michael was delighted.

Clara and Wolfgang gave a structure to Michael's life and a place he wanted to come home to. He also learned the joy of writing and receiving letters. The Schubert song "Die Taubenpost" became one of his favorites, and he would often end his lieder recitals with it. Clara was his constant in life.

Drum heg' ich sie auch so treu an der Brust,
Versichert des schönsten Gewinns;
Sie heisst – die Sehnsucht! Kennt ihr sie?
Die Botin treuen Sinns.
I cherish her as truly in my heart,
Certain of the fairest prize;
Her name is – Longing! Do you know her?
The messenger of constancy.

Clara and Michael had two more children, both boys, Ludwig and Franz. They decided to stay with the first names of composers. Every time He called one of them, he would sing the first line of a song by Beethoven or Schubert, and if the right one came, he got a treat. This was a wonderful way to teach them the great lieder by these men.

After their births, Michael decided to do less concertizing and perform mainly in Germany. Being able to spend time with the family was as important as singing. None of the children became interested in a career in music, which was fine. They realized that the time away from home that performing led to was hard on everyone. Michael would not retire completely, however, until 1912, when the boys were away at university, and Clara and he had a wonderful second honeymoon, at home alone.

The turn of the century was at hand and the world seemed to be changing daily, not always for the good. The Dreyfus Affair was covered in all the newspapers. Michael was outraged by the imprisonment of Zola. That an artist could not speak his own mind seemed impossible. For Michael the truth would come out at the trial and people could defend or condemn him as they wished. He feared that the whole event would spin out of control because of the growing anti-Semitism in both France and Germany. Many of the artists in Germany were Jewish, and Michael could not see what harm they were doing in Germany. If anything, these artists enhanced Germany's standing in the world.

In 1898, Empress Elisabeth of Bavaria was killed by an Italian anarchist, Luigi Lucheni. Michael rushed into our sitting room to tell Clara. "Our poor, mad, sick Empress has been killed by a madman, an anarchist. They say he is fighting against the ruling class. But this fragile woman could hurt no one and often showed the most remarkable concern for the common person. How would anarchy help anyone?"

"I heard she was traveling alone. Rumors have circulated that she was starving herself and wanted to drown. That is why she had an anchor tattooed on her arm. The poor soul, thinking that could weigh her down," Clara said as she rose to greet me.

Ludwig came home from school with a friend and the boy's parents, Herr and Frau Engel. We had invited them to dinner. As they came in, the boy's father overheard us and remarked, "Well, with people such as her in positions of power, it is no wonder people take to such extreme measures."

"Please come in and have a glass of wine before dinner." Clara always a wonderful hostess was trying to get everyone away from continuous subjects. She brought in wine glass and a bottle of wine which Michael opened. Ludwig and his friend went to Ludwig's room to play.

The dinner as always was wonderful. Clara had made roast duck with dumplings, carrots with rosemary and lots of butter, and a fresh loaf of bread. After dinner she served cheese plate with fruit. Michael invited everyone to the sitting room for Viennese coffee and chocolate.

Unfortunately, the subject assassination of Empress Elizabeth was brought up again. Michael asked his guest, "And how would you solve the problems of poverty, homelessness, and madness?"

Clara added, "As a professional man—I understand you are a doctor—do you never worry about how people with no money get medical treatment? If a man dies from illness or an accident, leaving his wife with no income and several children, how are they to survive and not end up on the streets? Berlin would quickly become a place where robbery, prostitution, and madness—" She was interrupted by Herr Engel.

"I assume they can go to Charity Hospital. It is world-class, and much research is being done there. They can get excellent care."

Frau Engel continued, "Yes, but there are Jewish doctors there. Not everyone trusts them or wants to be treated by them."

Michael shook his head and looked down at his hands. These were his guests, and he did not want to insult them. "More wine, anyone?"

"Sir, you sang the works of our greatest composer, Wagner, and knew his family. Did his writings and ideas have no impact on you? We are great because we are German. Jewish music and art are inferior. They cannot compare with Mozart, Beethoven, Schubert, our namesakes."

"Yes, yes. But Wagner's animosity toward Mendelssohn was due to his jealousy of Mendelssohn's popularity. Wagner befriended many Jews."

This did not stop the man. He continued in a tirade against the Jews. He believed they were polluting our German art and said that they did not understand our ties to the land and country, that their only loyalty was to other Jews, and that he found them to be disruptive in classes, always asking questions and interrupting the professors.

Michael could not believe what I was hearing. "But many have become as German as you, sir."

As the boys grew older, many of their friends' fathers held similar views. Franz was deeply affected by conversations he overheard when he went to friends' houses to play. To his parents dismay he eventually he joined a group of students who had begun to belittle and taunt the Jewish students.

Wolfgang learned of some of the activities of these students. He came home one day and asked to have a conversation with his father about Franz. "I do not know what to tell you, Father. All I know is that he hates the Jews and believes they are going to take over our economy, our arts, and our lives. He believes that the Jews will rule Germany."

"This is sure to pass," whispered Clara.

"Don't be so sure, Mother. He wants to be a lawyer, and one of his teachers told him about a chaplain, Adolf Streker, who has formed a group called the 'Anti-Semitic Voters Association.' I heard that he goes to the meetings with a father of one of his friends, who is a lawyer."

Michael walked away in utter disbelief. What could he say or do to change Franz's beliefs? Certainly, how Clara and he lived our lives would begin to dissuade him. He knew their Jewish friends and had met some of them in our house.

Ludwig was correct about Franz. The more he associated with those people, the more virulent he became in his anti-Semitism. One evening Franz brought some friends home and Michael overheard their conversation.

"Listen to what Luther says about the Jews: 'Therefore be on your guard against the Jews, knowing that wherever they have synagogues, nothing is found but a den of devils in which sheer self-glory, conceit, lies, blasphemy, and defaming of God and men are practiced most maliciously,'" one of his friends almost shouted with glee, reading from a magazine.

"Yes, we should visit a synagogue and throw a little mud at them along with jeers. I am sure we could gather a large group to do this. They should not be allowed to believe that their deeds go unnoticed and will not be punished," Franz replied.

Michael was horrified, but I dared not enter the room and interrupt them. That these words were coming from Franz's mouth made him wonder what he had not done right in raising him. He knew that Wolfgang and Ludwig were completely different, and they had been raised by the same parents. Surely there must be a reason. The foul language he heard from Franz's mouth made him want to slap him.

The next night Michael talked with both Wolfgang and Ludwig again about their brother.

"Father, I believe that the students he became friends with have fed this fire," Ludwig said. "They are all jealous and feel that they have deserved better from their teachers. Many Jews are the best students and work very hard. Some students believe things should be handed to them because of their families or names. I stayed out of Franz's affairs, and now I wish I had talked with him. I am not as optimistic as you that this is a youthful outburst that will fade over time. With an adult such as Streker indoctrinating them with all sorts of horrible literature about the Jews, there is not much to do. Some of the information is just false, but because it is published in journals it is taken as the truth. There is no science that will support the beliefs they profess."

Michael listened carefully to Ludwig but still felt he needed to talk with Franz. Wolfgang agreed that he should talk with him. After all, they were family. Certainly, Franz would see that such behavior was not appropriate and that as a member of the family he needed to seriously consider the consequences of his actions and words. He would certainly remember our Jewish friends and their children who came to the house.

When Michael did have the conversation, it turned ugly. Franz accused his father of supporting Christ killers, and he walked out of the house, never to return. He was seventeen. Clara would get letters from him, and Michael knew she secretly visited him. Some evenings she would just sit and cry and not tell Michael the reason why.

To say that Michael's final years are now filled with a broken heart does not give voice to the hurt he feel. It is as if a part of his heart has been removed and the empty space would never be filled again. No matter how much he loved Wolfgang, Ludwig, and Clara, there was still a missing part called Franz. He remembered the day he was born, the days I played horse with him and let me ride on my back, the evening bedtime stories, the birthdays, the

Christmases, and on and on. The memories only hurt more because he was reminded of what was and what he used to be. Michael sometimes thought that if he had died it would have been easier for him. He could lay him to rest and weep. Now he only weeps.

CHAPTER NINETEEN

Berlin and World War One

Franz was seventeen when he stormed out of my parents' house. It was 1911 and within four years his world was about to erupt into an apocalypse. When Germany declared war on Russia and France, he enlisted.

The German people were ecstatic and threw themselves wholeheartedly into a kind of patriotism that I had never seen. Inspired by the words of the Kaiser, that we were all Germans and all brothers, people took to the streets. In Potsdam the Kaiser dramatically raised his unsheathed sword and said he would not sheathe it until victory and honor were achieved. Did Franz care what the war was about? Not really. He read the newspapers and listened at bars to what the people were saying:

"This war is about Serbia. It will take only a few months to finish them off."

"We will dominate Europe and be the mightiest nation in the world."

"How can we not win? We are the greatest people."

"*Deutschland über alles!* Germany over all!"

People were shouting, singing, waving flags, and throwing hats into the air. Children sat on their fathers' shoulders waving and cheering. There was euphoria all over Germany. Franz could hear "A Mighty Fortress is our God" being sung, signaling that God was on Germany's side and God would create "a mighty fortress" around the German nation with the German people as the army. With God they were undefeatable.

There were voices of dissent in the government; they were disregarded, and war ensued. On the army's way to France, the army invaded and defeated Belgium. There was war in the East and in the West. Russia had come to the aid of the Serbians in the East, and a Western front now existed in France and Belgium.

Franz had no idea what awaited him. What did he know of war, of soldiering, of anything outside of his cozy life with a famous singer who loved him more than I would ever comprehend? Franz went home to inform his family of his momentary deployment to the Western front. He wore the uniform of a private in the III Corps Sixth Division from Brandenburg; it was there that he had enlisted in August. He did not go into the house but stood in the doorway to inform his parents that he would be leaving within a week. He wanted no tearful goodbyes at the train station. He told them he would write and let them know where he was but asked them not to write back. They could read about everything they needed to know in the newspapers. Cruel and heartless, yes.

Franz travelled by train and learned that the French and British had forced the German army to retreat. The army had reached the outskirts of Paris, but the combined forces of the French and British proved too much and they fell back to the Aisne River, where we built trenches to hold off the offensive. He was thrust into the First Battle of Ypres.

From the second week in October until November 22, 1914, the army fought, killing each other in numbers that sounded as if made up by some lunatic who was adding zeros to the number of dead. Several officers saw in Franz a cold and steely personality that did not flinch. Franz willingly marched towards enemy lines, often pushing fellow soldiers forward. He loved the closeness of death and the smell of battle. He was more alive than he had ever been.

The flare-up of smoke from men being hit by bullets and artillery created a land of dreams. The groans and distant screams did not scare me; they inspired me. Running through the smoke and dodging bullets gave me a sense of the surreal. Such bravery and sacrifice were heroic and sacred and not of the real world. He was not sure if this was patriotism that he had never felt before, or if some inner desire to be tested and face my immortality was being met. Franz didn't flinch when men were hit by bullets next to him, when bombs dropped a short distance from him in the trench, or when brain matter splattered on him. He felt a kind of sorrow for the dead, but like him they were soldiers, and this is what they did: fight and die. If one lived, it was because he was a fearless soldier of Germany. Achilles was alive again.

The First Battle of Ypres was as horrific as any found in Homer's *Iliad*. Franz had brought a copy of the epic with him for inspiration and courage. Unlike the other soldiers, he found the Bible offered nothing; it provided no solace or hope. The ancient Greek heroes' deeds, however, were an inspiration to him.

So the war cries of the Trojans rose through the broad army;

For the speech of all the men was not the same, nor was there one voice,

But the tongues of many were mixed in confusion; the men were summoned from many places.

These men Ares drove on, and gleaming-eyed Athena drove the Achaeans,

And Terror and Panic and Strife, raging insatiable,

the sister and companion of man-slaughtering Ares;

she is small when she first rises up, but in the end

she leans her head against the heavens even as she strides upon the earth.

She too hurled into their midst war-strife that levels all alike

As she advanced through the throng, multiplying the groans of men.

(Fagles, translation)

Yes, he was living the great epic. Achilles, Odysseus, Hector, and the others given life by Homer were important to him and prayer seemed of little use.

The rain and cold made the battlefield desolate. Trees, if there were any left, were leafless and at night looked like human skeletons. Craters were filled with mud and decaying bodies. If a wounded man crawled into a shell hole, he was soon to drown because of the water filling the hole. Planks of wood had to be laid so we could walk. If a man fell in the mud, he ran the risk of drowning in it if there was no one to help him out. Horses became stuck and had to be killed mercifully, ending their struggle and screams. All that the scene needed was Dürer's *The Four Horsemen of the Apocalypse,* and death harvesting the dead from the field.

At dawn the men could still hear the moans of the dying, a music certainly only the devil could compose. But in the light, they could not attempt a rescue. Besides, whose soldiers were dying? They were all in one grave now, Mother Earth. What a strange sound for spirits that would soon be angels. A chorus of enemies groaning their way into heaven. The victor was death not an army.

A new landscape was being formed that no one had ever seen and that no one would forget. To be here at these moments had an enormous effect on Franz. He was witnessing a new world being born. A world forged not only by men and steel but of guts and blood. This would spawn new men and ideas. The world could never be the same after these events.

The officers learned that Franz was studying to become a lawyer and saw that he was able to read and understand battle plans, compose reports, summarize documents from and to the generals in concise terms, and had the admiration of the soldiers he served with. He had often risked his life to help the wounded return to the trenches. He also encouraged those next to him not to lose heart; he would grab their shoulders and pull them forward with him. When his friends' hands were shaking too badly, he would write letters home for them, clean their guns and load them. He was determined to not let them despair and lose faith.

Franz's first official duty after I was promoted to *Unteroffizier*, sergeant, was to write a summary of the battle to take the Belgian city of Diksmuide on November 19.

In short, Germany's efforts resulted in a victory. The night before, they had pushed their line into assault position, and at dawn they began a bombardment that lasted until 13:00. The general assault then commenced. The French resistance was desperate, and their forces fired into their own town, killing civilians and soldiers. They had to retreat because of Germany's superior numbers and the spirit of the German soldiers. On November 11 and 12 there was heavy fighting and the situation remained unaltered. At 7:30 we commenced a two-and-a-half-hour bombardment followed by an infantry attack. The men made a good advance and by 10:00 had a strong position on the southern edge of Polygon Wood. The German army lost numerous officers and NCOs when they rushed into the open, but their spirit never wavered. The worst fighting occurred when they attempted to take a chateau. The enemy fired from windows with machine guns and rifles. The Fourth Army, with the others following suit, decided to stop the offensive on November 17. The men were exhausted due to the torrential rains and our loss of men. However, the time allowed us to construct trenches, wire entanglements, and rest billets to the rear. Belgian villages not affected by the war also afforded the men much needed rest. The result was that Germany had a secure line of defense and had moved their position forward.

As much as Franz missed being in the trenches and at the front, life amongst the officers was a pleasant change. The officers' dugouts were as nice as a poor person's home in Germany, and Franz was always offered a comfortable seat and a cup of so-called coffee. The trenches also had their own attraction. The men worked to make them "homey." They had chairs and tables on which they played cards, pictures of families pinned to the walls, and books to read. The trenches were dug deep underground with stairways leading to them. When boredom set in, men would line the trench walls with a kind of wood paneling. Bookshelves held books brought from home or confiscated from abandoned homes, and there were individual sleeping bays. Despite the lice, the rats, the horrible smells, men could play cards, drink coffee, and occasionally drink wine they procured from the villages.

The army had mastered the art of trench building. They zigzagged across the land, and there were forward and fallback trenches. Further back was for retreating troops and a second defense system. Communication trenches were built so information on changing situations could be obtained with some speed. There were several exits and escape routes, deep enough that the shelling had little effect on them.

On furloughs Franz went to his comrades' homes. They had great times, but there were also times of psychological distress. Some men found it difficult to be in a house, sleep in a bed, and be away from their comrades left on the front line. Franz didn't. He enjoyed meeting the girls, having home-cooked meals, telling of our heroic deeds, and spending time in the bars. He had great sympathy for his friends who suffered from the effects of being on the front. Men are not all the same, and their gifts and strengths are different. They were giving their lives for the fatherland, and their sacrifice was as great as losing limbs or parts of faces, paralysis, blindness. Death often was kinder.

The friendships forged between comrades were stronger than any family ties. They lived and died together, ate together, slept together, played and fought together. They knew each other's dreams and fears. The comfort the men gave each other was as loving as a mother's love. Although men cried for their mothers at the time of death, we were the ones who wrapped them, put their body parts together, and buried them. Franz took photos of my friends before burial to send to their families, if they wanted to see them. Not knowing where their sons, husbands, or boyfriends were buried or how they died was a great consternation. He wrote letters to accompany the letters of the commanding officers, hoping to give the families a sense of how important the sacrifice was to the soldiers with whom the men had served.

In 1917 the German army was still dug in and attempting to take Ypres, the only part of Belgium it did not occupy. A salient, or bulge which projected into German territory, had been created in the British line. Before the battle, the British had been able to detonate nineteen mines under our defenses. But because of the stupidity of their leadership, they did not attack, thus giving us time to reorganize and build concrete bunkers and machine-gun points. Because the land was flat, we could see that the assault was coming, and the bombardment, which lasted ten days, eliminated the element of surprise. On the first day of battle, July 31, 1917, the Entente did gain ground, but a torrential rain ensued, which reportedly was the worst to occur in seventy-five years. Everything halted. On August 16 the attacks resumed. Virtually nothing had changed. The troops' spirit never wavered and our junior officers held our men together.

The Third Battle of Ypres, Passchendaele, which lasted from July to November 1917, symbolized the entire war on the Western Front. The bravery of the German soldier will forever be a reminder of what the German spirit, discipline, unequaled defense strategy, and individual initiative are capable of accomplishing.

During the battle, images in Homer's *Iliad* again came to life. In the confusion, the voices of men from all the countries mingled together made a din of horror. Terror, panic, and struggle were seen on the faces of the men fighting for their lives. The landscape was one brought up from hell. Mud, barren trees, horses dying, men screaming, shell holes filled with water, and corpses met the eye wherever you looked.

Franz was wounded on September 26 during the Battle of Polygon Wood, earning him an Iron Cross. He was hit in my shoulder, arm, and leg, attempting to reach the enemy line after He had run out of ammunition. This was called bravery, but to run back would have been foolish. Franz did not want to die with a bullet in his back. He crawled back to his position after killing two enemy soldiers with his bare hands. He was "sent home" to recover and was unable to return until after the Entente had captured Passchendaele. Franz wondered if Field Marshall Haig believed gaining the village was worth the number of dead in his armies. There was virtually nothing left of the village, and there was no place for his troops to hide.

At Passchendaele, everyone was a casualty in some manner. Rifles clogged because of the mud, and hand-to-hand combat ensued. Men were trapped in muddy shell holes for days, unable to move because of massive machine-gun fire. Both sides helped wounded enemy soldiers to get medical attention, helping us keep what humanity we still had. Blood lust was rampant, however, and many killed just to kill, calling it "mercy killing." Human features were obscured by blood and mud mixing together. Only dull eyes emerged from a face; hands and feet looked like stumps of trees; and bodies sunk in mud looked like statues with their arms raised up to heaven. The machines of war made many men feel as if they were insects being killed—thrown up into the air and then deposited in parts for the living to walk over or use as shields. These were no longer men and friends. If we had thought of each individual as a friend, a loved one, or a soul, we would never have been able to advance. The din of battle was like a symphony created by machines instead of instruments. The composer was death and the performers men.

After Franz was deemed fit to return to duty, he was made an NCO and selected to be a member of a Stormtrooper squad. Training was intensive but Franz was physically and mentally fit. They had mock assaults using live ammunition to steel one's nerves. The goals were to be fast and light, carrying only what was necessary to break the enemy line at a weak point. After intensive shelling the men would attack weak areas, and like a tank the troops would roll over the trenches, and then speed into the rear areas, causing massive confusion which would paralyze the enemy troops. They carried hand grenades, flame throwers, and trench mortars, and as an NCO Franz could carry a rapid-fire pistol.

Franz was to be part of the Spring Offensive of 1918 called "Michael." The German army had gained five hundred thousand troops from the Eastern Front, and spirits were high. On the first day, March 21, the army dropped three thousand shells every minute for five hours. The bombardment focused on machine-gun posts and gun batteries close to the front and the headquarters and train stations near the rear. The first assault focused on the weakened areas, and a second assault of infantry would follow. Germans outnumbered the British and had the element of surprise. As a result, several of the British divisions were annihilated and created panic. It was as if Athena, goddess of war and wisdom, strode among the men, tossing bodies of men and animals into the air. Franz felt elation and horror simultaneously and loved it.

What was victory eventually turned to defeat. German troops had advanced so quickly, and so far, that their supplies could not be delivered. With no supplies the army had to stop. The success of the stormtroopers also became a defeat. We lost many of these elite soldiers, and they could not be replaced. In total between March and April the army lost two hundred and thirty thousand men, and to the men's utter dismay, General Ludendorff constantly was changing his war plans, leading to confusion amongst commanders. The army was unable to bring the Entente to the table to end the war. Exhausted and depleted, the army kept going.

Men could not believe that Germany would lose the war. Who could defeat the spirit and devotion of their troops, their training, their stormtroopers? But with an influenza outbreak and lack of supplies, even the most devout lost hope. Ludendorff would not listen to his senior advisors and did not pull back to regroup. The allies began negotiations on their own, and the army was left to finish the war.

In the end, Germany was a hated country, and we were forced to accept not justice but revenge. In response to the terms of the Treaty of Versailles, the navy scuttled its own ships. Men were found guilty because we protected our borders. However, the army Germany was allowed to keep was made up of career soldiers, and would not forget what they were forced to relinquish in money, land, and people. What they did not see was the phoenix that would arise from our ashes.

When the war was over, Franz returned home and continued his education, eventually obtaining a law license. His heart was not in the law, but he had to work to stay alive. Germany was in a depression that no one could see the way out of. Berlin had veterans walking the street asking for food and shelter because they could not work. Men were panhandling and living in dark alleys. The great city of Berlin was now a place of crime and misery.

Franz took on cases, but his defendants often had no means to pay. It seemed to him that the paying defendants were suing only to gain more money from those who could not afford to fight back.

Franz found a group of veterans to pass the evenings with. The discussions centered on the rise of new political groups, the rise of communism, and Jews. They all agreed on one thing: Germany needed a leader to make our Fatherland great again.

CHAPTER TWENTY

The Great War, Vienna

On Tuesday July 28, 1914, Franz Ferdinand, the heir to the throne, and his wife were assassinated by a Serbian nationalist named Gavrilo Princip, a presumed member of the Black Hand. The next day we all awoke to the news. We all now understood the resolve of Serbia to be a sovereign nation. Within the year we would see the whole world at war.

The Wolff family, since the 1700s, has always had at least one son in the military. Usually, they became high-ranking officers and lifelong soldiers. Otto Wolff often told his family of his time at the *Kriegschule*, the war school in Vienna and the army and how wonderful it was to be a soldier. The pride he had was enormous as well as his sense of duty and honor. These stories inspired his great-grandson and namesake to be a soldier. After the young Otto graduated from the Academy, he entered the *Kriegschule*.

Otto was an only son. Growing up he not only learned about army life, he also learned about the musical heritage of the family and the extended family he had in Southern Hungary, the Banat. Otto's father told me as much about them as I was interested in. Otto did learn about the famous violinist Johann Fritz and that he had a distant cousin named Michael. He is a famous singer and lives in Berlin. But Otto never met him or heard him sing, which as everyone says, is my loss. Several of his friends heard him and tell Otto that he is one of Germany's greatest singers. Otto didn't inherit any musical talent from his family, the army takes up most of his time. He does his only singing in the shower or with the other cadets when marching.

One month after the assassination Germany declared war. At the outbreak of war between Austria and Serbia, Otto was a captain and in charge of artillery training at the school. He knew he would be sent to either Italy or Serbia to defend the borders of Austria. He was sent to Italy for what would be named the *White War*. Like most young men who have not experienced war he thought that his vacations in the Alps would prepare him for the mountains of Italy and the war Germany was waging there. Otto also loved to ski and had done some hiking. The crisp air, the beauty of the wildflowers, and the occasional echo. But those memories are diminished by what he remembers about the war —death. Not the heroic deaths that he had heard about from his teachers, but brutal and pitiless death. Death from incompetent Italian commanders and the cruelty of nature. That he was able to survive was not due to any skill I had as a soldier, skier, or climber; rather, it was due to the deaths of others and the army's weapons and defensive abilities. He was to learn that he also had the ability to push from his mind what he saw, smelled, and heard on the battle fields. For months after he returned, it was not our defeat that invaded both his waking and dreaming worlds but the frozen bodies; the cries of trapped men; the quiet after an avalanche; the sounds of a sniper; the explosions of mines; flies in the blistering sun circling our wounded, who were afraid to move and waited to be picked off one by one by the enemy; the thud of bodies landing on the rocks; the dazed looks of men enduring what surely is hell.

When Otto arrived at the Dolomites, he was speechless. The magnificence and horror that struck him at his first sight of the Dolomites cannot be put into words. The landscape was one of God's wonders and should have instilled terror in those who thought this was a place for war. Temperatures were more than forty degrees below zero for months, and yet men were ordered to climb, dig, and tunnel in these mountains. They knew that they and the Italians were at the mercy of nature and war.

The weather was so cold that Otto remained in a state of constant shivering. Most of the men had never been exposed to temperatures like these, and they were unprepared to live under these circumstances. Many suffered from frostbite, with the inevitable loss of fingers and toes and eventually whole feet. Urine froze as it left the body. Any food they had was frozen, and although they thought it uneatable, was sucked on it for nourishment. The cooks did their best to keep fires going for cooking, but howling winds and snow extinguished them unless they were placed deep within the tunnels and caves. Those who died due to falls and avalanches we counted lucky because they did not have to wait in pain as rescuers searched for ways to get stretchers down the vertical faces of the mountains. We buried them in crevices.

Otto arrived in early October of 1915 at what he thought was the mature age of forty-five. He had a wife, Marie, and two sons, Otto and Hunter. Two battles had already been fought, and there was hope that the war would go in Austria's favor. They gained the high ground. We had better training and discipline, barbed wire, gas, and flame throwers. Otto heard, after he arrived, of the horrors that both sides had endured in the second battle in the Carso Plateau. The sun was the enemy then. One officer reported that the sun tormented the eyes, blinding them. Tongues became swollen from the lack of water, and the dehydration caused hallucinations. The daily water allowance was a liter and was often gone by daybreak. The smell of corpses caused vomiting, which worsened the dehydration. There could not have been a starker contrast to the conditions in the plateau than those in the upper Isonzo. At 2,000 meters there were electric storms, hailstorms, and freezing winds. Paths were so narrow that one false step led to death.

It was beyond my imagination that at Corso the Italians advanced in close-order drill formation with the officers raising their swords to encourage the troops. Austria was entrenched, and although outnumbered, it was like slaughtering animals. The Italians became entangled in the barbed wire and were left to die. However, those who reached our trenches made mincemeat out of the Austrians.

Otto fought in the Third Battle. As the Italians moved forward and we had troops behind the trenches, and when the enemy reached the trenches, we emerged from our dugouts and fought in savage hand-to-hand combat. No one ever got used to seeing the eyes of the men they killed as they were dying. Surprise, pain—and they asked for mercy even though they knew it was never granted. Our hands grew slick from the blood, and they remained bloodied for days. Otto grew used to the smell and was even able to eat when the blood from men mingled with the food. Some of the "boys" had a terrible time after such battles. They would shake for hours and not be able to look at anyone. The officers tried their best to encourage them.

The Italians never not found a way to cross our barbed wire. If they did breach the Austrian trenches, they were at a loss, and we were easily able to repel them back. The Austrian lines then moved up, and before the Italians could do anything with the ground they had made, were easily slaughtered.

The Austrian reserves were in better physical shape because they were placed far enough back to avoid the artillery strikes. Because the army had gained high ground they could aim at will. They called ourselves "The Masters of the Front." The men began to take advantage of the landscape and use grottos and caves as shelters, which could house up to one hundred men.

After the Third Battle was suspended, there was not a soldier who had not killed an Italians The Italians had been repelled three times and blamed their failure on the barbed wire.

Stalemate. After two winters, no one could move forward.

Otto and his men were moved in September of 1916 to Gorizia. On October 13, the Italians started their infantry attack. To Otto's horror, after the shelling there arose a massive army of almost one hundred thousand men. The Austrians opened fire on them as if we were at target practice. Machine guns showed Otto that this war was not about individual heroism but the dominance of weapons. Inches of ground would be gained, and mountains of men lost. Both sides groaned as they saw what was unleashed. Otto could hear some of my men asking if they could stop because their hands had been burnt by the repeated machine-gun firing. The ground drank up the blood as if it were fertilizer for the spring. What blooms would emerge from this blood? Otto could only hope that peace would blossom, and that this war would teach lessons gained from the hubris of men. Bodies were shelled deep into the earth as the shells dropped on what was called the "killing zone." As they lay covered in mud and blood, wounded and dying, Otto tried to talk with each of the men under my command. They wanted to know if they had served honorably and done their duty to their homeland. How could he tell them otherwise? No matter if they had served heroically or failed in their duty, they were honorable and loyal Austrians. No one could foresee the disasters that awaited at home after the war. There was nothing to do but continue and use everything we had in our arsenal.

To Otto's dismay the army was unable to replenish their troops and thus was always outnumbered. What they did receive were men of middle age with little or no training. The discipline Otto had achieved with his men was now in danger. It was the ethnic troops, the Slovenes, Croatians, and Bosnian Muslims, whose savagery became legend.

By the Tenth Battle, the Austrians were left alone to fight the Italians. The Germans had sent the majority of our troops to the Western Front. I was now a general and was sent to Caporetto. Otto's request for men and heavy batteries was sent to General Ludendorff. A combined offense of Germans and Austrians was planned.

Otto had learned that if men are to follow orders, they must see the courage of their commanding officer facing the same dangers as his men. But this was not a display of manliness, it was comradeship. Comradeship that encompasses loyalty, devotion, and courage. With these values Otto believed any army could win. However, the men were so weak from hunger that merely staying alive was all they could do. He was horrified to learn that some reserves had come to the battle only in their underwear and were told to take uniforms from the dead. And they were children. Otto had to be father and commander to them. He prayed with them, bandaged wounds, read them letters, ate with them; but cried for them in solitude. Who would avenge the deaths of these innocent children who fought for their homeland? What victory would bring them back? Would Otto be able to find the man he was before the war?

Austrian batteries opened up on October 24, 1917. Also, their arsenal of death included gas and Erwin Rommel. But the army lacked the will to annihilate and many men had lost the will to live.

The army's return home was not as we had imagined. Our families, happy to see us, soon realized we were not the sons, husbands, and fathers who had left. Some of the men were able to swallow the defeat and go on with life, but many, especially the physically wounded, could not. How do you run a printing press with no arms, how do you play the piano with fingers missing, how do you harvest a field with no legs? The list of casualties who were now unable to be productive citizens went on and on. Who feeds them, who tends them, who lives with them?

Otto's sons, Otto junior and Hunter, did not recognize him when he came through the door. His wife had met me at the train station and was trying her best to remain happy. What a word! What family member could be happy at what they saw in front of them? Otto had lost so much weight that Marie did not recognize his face. Otto's limp would be the least of her worries.

At home conversation was very difficult, and Otto often wandered off in his own thoughts in mid-sentence. Within a few months he would gain weight and be able to carry on a conversation. He was also able to smile and find enjoyment around the family dinner table with the boys. They were now seven and nine and were always asking questions about the war. There were stories that could make us all laugh. They loved the ones about us trying to put on entertainment for ourselves, dressing up as women and doing waltzes together, singing and forgetting the words and substituting off-color lyrics, and having snowball fights.

His boys favorite song was "Mein Michel, was willst du noch mehr?" ("My Michael, what more do you want?"). As the men had done, the boys added what they wanted after each verse. Chocolate cake, a toy train, hot chocolate with whipped cream, no school, a sailboat, and on and on. Their wants were endless and usually extravagant. The men had wanted a woman, a fuck, a drink, a warm bed, clothes with no lice, a shit hole far enough away not to smell, a uniform without blood, a large penis, hot coffee, their girlfriend—and their list was endless because they had nothing.

My Michael, what more do you want?
You have battalions and squadrons,
Batteries and machine guns,
You have the largest cannons.
My Michael, what more do you want?
You have two dozen monarchs,
Foot soldiers and priests,
An army so you can have a blessed sleep,
My Michael, what more do you want?
You have countless paragraphs of laws,
Your prisons are never empty,
You can have a nice nap in protective custody.
My Michael, what more do you want?
You have the highest taxes,
Your Junkers [wealthy landowners] toil so hard

Just to inflate the price of bread.
My Michael, what more do you want?
You have turnips and acorns,
And if you still want some more,
You can try to caress your belly.
My Michael, what more do you want?
You can drill and march
Crisscross round the barrack yard,
And then perish for your Kaiser.
My Michael, what more do you want?

Not far under the surface of these stories in his memory were the faces of those who once laughed and who became mangled and bloodied, lost in avalanches, decapitated in falls from the mountains, and had birds pick their eyes out, and bugs crawl from their orifices. The stories Ott told put flesh on these men again, and they returned to the land of the living for brief moments. Otto could remember every detail about their faces and could hear their voices. He knew their habits and fears. It was hard to push back the longing to be with them and to have died with them. How much easier death seemed now. Not glorious but peaceful death. "Living is harder than death"—Otto was not the first to say this, but he no longer laughed when he heard it said.

Otto would also tell his sons of the field hospitals where nurses and doctors, through a heroism of their own, patched up the men and send them to hospitals or home. After the patch up, which often was no more than a patch, or surgery, there was silence as they disrobed, there was drinking in the officers' tent, letters home to families, or long walks. Frostbite, or a shot to the arm or leg—these were the kinds of wounds a soldier wanted, bad enough to keep you out of the war but not kill you.

Otto felt most sorry for the boys who completely broke: shell shock. They were sent to mental institutions, and God only knows what they went through there. He had heard that the treatments were like torture. There was electric shock, and baths in ice, and they were screamed and yelled at by the doctors to "shape up" and "be a man."

The boys wanted to know all about the beautiful nurses and if the men fell in love with them. "Of course! How could they not? Here were these young maidens sitting by you day and night, providing everything you needed. You told them everything about yourself and they told you stories of their families, and eventually there was love," Otto told them. "I doubt if some of the men would have lived if it had not been for the kindness and care of these nurses. They gave the men a reason to live, a will to live. To some they actually appeared as angels."

No matter how Otto tried to occupy myself, he could not shake the war. Images always appeared; normal sounds became screams, rifle reports, shelling; smells permeated the house, and instead of bread baking he smelled gas. He would lie awake at night shivering or sweating, or running to find cover, or hitting some ghost that was only his wife. When he did talk about the war with other veterans, they had similar stories. These conversations always ended in a penetrating silence with each lost in our own hell.

Writing in the evenings became a kind of therapy for Otto. He had found that telling the stories somehow helped and he needed to tell the horrible ones. A way to remember what he had done and what had been sacrificed. He needed to feel proud and at the same time feel pity and guilt.

Diary

Angels formed From decomposing flesh With wings from flailing arms and coats That froze into ice

We talked of death as a grave matter, But it is not the grave, a place of rest. You found no spot of peace. No, you are comingled with the enemy As a heavenly choir, A new spiritual force, A new army forged from dirt, gas, manure. Body parts frozen become gates to St. Peter, Arches, columns, pews. Your hymns, formless words, muffled screams, Gasping and regurgitating. Antiphons are the refrains of machine guns, Glorias become the blasts of cannons. A heaven made from hell.

Death is not a democracy, It will take anyone with no vote needed. It is an anarchy.

I just want to know that I did something good When death surrounds me. I want to know that good has survived in me And in the world, That the part of me you loved is still worth loving.

Such small monuments for such an enormous sacrifice. These monuments give dates and names, They omit the person who cowered near me. A bullet ricocheted from the side of a mountain Into your skull. I saw nothing Hearing your voice which had been silenced Until it was safe Only for me.

They called it vertical sun, There was no escape from its flames. Our skin seared Tongues swelled Eyes melting. We prayed for death and water.

Why do they not dodge the shells and the bullets? Why do they march in a straight line? Why do they . . . No answers, only slaughter. Only ceaseless sounds of the war machines Burning hands, faces, lungs. I hear men shouting "Go back," "Go back," "Go back," A refrain that only ends in the gargantuan death Of our enemy, the other.

~

We will never be warm The cold has frozen our minds, bodies, and souls Numb to life

Duty is a strange word It is the opposite of freedom Yet it was duty we all died for Not for freedom Duty is not the same as glory Glory is from God Not from the hell of war Those men that died a glorious death Would be like Achilles And want nothing more but To return to a non-glorious life And live. Duty, a four-letter word, How many times did I shout it to the men? This four-letter word Along with more meaningless words Fatherland, Home To those who will have them carved above their heads In a place far from Home and Fatherland

~

During the winters Otto could not venture outside. His whole body froze, and all he could do or wanted to do was sit in a chair in front of the fireplace. It was during the cold months that Otto's mood changed drastically and he became 'difficult'. Marie finally gave up trying to get him out and "amongst the living." She made me soup, wrapped me in blankets, and gave me books to read. Sometimes his friends came to visit, and he was almost my old self. They talked about everything but the war. Occasionally they told me that some of the men from our unit had died of old wounds or natural causes, but several had taken their lives. We would take up a glass of schnaps we would sing "Ich hatt' einen Kameraden" ("I had a comrade") and then "Ein Prosit" ("cheers") and proceed to get so drunk we could not walk. Several times I woke up with my friends sleeping in chairs next to me and my wife bringing us dark, strong coffee.

Nightmares were constant, certain smells caused him vomit and he would not eat for days. The doctor was unable to help. He gave him tranquilizers and sleeping pills, but this made his feel and even more depressed. Eventually he stopped going to the doctor and threw away his pills.

Drinking became a drug that suppressed his anxiety and fears and he also found other means to provide him with moments of forgetfulness and exhilaration—the sordid kind. When the weather was pleasant, he began going to clubs and finding prostitutes. The prostitutes made him feel alive and he was able to release his anger. He paid them well and did not do too much harm. Like drink, they were a drug that had no name, and they all had the same.

As time went on, he would become aroused the moment I entered the club. The women Ihe sought were childlike, so he could relive life before the war when the girls were virginal and shy. When they had entered the room, he would have her sit on my lap, so he could imagine she was teasing me. They would not kiss me, so he kissed their necks, arms, and legs. He never undressed so he didn't feel vulnerable. He made them vulnerable. He tore their undergarments, held their hands so they could not move or touch him and he preferred to enter them from the back, so they could not see his face at the moment of climax and he could not see their indifference or loathing. After all, this was not love, it wasn't even ecstasy, it was violence. A violence that was inflicted by him in which I had the control. A violence in which he could linger and have all else disappear. He am not ashamed of this. It was necessary to go on and live. A complete forgetting, a complete merging into an unspeakable place where life and death are mingled.

When Otto and Hunter left for university, the house became a tomb with living persons. Husband and wife read the newspapers each morning over coffee. There was some talk, but it was about things, not about us. Sometimes a letter from one of the boys had arrived, and they would discuss that and talk about what to send them.

After the war, Germany suffered as horrifically Austria. They both lost land, owed money they would never be able to repay (how could they expect them to?); there was inflation, low wages, unemployment, and a society that was unable to deal with defeat. Of course scapegoat was found, the Jews. The clubs were filled with foul anti-Semitic jokes. People even wrote their hatred on the back of money. I came across one that read:

> Like the fungus and the lichens on the oak's trunk
> The Jews thrive on mankind's trunk.
> Where the Jews live in comfort
> The majority remain in poverty's grip.

These attempts were pathetic, placing blame on the doorstep of people who did not deserve it.

Even as his own household was now forced to sell some belongings to make ends meet, Otto still visited the clubs where he drank and found women. Otto would laugh and think, "At least I am keeping some businesses in money." He would return home, standing but reeking of beer, smoke, and sex. So be it! He was a living example of a hero for the German nation.

CHAPTER TWENTY-ONE

The Years Between the Wars, Yugoslavia

The men who served in the Austrian army during the Great War were more than downhearted about the defeat of Germany. They felt a strong connection to Germany serving with Germans during the war. A common language and culture also connected them. In the Vojvodina, ethnic Germans had also remained connected nationally and culturally to Germany. However, the German villages in Vojvodina were spared much of the violence and death.

After the war in October 1918, the Banat became part of the State of Slovenes, Croats, and Serbs. The next month we were part of the Kingdom of Serbs, Croats, and Slovenes when the State joined Serbia to form a Kingdom. In 1929 the Kingdom became Yugoslavia.

During these chaotic years, when people believed that a government would never be formed, life carried on. Nothing had changed in the villages, there were different borders, but the people were the same as well the ethnic differences. What was feared was instability and what would happen to the ethnic Germans living there. They had little or no voice in the politics of the region. The Serbians had entered the region after The Great War without consent.

The ethnic groups grasping for autonomy had no common identity amongst them. There were different religions, different languages, and different cultures. Many stayed "German" because they felt German. They also did not trust the government to make life better no matter what they did. They were a minority, a German in a foreign land.

To the younger children changing of the names of their village was confusing, but they continued to go to school and play with their friends. Another major changes was in the education of the children. If a school did not have at least thirty German students the teaching was done in the new language, Serbo-Croation. Only sixteen schools remained German. The children were learning a new language again. Hungarian was used in the past during the Magyarization period when Hungarian was the official language. The students had to deal with three languages: German, Hungarian and Serbo-Croation.

People talked in shops and on the streets about what would happen to the ethnic Germans in this newly formed Kingdom. They were living on a desirable piece of land for agriculture which all the different nationalities wanted. The major problem was how to keep the state of Yugoslav from falling apart.

On June 12, 1919, it was declared that a divided the Banat would cause economic ruin for the people living there and the division would mean the continuation of quarrels among the ethnic groups. The ethnic Germans feared soldiers who had deserted from the Austro-Hungarian army living in nearby forests who answered to no one. They were called green cadres. There were also no promises by either the Romanians or the Serbians to keep laws ensuring social justice and voting rights.

Even before the war, families had sent fathers and brothers to America to earn money and send it back home. Some families separated sending some of their children to be with relatives living in America. This caused heartache, with children not understanding why the family was being separated. Most families did not have the money to send everyone at once or even at all. But the promises of a new life in American were great. Parents wanted to give their children a chance at a better life.

American industries advertised for workers, promising a dollar a day in wages and a ticket to travel for eight dollars one way in steerage. Although the people were mostly farmers, these wages offered in America were an enticement. Families settled in tight groups in cities, allowing family ties and friendships to remain. Those who stayed behind believed that things would change economically and politically and did not want to leave our homes and a two-hundred-year history. Politically laws favoring the Serbs were being enacted. Serbians' desire to have an independent state was strong. Most ethnic Germans believed that they would become a part of a Serbian state. The majority of Germans were adamantly against this.

The Fritz Cabinet Shop had grown and was successful and provided the family with a good living. Many children from the family became apprentices in the shop and eventually had full-time work. The Pharmacy continued its work providing needed medicines and herbal remedies.

The agricultural reforms of 1918 were also a cause for concern. The state gave land to poor Serbians, thus forcing the ethnic Germans to lose their farms. They were forced to find other work or leave. Some were able to buy their land back from the Serbians who had no interest in cultivating it. No one could not understand why the Serbians did not value the land as we did. Germans were proud of our work ethic and desire to live off the land.

It was during these years that the ethnic Germans began to call themselves "Danube Swabians," further establishing an affinity with German. In sympathy with the Germans, they could not understand why Germany lost the war. Armies fought to the death. It was the generals who gave up, and the allies Austria and Hungary who sued for their own peace. Newspapers related how the Germans were not even invited to the peace negotiations and signed the document under protest. What the Entente did not realize was that they were only lighting a fire that would create an even greater Germany. To many the treaty was only a lull in the war. Others saw it as the eventual collapse of Germany and others blamed everything on the Serbs. More and more the ethnic Germans became enamored with their Germanness and the concepts of *Volk* and *Vaterland*. Emotionally most of all they felt tied to the earth, either where they now lived or where we had come from. Earth and blood were important concepts in their beliefs.

One evening a group of men were visiting the house of Dr, Joseph Knapp. People saw him as level-headed and a leader in the community. One man during the conversation about the land reform said "We came here as a people over two hundred years ago. We are not foreigners anymore."

"You know," another said, "I went to the formation of the Kulturbund in Novi Sad in June. I felt that we could still preserve our culture and still be loyal to Yugoslavia."

The conversation then turned to what was the most important element of their culture, the German language. A young man joined in and showed his frustration at all the changes in the official language. "It is now two years since the war ended. We have lost land, changed our official language again. We learned Hungarian and now have to learn Serbo-Croatian."

They all laughed when Dr. Knapp said, "I barely learned Hungarian. I am surely not going to be able to learn this language."

Other began to interrupt with their thoughts. "But all business is to be carried out in this language. Some of our friends are store owners. Out in the fields and in our houses, we still speak German."

"We were not even given meaningful representation when agrarian reforms were being drafted."

"And then the kick in the teeth, higher taxes."

"Some of us served in the Hungarian army and this is the thanks we get."

The Kulturbund had started a newspaper, the *Deutsches Volksblatt* (The German Folks' Paper), meant informed people about what was being said amongst leaders in the community.

Dieter Knapp was old enough to understand what was happening and feared the loss and his families means of living. He cut our one paragraph that spoke to the fears of people and also their identity. He took it home to show his father.

> We Swabians are a people of colonists and settled among
> neighbors of other tongues and of different bloods.
> Nevertheless, we feel ourselves not as foreigners in this land
> . . . since the ground upon which we stand, the landscape
> through which we pull our ploughs, was wrung from
> swamps and bogs by our forefathers. And this little spot of
> land . . . is everything to us, it is our German fatherland. .
> . . We seek to remain loyal to this tiny piece of earth, upon
> which the sweat clings to our brow, so long as we breathe,
> and likewise to the ruler, who holds his hand protectively
> over our Heimat.

The concerns expressed at the Knapp house were not unique. As a result branches of the Kulturbund appeared in many villages. They organized public lectures, music and folk festivals, and amateur theater performances as a way to foster the German culture. It also published song books and started libraries. Activities for the youth were prominent, as well as finding work for the unemployed and providing training courses. A hope was that if a unifying experience was provided, religious and ethnic differences would lessen. It also served to strengthen solidarity with Germany.

However, this would not be the only experience to which young people were exposed. A student activist group called the *Erneuerer*, the Renewers, and eventually the *Hitlerjugend*, Hitler Youth, would become popular, drawing my family into the Nazi ideology and army.

The brothers Dieter and Rudolf were twenty-five and twenty-seven in 1922, then they became active members of the *Kulturbund*. Once a place to eat, drink, dance, and be with friends, it began to become a political enclave. In 1924 Yugoslavia banned it for becoming involved in politics. The slogan was *Muttersprache, Heimat, Väterglaube* (mother tongue, homeland and ancestors' beliefs) was enough for people to question what happened in their gatherings. It could be seen as anti-Yugoslavian and nationalistic.

The brothers were both married and starting families. Dieter had one son, Markus, and Rudolf had two sons, who died at birth, and a daughter, Marta. In the fall of 1926 Dieter took his son Markus to his parents' house to their grandparents' house so they could babysit while Dieter went to a meeting.

"Of course, Dieter, we love having the little ones with us. Where are you going, and when do you think we you will get back?"

"Opa, I am going to a friend's house to meet with some young men who are back from school in Austria and Germany. They are excited about the events in Germany and want to bring us the information they have about a man called Adolf Hitler, who is head of a new political party. I think it is a good idea to know what is happening there, since we are ethnic Germans and have strong ties with Germany."

"Do you really want to get involved in all this political business? How is anything happening in Germany going to affect us? Our German Party here in Yugoslavia has as its motto *Staatstreu und volkstreu* (loyal to the state and to the people). We live here, not in Germany."

"How good do we have it here? Some of our land has been taken away, many are moving to America, and we have no voice in the government. We live in a country where we still are called a minority and are treated as such."

"Dieter, please stay away from the heat of youth. Do you remember hearing what happened to our relative Karl? His life was torn apart by his involvement with politics. Be happy we have been spared the real hardships of war and revolution."

"I know you mean well, but I cannot let the world pass me by. You are older and can only see the past. I can see the future. If Germany can recover, we may have its support and its development industries and agricultural advancements. Germany needs our wheat and hemp. We suffered when the war closed railroads and we could not ship our goods."

In an exasperated tone Dr. Knapp "Do what you must, Dieter. But I have always felt that the fighting stopped in 1918 but I don't think the war is over. There is much hatred around. We may all get along, but we certainly don't love each other or trust each other."

Still try to win his grandfather over to understanding his position, Dieter replied, "What would be wrong with us having the protection of Germany? We fought on their side during the war. Being able to sell wheat and hemp to them would help us economically. Besides, I am going only to hear what they say."

Rising to talk Markus from Dieter Annika Knapp said, "Go ahead. But don't go along with the crowd and agree to things you don't know anything about."

"I won't" Dieter added with a note of irritation in his voice. "You know my father never lets me have my own opinions and ideas. I hoped that for once I could be involved in something important and make life better for our children."

At the start of the meeting a young student by the name of Georg rose and said, "Have you heard of Edmund Steinacker? He writes under the name of Sincerus. He formed the Hungarian German People's Party in 1906."

"It's 1926! What has he been doing for the last twenty years?!" a friend laughed loudly.

"His friend Professor Bleyer has started the Volksbildungsverin Society (The People's Education Society) to help us educate our children in German.

Almost one hundred percent of our teachers are Hungarian! Some children in the Banat are not taught to read or write German. How are we to become valued and above the idea that we are a dim-witted people unless we have a good education for our children."

An slightly older man of thirty rose and agreed saying, "Yes, he is right. We are unable to assert ourselves because of our language. I heard that in court a man couldn't be cross-examined because he asked for it to be questioned in German. The court considered him unpatriotic."

Dieter felt brave enough to add to the conversation. "My family has always been farmers. We came here as German farmers and we made this area livable and, in fact necessary. We provide their food."

"We should honor our ancestors and remain true to what they were, Germans. We are still a People no matter where we are living," said another student.

A heated discussion followed with some claiming they were all German and must remain so. Other saying our future lays with Hungary now that we no longer have the protection of the Astro-Hungarian Empire. Many felt we should fight to our statehood as the Serbs and Croats were doing.

A man in the back of the room stood, a veteran of the war, and loudly proclaimed, "I fought for Germany, and I learned what Germany was. Their army was better equipped than Hungarian army and they are a powerful nation. It is not their fault we were defeated. I think it would be good us align ourselves with Germany."

Many shouted 'yes' in agreement and there was applause. From all sides people started talking. "Our neighbors will be more than happy to gobble us up and then we won't have a choice to determine who we are" and "Who will defend us? We need the support of Germany. I tell you; they will one day have an army again," two of the loudest voices shouted. But they were expressing what the general sentiment was.

The discussion went on util well after midnight. Dieter needed to get home. No minds were going to be changed that night. But the Awakeners were gathering support. Eventually decisions would be made for people and not let them decide for themselves. The main question, "Who are We"? remained.

When Dieter returned, very excited and agitated, he did not talk much about the meeting. He was hesitant to talk about the meeting and that he agreed with most of the young men there.r ideas. He did tell his grandparent that the group themselves Awakeners, *Erneuerers*. Dieter understood that if the youth began to think differently, then the future would be different.

Dieter met weekly with his friends at the Kulturbund.

CHAPTER TWENTY-ONE

Part Two

Wer in Europa die Fackel des Krieges anzündet,
kann sich nur Chaos wünschen.
Whoever lights the torch of war in Europe
can wish for nothing but chaos.
—Adolf Hitler

"Franz, have you heard about this new political party started in Munich? It's called the German Workers' Party, DAP for short. A friend of mine went to one of their meetings and heard a man, Adolf something, speak about the Versailles treaty. Here, I have a letter from him with a couple of quotes." Since returning from the war Franz Müller kept company with far-right people and politics.

His friend Ernst got his letter out and read: "As long as the earth has existed, no people have ever been forced to declare themselves willing to sign such a shameful treaty."

Ernst continued reading that the group blamed the finance minister, Erzberger, a Jew for the war and our problems. "At another meeting, Hitler" (the man named Adolf) "also spoke of 'the Jews, who alone are profiting from it and don't shy away from inciting civil war with their rabble-rousing and base agitation.' He also demanded a stop to Jewish immigration and that Germany be only for Germans."

181

Franz's group of friends decided to travel to Munich to hear this Hitler in person. The Hofbräuhaus was the meeting place, and everyone was packed in with no room. It was February 24, 1920. The rise of NSDAP, the National Socialist German Workers' Party—the Nazi party.

More and more people were attending his speeches, and they were frenetic by the time he finished. Franz and a few of his friends decided to stay in Munich where they took menial jobs and lived together in a rundown apartment. The atmosphere was electric.

After the September 18, 1922, speech several of us gathered at a local coffee house to hash over Hitler's points. The conversation started with Franz recounting the line he most admired. "I agree from the bottom of my heart that vengeance is needed on those who betrayed us at Versailles. Isn't this close to what he said, how after two million Germans died in vain,we sat down afterwards at the same table as friends? We should not pardon them but demand vengeance."

There were shouts of "Yes! Yes!" "We should string them up in the streets!"

"Yes, I watched too many suffer and die to be told I need to accept that damn treaty and to lie down and take defeat," Franz added, and pounding on the table. His face was red from emotion. He could feel the excitement he felt during battle. "We didn't start the war, but we could have won if the damn generals had not given up. I admit I was excited about going to war, and that it turned me into the man I am, but I see vengeance as necessary to regaining our dignity."

Others who were at the speech joined us. Several were veterans and wore there medals on their coats. "Yes, did you hear that he wanted our heroes honored by having our streets named after them? Yes! Let's tear down those Jewish street names."

It had now become a crowd. People broke up into groups and discussion began to center on the 'Jews'. Several mentioned Hitler's comment about the expulsion of all Jewish people who had come to Germany since 1914. "They are all capitalists, and tricksters who make their money on the stock market."

Franz added to the mode agreeing with Hitler's statement about the Jews causing disunity was true. "But what is his solution to the Jewish problem? To expel all Jews? How is that going to be achieved? Do we just kick them out of their houses and give them free train tickets to somewhere else?"

There was laughter and someone in the back shouted, "That is not a bad idea, my friend. Germans would then have a place to live and work. We could just take over their businesses."

Another man said, "We must also rid our culture of their ideas. We do not need their books, art, or music. We need to hear more Beethoven, Schubert, read more Goethe and Schiller, and get rid of the art by Otto Dix."

My friends shouted "*Ja, Ja*, what horrible art."

Franz knew the art of Otto Dix's. Those who had spent months at the front knew that his images were true. He was unsure what made his art bad. Could seeing paintings cause a society to become as decadent as Berlin was? The culture of decadence was also being addressed by Hitler. Franz agreed that Hitler was out to clean the streets of the prostitutes, those that Dix painted. Get rid of the diseases caused by them, end homosexuality, and other perversions of the flesh. Hitler understood that people needed to be surrounded by art that praised and uplifted the German nation and spirit.

The men all agreed that what was needed was will, courage, and energy; the exact words of the speech. One man immediately said, "*Ja*, I wrote part of that sentence down. 'Where then can any strength be found? . . . It is to be found, as always, in the great masses! Their energy is slumbering, and it only awaits the man who will summon it from its present slumber and will hurl it into the great battle for the destiny of the German race.'"

This man had touched the soul of these people. He was tapping into their feelings about the war and the Versailles Treaty, He was giving the people a voice. There was an energy in the room was palpable. believed that Germany could rise above defeat feeling this kind of energy. Did we have the will and the courage? Is this the man who would lead the battle for our destiny?

Hitler was offering hope to the people. His speeches reached the people because he told them what they wanted to hear. The way he said things was as important as how he said them. He was an ordinary man who fought for his country and was now fighting for his country's soul. Germany had to become great again and he was the man to make this happen. His speeches became events that everyone wanted to be a part of. There were flags, bands, and parades exciting the audience and preparing them for his entrance. Before the war Germans were people who valued "orderliness, cleanliness, and precision," and honest and dutiful people. Now they felt they were ruled by a republic that was criminal and run by Jews. There would be no more classes but a people with workers of one ethnicity. One line that was emblazoned into my being was from a speech in October 1920: "People who work with their heads and those who work with their hands need to realize that they belong together and that only together can we get our people back on their feet again." Genius.

Franz and his friends all joined the Nazi Party. They could see a future. A future who needed an army of believers. They all volunteered for jobs. Franz wrote pamphlets and flyers for people and distributed them around Munich. He also wrote articles for the newspaper that a man named Rosenberg had established, the *Völkischer Beobachter*, the *People's Observer*. Hitler called it "the most hated paper in the land," because it spoke truth to the German people in plain German. Hitler was often at the paper's office, and it was here that Franz began to know him better and spend time talking with him. We weren't friends, but he knew who I was and knew that I agreed with all his ideas.

Franz left his law firm and worked pro bono to have money. His work at the paper and with the NSDAP was as exciting to him as my days before the war. He was going to make a difference and be involved in the formation of a new government.

However much he believed in the party he did not join the coup d'état that Hitler planned. Franz felt that the veterans who made up the SA, a paramilitary organization that Hitler founded, were a bunch of thugs. They were not the kind of soldiers that represented the army he had belonged to. The failure of the *putsch* in 1923 and Hitler's ensuing imprisonment put many of the party's plans on hold. But during his time in prison, Hitler wrote *Mein Kampf*. Franz bought it immediately when it was published and read it several times, hoping to understand where he came from and where he would lead Germany. After his release from prison, Hitler was banned from public speaking, but he continued to speak behind locked doors. Prison had changed him: he had become austere.

Franz moved up the ladder of importance and was getting closer to Hitler's inner circle. He felt that eventually he would find a place of importance within the party. Hitler's inner circle included Alfred Rosenberg, Heinrich Himmler, Hermann Göring, Joseph Goebbels, and Ernst Röhm.

Franz sat close to Himmler at meetings and parties and tried to engage him in conversation. He told Himmler of his experiences in the war and how he would never forget the sacrifices of our youth. Himmer listened to the stories, nodding his head and saying, "Yes, such a sacrifice. This is what we will need in the future to make Germany great again."

In 1927 Himmler was named Deputy *Reichsführer-SS*. As a tall, blonde, athletic man, I would have had no problems if I decided to join their ranks. By 1933 their ranks had swelled to fifty thousand members. Franz wanted to fight, be a soldier again. He watched Hitler closely at all meetings and observed his dealings with his inner circle. Hitler was an odd mixture of traits that were often contradictory. The inner circle was made up of men who would have never been accepted into the SS. They were fat, frail, and looked Jewish, and Goebbels had a right foot that turned out awkwardly and seemed smaller than the left. It seemed to me that Hitler surrounded by people who were "less" than he was, making him their superior. He blamed everyone around him for mistakes that were his, and he could be a bully. Franz saw enormous hatred in him, and his need for revenge seemed unquenchable. He could also be gracious and engaging, as well as affectionate to children. His oratory was dazzling.

He was able to gain power and thus superiority by his words. I heard him claim that the masses were like women who could and should be seduced by words. He was able to express the deepest unspoken desires and needs of the people and convince them that these were also his. He embodied the primitive need for aggression and control, with the ideals of the German people's past glories. The complex became simple, and he gave quick solutions to problems. But was his ability to evoke the power of myth enough to create a new government and super race of Germans? Were hatred and revenge to be his guiding forces for the rise of Germany? He saw himself as Germany and wanted the people to see that Hitler and Germany were one, along with hatred and revenge.

In 1933 Hitler was named Chancellor of Germany and he announced his objective of securing *Lebensraum*, living space for the German people. Events moved very quickly, Franz could see war. Many evenings were spent in beer houses listening to speeches, hearing people argue about everything possible, and learning about how the world was perceiving Hitler. Hitler was clear about what he wanted and how he was going to get it. The German people are behind him, and they will do what he wants.

"Franz, do you think Europe understands what Hitler wants?"

"He has been very clear about what he wants for Germany. Are they not listening?"

"No, I don't think so. They will want peace at any price. They can't possibly understand our need for revenge and our hatred of what we have had to endure."

"You may be right, Franz, but how is your will, courage, and energy after the 'war to end all wars'?"

With an earnest voice Franz replied, "You know, I loved war and would gladly go back."

We didn't have to wait long for events to change again in Hitler's favor. Hindenburg died the next month, and Hitler named himself President, calling himself *Führer,* and instated conscription in 1935. He made his first move against the Jews in the Nuremburg Laws in September of 1935. And with the occupation of the Rhineland in 1936, they all knew that war was not far off.

CHAPTER TWENTY-THREE

Hitler Youth

Serbia

It was 1939, Markus was as sixteen. His father, Dieter Knapp, always attended the meetings at the *Kulturbund* and he always eagerly awaited his return, to learn more news of Germany and Adolf Hitler. Within the community there were families who shied away from the meetings. There were strong divisions amongst families about what the *Kulturbund* was doing and its purpose. The older generation did not want to entertain the ideas of the Nazis, while the younger generation saw the Nazis as a way to assert their Germanness, obtain financial and educational help from Germany, and improve lives.

By 1940 there were Hitler Youth groups in most of the villages which Marcus joined of the boys in the villages had also joined and were enthusiastic about the activities, and they listened to the lectures about National Socialism even if they didn't understand or care. Camping, marching, drills, mock battles, and other activities prepared us for the military. Our schools, also, were undergoing changes. We usually started the morning off saying *Heil Hitler,* there were new science courses in "race science," and geography was about the lands taken from Germany. In history we were taught to blame the Jews for the Treaty of Versailles and the hyperinflation of 1923. My favorite change was that gym was held for two hours every day. It extremely important to the leaders and if one failed, they were often expelled.

"Father, today I learned how Jewish people caused us to lose the war."

Marcus's father, who loved to ask about what he learned in school, said, "And how did the Jews do that?"

"As you know, they are mainly bankers and financiers, and they sought profits from the war, like from our guns and ammunitions. They are capitalists and communists against nationalism and socialism. They were also responsible for the Versailles treaty. I'm not sure what that all means, but they are our enemies and becoming strong against us. I think the teacher also said they are all intellectuals, and Hitler admires strong, physically fit people."

His father nodded. "You are right, Markus. You seem to be learning a lot. How do you hope to utilize your knowledge?"

"Oh, there were also some posters up at school. I wrote down what one said: 'Agricultural labor is harvest labor. German soil is our common, greatest, and holiest possession. To till the soil and bring in the harvest assures the life and fighting strength of the people.' I hope to use what I learn to make us a welcome part of the German Reich and do what's necessary to bring about our ascension."

His Father agreed and said, "We are very important to Hitler now. We are the breadbasket of the world. The farmers here in Vojvodina are closer to the soil than many others. We came here two hundred years ago to make this land fertile, and now we can give back to our fatherland."

Marcus asked his father what stories he knew about their ancestors. What little Dieter knew about the first Fritz family and their hardships he related. They had some famous musicians who had lived or were still living in Austria and Germany. His father thought one was a violinist who had studied with Haydn, and another was a singer whose son fought for Germany in the war. Dieter showed Marcus a Bible and poems of Goethe that had been passed down through the family.

"Is Goethe okay to read?"

"Yes, Markus, he is not one of those Jewish writers." Marcus asked if he could keep the book of poems and took it with him on Hitler Youth camping trips.

Many books had been banned, especially in the sciences. The students did not understand what Jewish science, music, or literature was, but they knew that it was different from what we were taught in schools and was often referred to as decadent.

Although Marcus was physically exhausted at the end of each day of the spring camping trip, he had time to sit and read some of the poems. One evening he found a tree to rest against and flipped through the pages until something caught his attention. There was a full moon, and he saw the poem "An den Mond", to the moon.

He tried to understand the poem. "Yes, the moon does fill the bush and valley and its light is not that of the sun. "Misty" is a wonderful way to describe it. The poet said the moon at last set his soul free. As he thought, he realized that there is a quietness, a peace that we all feel in moonlight. Is it this peace that makes my soul free? Is my soul not free all the time?" The language of the poem was not concrete, and therefore it was difficult to understand the exact meaning. The trumpet signaled *Zapfenstreich* (curfew) and he ran quickly back to his tent. He decided to ask his teacher about the poem when he returned to school. It somehow gave him comfort.

When he asked my teacher about Goethe and his poetry, the teacher was eager to answer Marcus's questions. "Goethe is one of Germany's greatest treasures. His poems about nature are odes to our native land and the beauty of it. Yes, they do give comfort. Do you know why he wrote this poem?"

Marcus shook his head and said no, and they read the poem together, slowly. Marcus learned that it wasn't just about nature but about the suicide of a young girl whom Goethe knew. She drowned herself in a lake near his cottage. He was devastated and wrote the poem.

"So, Markus, why does he start with the moon?"

"Maybe it is because at night we think of death."

"That is an excellent start, Markus. And what would some other reasons be?'

The discussion lasted about an hour, and he promised the teacher that he would continue reading the poetry. They met several times again, and the conversations became important to Marcus. He was learning the greatness of German culture and what it gave the world. Germany had created a Youth Theater Series that had put on plays of Schiller. Although Marcus could not go, he read the plays and poems of Schiller. Marcus went to a friend's house that had a record player to listen to Beethoven's Ninth Symphony and hear how Beethoven had set Schiller's "Ode to Joy". He would remember the music and poem for the rest of his life.

His cousin, Marta, had studied to be a nurse in Timisoara. She had married the pastor of the Lutheran church in Schowe, Ernst Gottlieb. She and her husband were very concerned about the war that had started with Germany taking over Austria and invading Poland. Ernst had lived in Germany during the Great War, before taking the pulpit call in Schowe. He often talked about what he felt were the evils of war, and what war did to the soldiers and their families. The congregation became very worried that with his talk and sermons he would cause problems for himself and Marta. Marcus's family distanced themselves from them, knowing that their talk was considered by many to be treason.

Germany considered its culture to be centered around the myths of our ancient warriors. Marcus and his father shared dreams of being warriors for Germany and creating a German Empire that would last for a thousand years. This new empire would end ethnic divisions between Serbs and Germans, and end the mistreatment the Germans had suffered being shuffled around between Hungary, Yugoslavia, and Serbia. Marcus's family wanted to be a part of Germany and receive all the benefits that Hitler was providing.

Marcus's father had many fights with neighbors and family over the Hitler Youth group and our activities.

"Have you heard about the Brownshirts in Germany?" my uncle said. "They go around murdering people who are against Hitler: the communists and the Jews. This is not how government function. We elect our officials and have open and free debate and dialogue. He wants to do away with democracy and turn Germany into a totalitarian society."

Dieter, trying not to raise his voice, said, "I would rather have a state that can control the chaos that the Weimar government has created. We need order. Some heavy-handed means are necessary."

"Dieter, I can't believe you are saying this. In the past—"

Dieter cut him off: "In the past we have had our land taken away. Our colonies have been divided up between nations. We have high taxes. And we have reasons to fear the Serbs and the Jews."

"But certainly, murder is not the way. Hitler wants a war of annihilation. I have been reading his speeches in the German newspapers. He does not hide his beliefs. Do you agree with murder?" With this last sentence Marcus's uncle rose as if to hit his father.

His father rose also but turned his back to get more beer and said, "Yes! It is the only way to cleanse our society of the vermin that has infected it."

My uncle then listed the names of the Jewish people who lived near us. "Do you mean to murder our neighbors and friends?"

"What makes you think they are our friends? Do they invite us in for a drink and dinner? Do they—"

My uncle now interrupted my father and stood within an arm's length of him. "No, but our children play together. We benefit from their shops."

The argument got more heated, and my father stormed out of my uncle's house. They were never to speak again.

Because Marcus's had stopped going to church, we rarely saw his cousin, Marta, and her husband, Ernst. They learned that they were helping Jewish families emigrate to France and the Netherlands. Marcus and his father both agreed that at least they were getting rid of Jews.

In April 1941, Germany occupied Serbia and quickly defeated an unprepared and ill-equipped army. In March 1942, Marcus joined the newly formed Waffen-SS Prinz Eugen division.

CHAPTER TWENTY-FOUR

Prinz Eugen Division

Marcus's unit was called the *SS-Freiwilligen Gebirgs* division, the SS Volunteer Mountain Division. The commander was Artur Phelps, an ethnic German from Transylvania. On April 1, 1942, the men received their formal name, the Seventh Waffen-SS Volunteer Mountain Division Prinz Eugen.1 They were assigned the old Nordic symbol of the Odal, signifying blood unity, family, and kinship. The uniforms also carried the Edelwiess emblem, Prinz Eugen and lightening strokes on our collars, the death head and the national emblem for the SS on our hats. Yes, the members of the division believed they were united with Germany by our blood. They were no longer citizens of any other nation; they were part of the German Reich. Their oath was: "I vow to you, Adolf Hitler, as Führer and chancellor of the German Reich, loyalty and bravery. I vow to you, and to the leaders that you set for me, absolute allegiance until death. So help me God."

Commander Artur Phleps, although called him Papa Phleps, was rigorous and stern. The training was difficult and necessary. During the war he had served in the Imperial Army of the Austro-Hungarian Empire and was known for his excellence in mountain warfare. Marcus was glad that the Hitler Youth group had demanded so much of physically. As a mountain division they had to be able to climb and descend mountains while carrying materials

---

1   Ian Baxter in *Images of War 7th SS Mountain Division Prinz Eugen at War* lists the date as July, 1943 when they were moved to the Dalmatian Coast

and heavy packs. By the end of the day all the men were all exhausted but, felt good since each day things were getting easier.

More men were needed in the division to achieve our goals of wiping out the Serbian Chetniks , so all men in the Banat were conscripted. The ranks eventually swelled to 21,500 troops. Since most of our recruits were peasants, their transition to soldiers was often difficult. The sight of a man learning to drive a motor vehicle rather than one led by horses often drew laughter from the onlookers. For others the challenge was learning to ride a horse. Strict discipline was required, to teach the troops how to ration water and deal with vertigo. Also necessary was training in using the weapons and understanding the tactics of the Chetniks and Communists, who were fighting not only us but each other. We would become known for our thoroughness of eliminating all sympathizers, spies, and chetniks. Their song speaks to their dedication to destroy the Serbs.

> Prinz Eugen, the noble troop,
> it must scuffle with Serbs,
> our trash division!
> And many Serbian skulls,
> and many Serbian maids
> will I soon see fallen . . .

The first operation was against the Serbian forces under General Draza Mihailovich's commander, Major Dragutin Keserovic, in the Kopaonik Mountains of Kriva Reka. Himmler visited us to observe our operations because he deemed this so important.

"I am pleased with your attitude and training" Himmler said when addressing us. He then promoted several of us. Marcus was promoted to the rank of Sergeant, a junior squad leader, because of his initiative during training and was seen as a model by many officers. He wrote home to my father of the great news.

Phleps' first orders were given on October 5 for an attack on the Kriva Reka area. The troops were ordered to treat all people as sympathizers and therefore enemy. The men knew what that meant, kill them. The area was the headquarters of Keserovic and it had to be destroyed. "Every man in Division

'Prinz Eugen' will fight victoriously wherever the combat takes them. We now lay the groundwork for future operations. The division must fight to destroy our enemy, eliminate his headquarter and maintain the peace. Forward, Prinz Eugen!"

Marcus felt a thrill and a rush of excitement. As they marched forward many saw how the forests and lack of roads would hinder their movements. The men had been divided up into four groups to encircle the chetniks. The chetniks were outnumbered and division felt confident that they would succeed. What gave them pause was the fact that they could be anywhere, and they would not see the enemy. When they began pincer movement, they encounter only small numbers of chetniks who could retreat and move very quickly out of area of combat. They were able to pick us off because of their knowledge of the area and ability to hide.

The Prinz Eugen division lost, and it was unbelievable to Marcus. Even when he learned that there had been spies who had learned of their plans guarantying their loss, Marcus was unable hide his utter disappointment.

"Markus, you have survived to fight another day. Stay strong. This is only one battle out of many", the Lieutenant told me."

"Yes sir" was all he could answer.

"Remember we were able to punish the village and word of this will spread and create fear."

They had killed 690 civilians in Kriva Reka, burned the village, and killed 46 men, women and children in church they blew up. Some of our men had a difficult time with this punishment, but Marcus knew it was necessary to defeat chetniks.

To Marcus's amazement, the men were ordered to 'refrain' from killing civilians and burning their villages without cause. Our cause was the elimination of any Serbian who could fight against us. The battalion commander, Richard Kaaserer, was dismissed from the SS. Many of the men felt that his dismissal was warranted. "We are not here to kill innocent women and children. This action will not provoke fear but hatred from the people and provide more enemy soldiers," my friend Horst said to me. "We are not murderers. My father never did things like this during the war. The killing of the enemy was slaughter enough for him."

"Horst, we must see everyone as the enemy. These villages have spies, and the civilians will kill us as quickly as the soldiers." Our methods would last throughout the war.

The Wehrmacht also proved a deadly force in Serbia. In Pancevo nine German soldiers had been killed. This was the division's command post. Standortkommandant, Site Commander, Bandelow had issued the following statement: "There have been repeated attacks and sniping against German soldiers in violation against internal law. For every wounded or killed German soldier 10 Serbs will be hanged. If this doesn't stop the sniping, we will double the number to 20." A total of 36 Serbians were killed. Marcus believed that the soldiers were doing nothing that hadn't been accepted elsewhere. The most complete liquidation of people took place in Kragujevac as a reprisal for insurgent attacks. Between the months of September and October of 1941, it was ordered that one hundred Serbian men and boys be executed for the killing of one German soldier and fifty for every soldier wounded. This amounted to the execution of 7000 men and boys. Prinz Eugen's reprisals paled in comparison, they had nothing to feel guilty about.

~

"Prinz Eugen" by Otto Kumm

Otto Kumm, the second commander of the 7 SS mountain Division Prinz Eugen, wrote a history of the division. In it he praises the men. He writes movingly of their courage and commitment. "Their commitment, their sacrifice, their bravery, and their freedom of their people." (Preface page viii) He states clearly that the division did not commit any acts or war crimes and that these crimes were undocumented. (270) Kumm believed that the charges against the men "served as an alibi to divert attention from crimes committed by the partisans themselves." (270) As evidence that they did not commit atrocities he relates an incident in Montenegro that supposedly killed two women by "slitting their bellies open." (270) The soldier, Ostuf, Joachim Krah, had never spent time in in Montenegro.

However, it was widely known, and is still talked about today in Serbia, that there was an order from Hitler that for every German soldier wounded fifty hostages were to be executed and for every German soldier killed one hundred hostages were to be killed. It was events such as these that brought members of the division before the Nuremberg Tribunal.

In the transcript of the trial the following was used to describe the division: "The Eugen Division left behind scenes of conflagration and devastation and the bodies of innocent men, women and children who had been burned in the houses." (Volume twenty, the 196th day, Tuesday August 6, 1946. The trial relates that in Montenegro that the victims were shot and slaughtered, and that torture was a part of this purge operation. General Phelps, the first commander of the division, was indicted.

CHAPTER TWENTY-FIVE

Vojvodina, Yugoslavia, 1944
Rache ist die neue Unrecht
Revenge is the new wrong
—German Proverb

Когда гнев и Месть женятся их
дочь жестокость
When anger and revenge marry, their daughter is cruelty
—*Russian Proverb*

Why all this suffering? How could we have been so blind? Why did I just follow along, believing right would prevail? Did we deserve this? These and many more questions will haunt people from the Banat for the rest of their lives. They also wondered if their relatives in America and Canada know what has happened to their *Heimat,* home, and their families in Vojvodina, Austria, and Germany. They were spared, while ethnic Germans reaped a revenge of Biblical proportions. Between Tito's and Russia's revenge the ethnic Germans, called "Danube Swabians," were almost wiped out as a people, and the Allies seemed to turn away. People wondered at the time if they even cared what was happening. Did they believe we deserved our fate? Our destruction started in the autumn of 1944; we call it Bloody Autumn.

Romania had changed sides and was with the Allies while the *Wehrmacht,* the regular German army, was retreating from the Eastern Front. Germany had been bombed into rubble. The ethnic Germans had heard that the

Russians would make their way to Berlin through their villages. Tito's army was also to be feared as they would surely seek revenge for the war carried out against the Partisans and the Chetniks. Hope was that Germany would have the Wehrmacht protect them, or that their sons and fathers who were in the SS-Waffen Prinz Eugen Division would be sent home to help. But there was to be no military help from the country they gave their men to.

Villagers heard that they needed to evacuate the towns, to leave with no place to go but Austria or Germany, as soon as an evacuation could be organized. The task of preparing was given to Dr. Jakob Awender, leader of the Renewers. The plan was simple. There were to be five groups with fifty-three marching columns. Each column was to have a leader, an escort, a doctor, a midwife, and a car with medical supplies, spare parts, archival materials, our parish books, coal and gasoline. But we were to find out that Hitler gave a 'secret 'order not to start the evacuation.

Many people decided to stay. They could not believe that Germany would not protect them. By October 1945 the Serbian Banat was occupied by Tito's partisans and Soviet troops. Serbians began to take over houses and violence ensued.

Even when Yugoslavia began to expel them, rather than evacuate us, terms which are very different, the occupation authorities in Austria and Germany only accepted a few because of limited transportation. It was not until 1951 that what remained of these people were able to go to Germany.

Marta hoped that her cousin, Markus, was safe. She heard he was helping German troops in their retreat. "And what happens to our troops when the Germans are gone, and they are left? Can they retreat with them? Will they be allowed to come home?" I asked Ernst.

"Marta, I don't know. I hate to sound angry and cynical, but this is what Markus wanted, and now he will reap what he has sown with Himmler and his gang."

Marta could not believe that Ernst was saying this. She knew he hated that many young men had turned to Nazi ideologies, but now both Marta and Ernst knew they were going to be left to the Russians.

"Why will they not allow them to return home and help us? We counted on the protection of Germany. Now we are left to face the Russian army and Tito's partisans by ourselves.

Very quickly Marta and Ernst began to learn what awaited them if we did not evacuate. Those stayed foolishly believed that it could not be as bad as the reports we had heard about the war itself and its final days. This was their home, and their family had been here for two centuries. They loved the land and life they had created here. There was no way for people to know what awaited them.

Ernst was a pastor, and he wanted to stay to provide spiritual support. Marta wanted to stay and help the elderly and infants; they were the most vulnerable and would suffer the most from any disasters. Starting on September 27, hundreds began making their trek through Torschau from the village of Jarek.

People began to hear terrible stories, as refugees from villages to the north and east trekked through to "safety," wherever that might be. Who would take them in? The Partisans, whom the Prinz Eugen troops had fought, were ruthless in their revenge. People were told of a party in which a large group of German men were killed, cut up into pieces, and placed in a pile in the center of room, around which the Partisans danced. People recounted seeing a brown crust on the streets that was the blood of the murdered; it could not be washed away. Boys around the age of twelve were taken to rooms and shot. Because so many of the men were still fighting in the war, these brutal attacks were levied at the young, women, and elderly. Homes were confiscated and looted. Everything of any value was taken. We had buried our most treasured items, but they found these too. Our homes became their places to sleep, eat, and drink.

Women killed their daughters and then committed suicide. One grandmother threw her granddaughter down a well and jumped after her. The grandmother was saved by horrified neighbors, but the young girl died, having been trapped under the large skirts of her grandmother's dress. Girls as young as nine were raped to death. A beautiful young woman was savagely beaten for hours, stripped naked, and then her entire naked body was burned by a household iron. She died two days later, after suffering unbelievable pain.

Some fifteen hundred did flee, however, hoping to go to Germany and blend in with the local population. When wagons by the hundred appeared on our streets, we stared and cried. The children could not understand what was happening. As the people left, the local organist played, for the last time, the hymn "Entrust all your Days and Burdens." As time progressed, people realized how horrible the decisions were going to be. Leave everything behind in the hopes of finding safety or stay and meet certain death. The Partisans had destroyed bridges and blocked roads, trapping people. Austria did not want the refugees, thinking that they were gypsies, and there was literally no place in Germany for the refugees to find a place to live. Those who had relatives in America could not emigrate, because all legal papers were being destroyed. Each person also had to have a relative who would guarantee them a job and lodging.

In November 1944 the AVNOJ Laws were passed in Yugoslavia. The Danube Swabians were declared outlaws with no rights, and all possessions were to be confiscated. This meant clothing, furniture, dishes, bedding, linens, silverware. Panic broke out at railway stations, and those hoping to travel by train might be bombed by Allied bombers. Children screamed and cried when they accidently dropped their mothers' hands. Mothers yelled their children's names. The heat and the number of people jammed into the cars, along with the lack of food, caused many deaths.

Ernst and Marta spent sleepless nights trying to decide whether to stay or leave. A decision was not reached in time. On October 7 and 8 the village of Jarek was plundered. The inhabitants had been moved or killed. The evacuated village would be made into a concentration camp, a death camp. Partisans had agreed with their communist brothers to resettle all able-bodied men in Russia. This resulted in separated families and abandoned children, when thousands of people were sent to work camps as reparation for what the Germans had done to Russia during the war. They not only demanded work but also the land and the bodies of the women. As the physical landscape in Europe was destroyed by the war, the physical bodies of women and girls were raped and destroyed. People were at the mercy of the Partisans and the Russians and there was no mercy, only savagery and barbarity. Infants were kidnapped from their parents and sent to Serbia to be repatriated.

Between the Russians heading for Berlin and the Partisans, the ethnic Germans were caught in a cauldron that had no escape and were experiencing hell, the only way out being death or deportation to another hell in Soviet work camps. Then, in December of 1944, two types of concentration camps were started by the Serbians: forced labor camps and death camps, where all died of starvation and torture. The plundered village of Jarek became a death camp.

The Jarek camp was formed on December 2, 1944. Ernst and Marta were separated. Ernst was transported to Russia and Marta was sent to Jarek. In Schowe the people were taken to restaurants and crammed together for three days. They were then taken to Jarek or to Russia, shipped in cattle cars that were nailed shut, with no winter clothing and no food or water. Serbians wanted some of the young women to stay and do work that was needed in Serbia. If, however, a mother was taken and forced to leave her children, it was up to the people in the Jarek concentration camp to raise the children. Some infants who were not weaned died of starvation. It was not long before typhus broke out because of the lice. Whatever people could catch was eaten, otherwise they were given soup made of dried bean straw, cooked in water with all the filth and bugs and seed corn, twice a day. At sunrise they were taken to the fields to work. Work hastened death. If someone dropped from sickness or exhaustion, they were left there to die or were shot. The life expectancy was two weeks.

Marta was allowed to stay in the death camp and not be moved to a work camp even though she was considered young and well enough to work in Russia, because she was a nurse and could help with the children. Many had developed boils that leaked an odorous green pus. Marta bundled the infants with clothes rinsed in chamomile tea. There were never enough clean clothes to use as diapers, and the babies developed terrible rashes. She made an ointment from lard and mint for their bottoms and tried to keep them as dry as possible. Diarrhea scourged the children and diapers were of no use. The littlest ones dehydrated so quickly that nothing could be done to save them. Mothers were starving and could no longer breastfeed their infants. Many infants sucked so vigorously that eventually all they could take from their mothers' breasts was blood. Eventually the babies became mute and limp, having died in their mothers' arms. Mothers prayed: "Please, God, do not forget me." Broken and starving themselves, many women never recovered from their loss.

There was also a children's home for those who were orphaned by their parents' deaths or deportation to Russia. They would sit for hours in the corners, completely devoid of any emotion. They had no tears when their friends or other relatives died. The youngest ones were taken to a government home where they would be "Slavinized." All traces of former lives were to be erased and eradicated. With our deaths, our language, our culture, everything would be wiped from existence. It would be as if we never lived and we will never live again. Twenty children died each day.

Marta also helped the dying and elderly who were too weak to stand or move. There was a room at the camp with straw covering the floor where the sick lay. This horrible place was called the infirmary, or the antechamber of death. All Marta was able to do was relieve some of their suffering by brushing away the lice that were running all over their faces and placing new straw underneath them because of diarrhea. I never will forget one old woman yelling to me to stop the dogs from biting her feet. When she went over and removed her threadbare blanket, I saw that rats had started to eat her toes.

When Marta could, she dspent time with people who were in worse shape than she was, talking about happier times. Many of these people were Marta's relatives, and to see them dying in such circumstances would often make her vomit. She could not bear to look at their open wounds, their infected eyes, the lice, their vomit which was only bile, the smell of decay and dirt, their knotted joints, their hunched backs, their smile-less faces, their hairless bodies. They didn't look like the cheerful people whose houses she ran through as a child or who shared meals with her family. Their skeletal bodies had lost all their unique physical characteristics. They were bones with swollen stomachs. Many had had their heads shaven, and one could not tell if they were female or male. Most others were members of Ernst's congregation. She prayed with and for them and sang hymns. Marta told them the story of Bach's death and how he sang the hymn "Vor deinen Thron tret' ich hiermit" ("Before Thy Throne I Now Appear") on his deathbed. Most often they asked to sing with her the last verse of "O Haupt voll Blut und Wunden" ("O Sacred Head, Now Wounded"). It was as if they knew when it was their last moment and wanted to be reminded that their suffering was also Christ's suffering. The music and words made their pain easier at the end. They looked up, their eyes now peaceful. Their limbs relaxed, and death was truly a release. I prayed that I would have such faith at my end. All Marta could see was suffering and torment, not Jesus's face, and her faith seemed incapable of holding on to Christ. She felt powerless against the forces who only wanted to see Germans suffer and die. Being powerless made her give up all hope and she dared not think of Ernst. That would be too much.

> Be Thou my consolation, my shield when I must die;
> Remind me of Thy passion when my last hour draws nigh.
> My eyes shall then behold Thee, upon Thy cross will dwell.
> My heart by faith enfolds Thee. Who dieth thus dies well.

There were extremely malicious and sadistic guards at Jarek. One was a woman by the name of Jana. She had become a Partisan in 1943. She would pull women by their hair and then drag them for many feet. The women's bodies were often raw where she had whipped them with her riding crop. Not even the children were spared. She made them pluck out grass in the meadows with their hands and would run over them with her horse all the while hitting them in the head. One could often hear her complain that not enough people had died.

On Good Friday she ordered the streets to be cleaned and the grass plucked by our fingers. The job had to be completed in two hours, and when it was not completed her whip came out. On Easter another pastor from Schowe was forced to clean all the toilets. One pastor was beaten beyond recognition because he would not stop ministering to people.

Her worst abuse was for those living. When a person died, she would stomp on their chests, yelling: "So, German, have you bitten the dust?" The living saw their loved ones desecrated. Nothing was beneath her.

Eventually, everyone was awaiting death. They had wounds all over our bodies, and the children's heads and bodies were swollen. No one had no strength to help each other. All they had their own life hanging by a thread. The savagery and brutality with which people were treated had no end. I cannot talk of some of the things that were done to the children. If the children were dead, there would be no more Germans.

One night Marta escaped with a boy of twelve who was still able to walk. During the day they hid in the fields and in ditches filled with fecal matter. At night they walked, continuing on a trek to Austria. Marta would see forever the dead and the dying, the crying children, the mourning mothers, the suicides. She had learned about the brutality of humanity and the beast called revenge. She had no home to return to and had no hope for what she and the boy would find. Why would those who won the war be any different?

⁓

Note:

The Jarek camp closed during the Holy Week of 1945. The total number of people who died there is not known. The estimate is around five thousand people. There is a marker at the mass grave site, placed there by the Serbian government on May 6, 2017.

CHAPTER TWENTY-SIX

I have a tale to tell I shall also ring the bell
When you start believing
When you start hearing
Maybe it's my turn now.
—Herta Müller, whose Banat village was destroyed
by the Russians and Tito.

The boy's name was Peter. He told Marta that all his family had died at Jarek. Appearing neither sad nor angry, he escaped with Marrta because there were no other options. He was numb and unable to comprehend what had happened or was happening. He was underweight and had lice. Bruises and wounds he had received from Jana and the other guards covered his body. Marta told him that she would be his mother from now on and find them a safe place to start a new life. That night they hid in the large open field outside Jarek where they had dug a mass grave. She sensed no one cared if they escaped. With no winter clothing or food, how would someone survive in December? The few souls remaining were being transferred to another death camp.

At sunrise they began their trek, they talked about how we didn't want to leave their homes, where family and happy times had existed. It was wonderful and sad to reminisce about how beautiful the fields, yards, homes, streets, and churches were. Marta told him her husband was a pastor at a Lutheran church; Peter was Reformed. "We can choose together which church we want to go to when we find our new home," she said. "What is important is that we live not what church we go to."

"But don't you think that in Austria everyone is Catholic? My parents told me that the very first colonists were Catholic because Maria Theresa was Catholic," Peter said.

Intrigued that he knew this, Marta asked, "Peter, what else do you know about the original settlements and the people?"

"My grandfather told me that our family came to the Banat when it was opened for Protestant settlers. I have heard about 'all the hard work' that had to be done and how happy they were to have their own land. I never heard them talk about being German, only that they came from Germany and now considered themselves Austrian or Hungarian, I can't remember. I remember asking why we all spoke in German if we weren't German, and they told me: because that was our native language and where our culture and roots are from. I didn't understand, but I also probably didn't care. I felt safe and secure, until the war." Peter stopped talking and became withdrawn. I tried to bring him back to his pleasant memories, and I asked about his favorite foods.

"Oh, the strudel and the sausage, of course!" he said. "I remember the whole family gathered to make the sausage from the newly slaughtered pigs. It was a huge party, actually. I ate until I was sick. Even now I can smell the spices and hear the sizzling of the sausages. The men made the sausage and the women the strudel: apple, poppy seed, cherry, and almond. I could never learn how to make the sheets of the paper-thin dough. I tried but failed every time. All the women would laugh and say, 'Ach, Peter this is women's work, go help the men.'"

"Oh, Peter, I used to love the dumplings and paprikash. The meat fell off the bones, and my grandmother added chicken liver to the dumplings."

"Do you think we will ever have those foods again, Marta?"

"I'm sure we will, we are going to Germany."

They walked for hours about what they knew of the history of their ancestors. Marta told him she had the family Bible with her family's births and deaths were recorded in it.

"My mother did the same thing."

"I think that's part of the nature of mothers: to keep our history. How else are we to know who we are? We all have pasts, and we are a part of all those people who came before us."

"There are people I don't want to be a part of," Peter said with great seriousness. "My uncle was always mean to me. I think he didn't like me because he didn't have a son. I would often hear him say that one needed a son to carry on the family name."

"How did you think women carry on the family name? When we marry we lose our family's name."

"Do you think that's why you put the names in the Bible? My mother always said I was so much like her family, the Schmidt family. I have the same eyes and hair color of my grandfather."

She began to wonder if he was related to the Schmidts in her family. The villages were small, so she thought just maybe.

The memory of this brought tears to Peter's eyes. He finally let his grief out. Now some healing might occur. "I will never forgive them for killing my grandfather. They took him out with a bunch of old men who couldn't work anymore, and they made them dig a hole and take off all their clothes, and then they shot them. I hate them! What did those old men ever do? All they ever did was get together on Sunday afternoons and sing old German songs and drink. They were not even born in Germany." Peter began to tear at his hair and yell. He fell on the ground and curled up into a ball.

Marta got him to stand, and they walked over to a beautiful tree and sat underneath it. "Peter, you will always have your grandfather with you. He is inside and no one can take that away. It is spring, and the world will soon become whole again." Peter was both child and man because of his experiences at Jarek. He had gained an understanding of the world of men and what they are capable of doing. I had never before seen a woman like Jana, and I wondered how she had become such a horrible person. Women give and nourish life; they do not destroy it.

"How can you believe that?" Peter said. "The war tore everything apart. People and land. And if the person lives, he is not the same. I will never feel free and hopeful again. I had hope that . . ." He became silent again and started to cry. He was crying so much because he had not cried before this time. He had stored all these tears and only released them when he was safe.

Never were those terrible people at Jarek to see him cry; he would not give them the satisfaction of knowing how he felt. He had turned into a stone. Now the stone was cracking.

"Peter, it's good that you are crying and feeling these things. It would be wrong if you couldn't feel. Do you think there are people who have survived the ordeals and suffering that we have and feel differently? What kind of person would not hate after all this? Jesus. He didn't hate the people who tortured and killed him. I know my husband would be saying this even—"

"Yes, but he was God! I am not! How can I ever go back to church and listen to 'forgive your enemies'? The whole world hates the Germans because of this war. Even if we had no part in what the Nazis did, we will all be accused. I will never be able to feel safe around Russians and the Serbians. They believe we are all the same and deserve the same. Have you heard what the Wehrmacht did in Russia?"

Marta had but did not tell him because he still had not seen or experienced the worst of what people can do. How many lives, how much destruction, how much torture can we any endure?

"We cannot live with hate in our hearts, Peter. There must be a better way, even if we can't see it now. Certainly, we will meet kind and loving people again."

"I don't think so. Our neighbors were never really our friends. I think they only tolerated us until they had the chance to rid themselves of us. I used to believe that *Heimat* was more than our house. It was a home, a place of shared love and people taking care of each other. Now I think there is no such place as a *Heimat*."

After Peter had cried for a long time, he fell asleep in Marta's lap. She had no answers to these questions, because she too carried hate. How many friends and relatives did she have to see die by people's cruelty? One death would have been more than enough. If she could never forget, maybe she also could never forgive. Such a terrible world to live in. Everything people owned was gone—house, land, relatives, food, clothing, our language, our culture, and most importantly spirit. Marta had never known such hate, and now she did, within herself and within humanity. Did Marta see this hate and do nothing? Where were they when the Jews were taken from their village? Some of the men helped get them on the trains. Where were they now—in Russian work camps, or in German work camps? She thought dead. She had ignored so much, believing that all would be well.

When Peter awoke, he asked if there was any food. "Do you think we will ever be full again? I saw people eating cats and other animals. I couldn't, it made me sick. So maybe I wasn't as hungry as they were."

"I picked up a couple of apples when we were walking past that farm behind us. Why don't we go back and ask them if they have anything they can share?" Marta had no idea where they were.

The farmers were not happy to see us and would not let us in. Not knowing what our fate had been, or whether we were gypsies, Serbs, or Germans, they feared us. They told them we were fleeing Tito and the Russians and needed food and knowledge about how to get to Germany.

"Have you seen any groups traveling or know of a safe route to take to Austria?" Marta asked. They told us we were near the border and gave us bread and water. They said that some refugees had managed to get to the Austrian border, but many were being turned back.

"But we have no place to go back to," Peter blurted out.

"Sorry," the woman said. "This is not our problem. Look for a train station. I have heard they are transporting people to Germany, if you can get into one of the cars."

Marta had seen in her family Bible that she had a relative by the name of Michael Müller with three sons living in Berlin. He was a famous singer, so she thought they might have some luck finding one his sons.

It took several weeks to find a train we could board that would take us to Germany. The train became another nightmare. For the weeks that they searched and waited for a train, finding food was difficult. They often picked up food that had been dropped and was starting to rot. By picking off the rotting sections, they could salvage pieces. Also, there were trees with some fruit. Peter would often have to climb quite high to reach it, since the lower branches had been plucked of all fruit. They also ate flowers and herbs. Water was the most difficult to find. Much of it was polluted with animal and human waste or garbage. Sometimes they found a small barrel of rainwater that did not look as if it had been contaminated.

The train cars were cattle cars and were freezing and full of people who were sick. The people inside were not allowed to start even a small fire to keep warm. There were no toilets and no straw to sleep on. When the train stopped, the dying and dead were taken out and laid in a field. There was no way to save those who were certain to die, so their fate was the same as the dead. Marta believed the journey of sorrow was over. She said prayers for their peace and thanked God she did not have to watch more children die. The train car was mainly inhabited by women and the elderly. Peter was mute through most of the days we travelled. He spoke only when spoken to and seemed to go deeper and deeper into his own thoughts. I feared what those were and did not ask him.

The train halted at the outskirts of Berlin. Her hopes were to find the Müller family, but I had no idea if any of them were alive or if they had any knowledge of their family in Vojvodina. My mother had sent letters to our relatives in Vienna and Berlin, and she had kept letters that people had sent us. Not ever paying attention, I knew no addresses or places of work.

Walking into Berlin after disembarking from the train, Marta was unprepared for what she saw. There had not been heavy bombing in the Vojvodina, so to see the remains of Berlin was a shock. The villages were not large cities, and this massive destruction was beyond anything she could have imagined. The spectacle of destruction caused her to stop and lean against a wall. Marta was surprised by the calm that permeated the city. Berliners had resigned themselves to what was about to occur. They greeted each other with the words *"Bleib übrig!"*—"Remain!" or "Survive!" The Russians were at the door, and their revenge would be horrendous, if the terror taking place in the city was any indication.

The weather also was a harbinger of events—heavy rain and wet snow. Life was to be drenched in violence again. We managed to find shelter in a bombed-out apartment that had three walls. It had a stove of sorts. Peter went out to beg and scavenge for food. Marta broke up the remaining pieces of furniture in hopes of lighting a fire. She found some straw and a broken mirror. Hopefully in the next day or so the sun would be in the sky for them to start a fire with the mirror. Peter came back with some potatoes, bread, and a friend who said he could help us locate food and matches if he could stay with us. His name was Walter. His father was in the Wehrmacht and his mother had died in a bombing. He said they could come back to his house since it was in better shape than our three-walled shelter.

He lent Marta his mother's clothing. He knew she would not return them, but she promised that she would give him something in return. "If we could be a family, that would be wonderful," he said.

Marta spent my days trying to locate information about her relative Michael Müller, and the boys foraged for anything they could find. They brought home news of the Russian army and how close to Berlin they were, and how many troops there were. They also brought back new of what the Wehrmacht was doing to defend Berlin and any other pieces of information that would give them hope.

Eventually they had several more people staying in the apartment, who all provided something for the common good. They gathered in the basement during aid raids. There was no privacy, but they were living.

Marta also went to the hospitals that were still functioning, offering help. But on February 3 Berlin was hit by a United States bombing attack. There were dead and dying everywhere. Marta ran from street to street, helping those she could. Three thousand Berliners died in the raid. She had learned to only help those who could survive and could walk or be carried to shelter. Those with chest, head, or stomach wounds would not survive. The wounded begged the people who walked by for water, for help, or to shoot them. When she returned home that evening, she did not even wash or remove her clothing but, sat down on a chair and immediately fell asleep.

The next morning, Marta realized that Peter was gone. Walter searched for him for days. He was eventually found under some rubble only a few feet from the hospital where Marta volunteered. She never knew why he was coming to the hospital, perhaps to look for her. Another loss. Another life. Another forgotten story of suffering. After Peter's death Marta saw less and less of Walter. Hopeless was the only feeling she felt. She knew that things would get worse and wondered if she could find the strength to search for Michael or his sons. In a way, she was glad I didn't have the responsibility of Pete. She prayed that she could banish this thought, but knew it was taking everything she could muster to care for herself. She was sure that she was anemic and possibly had scurvy.

Rumors circulated that the Russians had been raping all the women and girls in the areas they entered and captured. Women did not talk about this, but all knew what awaited, with only children and old men to guard them they were on our own. The women worked at rebuilding Berlin carrying buckets of water, bartering for food, mending clothing, dusting and cleaning up from the bombings the streets and rooms, calming the children, soothing the dying, and repairing anything that could give comfort. Marta's refuge was the books she was able to find. At least she could go to another world when reading them.

Food was getting scarcer. The people in the room with Marta remained civilized and shared, although resentment was brewing toward those who provided less. Occasionally they were able to get some wine to share when they prepared a fest from vegetables and some meat for a soup. "This is better than anything we had at Jarek," Marta offered as praise for a good dinner. The irony of this statement was not lost on anyone. All started to laugh. They cried and asked if anyone needed more salt. Sometimes they had small amounts of sugar and flour. Even a morsel of dessert brought laughter and joy to everyone. The children were given more, knowing that this might be the only joy they would have for days. Marta told them stories from her home but refrained from telling those that dealt with the arrival of the Russians, not wanting to create fear. They had enough to worry about and did not need to imagine what could happen.

The call for more men to win the war and save Berlin was issued. Mothers watched with a grief that was unbearable as their youngest sons were taken to be in the army to defend Berlin. They knew the boys were being sacrificed and that their husbands and older sons would probably not return. Bitterness like bile stuck in everyone's throat after Goebbels's speech when he stated, "Each mother who has given birth to a child has struck a blow for the future of our people." One woman living with us laughed hysterically and said, "We will not be impregnated by good German men but by savage Russians."

No one in the small apartment celebrated Hitler's birthday. Not a day had gone by that we did not hear of suicides, death from starvation, and madness. On April 23 we heard that Russian siege guns were entering the city. I argued with a man who believed that Wenck's army would come and rescue us. His reply: "Our only hope is that the Americans will get here first, and we can surrender to them. They at least act like human beings. They will at least allow us to survive. We still might be able to be Germans and not scattered to the ends of the earth. I cannot believe that Russia will let a single one of us live." With typical Berlin humor, one man referred to Berlin as the *Reichsscheiterhaufen,* the Reich's funeral pyre.

April 26 began with fighting in the streets, Germans looting bombed stores and taking anything even if it was of no use. Nights were bestial as Russians raped old and young women. Russian troops searched every house and cellar, using flame throwers to burn everyone and everything in their way, and the rain made the smell of burning worse.

On April 30 the following announcement was given by Admiral Dönitz on the radio:

> German men and women, soldiers of the German
> Wehrmacht, our Führer, Adolf Hitler, has fallen. In deepest
> sorrow and reverence the German people bow. He recog-
> nized the terrible danger of Bolshevism at an early date and
> dedicated his existence to this struggle. The end of this,
> his struggle, and of his unswerving straight path of life, is
> marked by his heroic death in the capital of the Reich. His
> life was one single service for Germany. His action in fight-
> ing against the Bolshevist springtide was waged beyond
> that, for Europe and the entire civilized world. The Führer
> has appointed me his successor. Conscious of this responsi-
> bility I am taking over the leadership of the German people
> in this grave hour of destiny.

On May 2 there was a silence in Berlin. General Weidling had met with Russian General Chuikov, giving him the following announcement and to be read to the German army:

> On 30 April 1945, the Führer committed suicide, and thus
> abandoned those who had sworn loyalty to him. According
> to the Führer's order, you German soldiers would have
> had to go on fighting for Berlin despite the fact that our
> ammunition has run out and despite the general situation
> which makes our further resistance meaningless. I order the
> immediate cessation of resistance. Every hour you keep on

fighting prolongs the suffering of the civilians in Berlin and of our wounded. Together with the commander-in-chief of the Soviet forces I order you to stop fighting immediately. Weidling, General of Artillery, former District Commandant in the defense of Berlin.

The silence hung black and heavy, like a pall over a coffin; there was no longer protection by the military or Home Guard. Most people hovered in our basement shelters as we waited, listening to the roar of tanks and artillery on the streets. Marta and her friends could hear Russian soldiers running up and down their steps and across rooftops. Eventually found the basement. They heard them call *"Komm,"*(come), which was misunderstood at first. They thought they were going to give food. What it meant was an invitation to rape. There was not a woman or girl in Berlin who had not been raped multiple times. You did not ask a woman *if,* if you had the courage, you asked *how many*. Everyone tried to protect the youngest but could not fight off the men, strong from battle.

Marta realized that if she did not try to go west, she would be trapped with the Russians. She had no idea how far into Berlin or Germany the Russians had advanced and did not know where the Allies were. She knew she could not stay long and would do anything to flee to the other Allies. Her only hope was to get away from the Russians and their brutality and revenge.

The Germans also feared the communists. When a local election was held in 1946, there was a massive anticommunist protest vote. Moving between the Soviet zone in the eastern part of the city and the Allied zones in the west was easier than she thought, but she needed a job and a place to live. Each day she traveled to the west and asked Germans about the hospitals and visited them, hoping to find employment. Eventually she found one and earned enough money to buy food rations. She knew how to live with little food and saved as much as I could to find housing.

Little by little, the women of Berlin were rebuilding the city. Working by hand and with outdated tools, they removed debris, mortared bricks together, built walls, and erected homes. No one knew whether the women who were working to rebuild Berlin where wealthy or poor. They all looked alike and did the same back-breaking work. There were a few who complained, but they received no sympathy. Food became the primary concern in the Eastern Zone in 1948. From June 24 until May 12, 1949, the Soviets blockaded American efforts to supply food to Berlin. It was then, tired of starvation and the lasting physical problems caused by starvation, Marta decided to move permanently to the Western Zone. Some of the nurses in the hospital where she worked were living together and had room for one more. She told them I could not offer much money for rent because of her salary, and they answered, "What makes you think we make more than you?" She moved in. No one asked questions about one another's lives before the war or what had happened during the war. They ate, slept, and started over. These single women became Germany's future.

Marta began asking around the hospital if anyone knew of the singer Michael Müller. Several had heard of him but did not know what had happened to him or his family. Someone told me that one of his sons was a violinist and instrument maker but didn't know his name. I began searching for a Müller who made instruments in Berlin.

In 1959 I found him. His name was Wolfgang Müller and he was the son of Michael. He invited me over. His apartment was near his shop, and both were remarkably intact. Business was almost nonexistent. Who could afford an instrument, and who had time to play one? He repaired instruments for the opera orchestra and the Berlin Philharmonic, both of which were operating again.

They had several dinners together and he told Marta all he knew of his family of musicians, starting with Johann Fritz.

"Yes, I did inherit his violin, and I have been able to keep it safe. It is a treasure for our family and for Germany. What a life he must have had, knowing Haydn and Beethoven, playing for Maria Theresa, and I heard he played in the orchestra for the premiere of Beethoven's Ninth. I understand they are doing a performance of it this week. Would you like to go with me? Furtwängler is conducting."

"I would love to. I have never heard an orchestral concert of classical music. How much are the tickets? I don't have much money."

"Don't worry. Many of the orchestra members give me free tickets for doing repair work. I find the beautiful music more filling than food. It fills my spirit and gives me reason to go on and be German. I will get two and we can go Saturday night. Have you heard the story of their last wartime concert?"

I shook my head, no, and he related the following story.

"The program included the Beethoven Violin Concerto and the final of Wagner's *Götterdämmerung* ("The Twilight of the Gods") and Brünnhilde's Immolation Scene. And if this was not prophetic enough, Hitler Youth were stationed in the theater to give cyanide capsules to audience members who wanted to commit suicide rather than face the Russian Army. I was not there. I think I would have begun to tear my hair out in utter despair, regret, and fear. But what music!"

Marta was silent. Remembering all the suicides she had seen at Jarek because of Hitler and the Russians brought back too many memories. Wolfgang looked at her as he had surely seen her face go white. "Have I said something that has offended you? I'm so sorry."

"No, it's fine. I haven't told you about my last days in our homeland in Serbia where I was in one of Tito's concentration camps. I saw many horrible suicides. Women protecting their daughters from rape. I want to forget. I wonder if the Germans understand what hell they released in all of Europe. Or if they realize they have made the German people victims of their hate. But, please, let's not talk of this. We can share beautiful family memories with each other and hear spiritual and transcending music."

Wolfgang bowed his head and kissed her hand. "I too have lost my whole family in horrible ways. But now we have each other, and we are family. Can we ask for much more?"

"No. There is nothing more. Maybe I can find a home again and feel as if I belong somewhere beautiful."

The concert was miraculous. It seemed as if the members of the orchestra were praying that new life and new hope were to be theirs. When the voices entered, it was as if heaven were pouring down on us music to give us strength. I believed that by giving this glorious music to our people and to the world, we could even assuage our guilt. Surely Beethoven saw the world differently than the Germans had when they allowed Nazism to prevail. Beethoven spoke of all of us being brothers and living together in joy. How did we wander so far from this truth?

Wolfgang had an extra room in his apartment, and I moved in. I continued to work as a nurse and helped him with his shop. Wolfgang eventually gave Johann's violin to a music museum with some of the scores Johann had kept from Beethoven and Haydn. They spent their evenings listening to music and reading Goethe. Marta's mind was exploring ideas and thoughts that were new to her, and eventually my life was mending. These concepts of music being a philosophy and a language that could change the world were difficult at first, but Wolfgang was patient. She loved the poetry of Goethe, especially the Mignon poems. Wolfgang played Schubert and Hugo Wolf settings of the poems. Often, she could not sleep because the music kept running through my mind.

Marta would never feel at home in Berlin and would never forget the past, but she would not let the past define her future or who she was. Home was hidden someplace deep in her heart; it was a vague memory like a song she had once heard.

Marta often listened to Strauss's *Four Last Songs* and cry, because the poet Eichendorff understood that we tire of our journey, and the poet stops to reflect on the beauty and peace that exist once we find death.

Marta found a book of poems written by refugees. One, "You Are Still Part of Me," ends this way:

> And we, the last of our kind, wander homeless,
> Strewn about like seaweed after the storm,
> Driven aimlessly like the autumn leaves, —
> Heavenly Father, You alone know our desolation!

END

NOTE: Statistics

There is disagreement amongst experts regarding the numbers of ethnic Germans who died in or were deported, or expelled, from Yugoslavia. It has been reported that prior to the end of the war, 80,000 ethnic Germans from Yugoslavia had been drafted into the German army and another 215,000 to 245,000 had been evacuated to Germany for labor purposes. There were 200,000 to 250,000 remaining ethnic Germans in Yugoslavia at the war's end. In 1944, Partisans killed about 2,000 ethnic German intellectuals and leaders. During Blood Autumn in 1944, around 12,000 able-bodied men and women were deported to Russian labor camps, of whom 2,000 died. Between 1945 and 1948, approximately 51,000 children, women, and men died.

Selected Bibliography

The books listed below were used as part of my research. They are mostly academic in nature but are well worth the time and effort to read. They are all in print and can be purchased easily.

Anonymous. *A Woman in Berlin* (a diary).

de Zayas, Alfred-Maurice. *A Terrible Revenge: The Ethnic Cleansing of the East European Germans* (includes the poem "You Are Still Part of Me.")

—————. *Nemesis at Potsdam.*

Janjetović, Zoran. *Between Hitler and Tito: The Disappearance of the Vojvodina Germans.*

Jünger, Ernst. *Storm of Steel.*

Keeling, Ralph Franklin. *Gruesome Harvest.*

Le Bor, Adam, and Roger Boyes. *Seduced by Hitler: the choices of a nation and the ethics of survival.*

Lowe, Keith. *Savage Continent: Europe in the Aftermath of World War II.*

MacDonogh, Giles. *After the Reich: The Brutal History of the Allied Occupation.*

Moeller, Robert G. *War Stories: The Search for a Usable Past in the Federal Republic of Germany.*

Zakić, Mirna. *Ethnic Germans and National Socialism in Yugoslavia in World War II.*

CPSIA information can be obtained
at www.ICGtesting.com
Printed in the USA
JSHW020038030622
26596JS00002B/10